THE
HANGMAN'S
HANDYMAN

THE HANGMAN'S HANDYMAN

by

Hake Talbot

RAMBLE HOUSE

ISBN 13: 978-1-60543-358-5

ISBN 10: 1-60543-358-6

Published: 2005, 2009 by Ramble House
Cover Art: Gavin L. O'Keefe
Preparation: Fender Tucker

TO MISS TITMOUSE

THE HANGMAN'S HANDYMAN

An Island Called The Kraken

THE CRASH OF THE SEA on the rocks was the first sound Nancy heard. She found herself, still dressed in her evening gown, lying across the foot of the bed. It was nearly a minute before she realized she was in the room given her on her arrival at The Kraken that afternoon. The girl pulled herself to her feet and groped her way toward the dim outline of the window. The wind that had lashed the Carolina coast since sundown was beginning to die, but the night was still dark. Nothing could be seen but the white crests of the breakers below.

Nancy stood for a minute gazing out into the night, wondering idly what time it was and why she had not undressed. All at once she became aware of the fact that she had no answer to these questions or to a dozen others. Everything that had happened since dinner was as blank as though she had fainted at the table and been carried up to bed.

Earlier events seemed clear enough: the end of the long drive from New York; the shining mahogany speedboat; the island itself, so curiously named The Kraken, and seeming strangely rocky against the low shore only a quarter of a mile away; the great stone house; the unexpected nature of her fellow house guests; the storm, with its attendant doubts for Rogan's safety; and the curious incident of the broken mirror.

Yes, all that stood out sharply in her mind. She could even recall the beginning of dinner, with Jack Frant's lean little figure looking so out of place at the head of the table, his seven guests ranged on both sides of him, and the five empty chairs. Nancy winced at the picture. Somehow those vacant chairs seemed more ominous than if all thirteen places had been filled. Her last definite memory was of Jack's high-pitched laughter when Evan had knocked over the salt cellar. After that there were only occasional flashes— old Miss Makepeace's acid smile—the black faces of the Negro servants— meaningless words—and then nothing. Yet if she had fainted at dinner, why had no one taken care of her? She could not believe she had been merely carried upstairs and dumped on the bed like a bundle of soiled clothes, but what other explanation was possible?

Well, the answer certainly was not to be found here. With growing alarm Nancy felt her way to the door and pulled it open. A faint glow from her right illuminated the four-foot corridor, and she followed it to emerge upon the wooden gallery built along one wall of the main room of the house—a room so huge that the candles placed on a table in its center did little more than call attention to the shadow-haunted darkness which pressed in upon them. Except for the candles and an occasional hiss from the burning driftwood in the great fireplace, there was no sign of life.

As the girl turned to the stairs that led down on her right, a low-toned clock struck somewhere in the depths of the ancient house. Mechanically she counted the strokes—ten of them. Dinner would have been over about nine, so she must have been unconscious all that time. Suddenly, the full implication of the hour struck her. If it were only ten o'clock, where were the other members of the house party? Normally they would be here, grouped around the fire, playing cards, or strumming the piano. Even if they were in the library, there would at least be more lights and the sound of voices. Instead she found only four candles and a dying fire.

Hesitantly Nancy crept down the stairs and had almost reached the center of the room when she heard the thud of the knocker beating against the main door. The shock to the already frightened girl was so great that she was forced to clutch the edge of the table to steady herself. In a few seconds her sturdy common sense came to her rescue. She had wanted company—well, here it was. If some evil were abroad on The Kraken it would be in the house, not out in the storm. She picked up one of the candles and moved forward, holding it before her like a shield.

Then, leaving the inner door of the vestibule wide behind her, she opened the outer door.

Seen in that flickering light, the man who stood there bulked enormous. He was clad in dripping oilskins, and the sou'wester cast a mask of shadow over the upper part of his dark face.

"Please, ma'am, would you have half a bed for a poor shipwrecked sailor that got crowded out of Davy Jones' locker?"

Nancy felt her small stock of courage drain away. Then to her relief she heard a chuckle that she recognized, her candle was caught as it fell, the man's sou'wester was jerked off and she looked up into his laughing eyes.

"Rogan Kincaid!"

"Remember me? I was afraid you wouldn't."

"I couldn't see you at first. I'm—I'm awfully glad you're here."

"Thanks. I'm glad to get here. There've been times in the last few hours when I didn't expect to make it." He glanced into the darkness beyond her. "This is Frant's island, isn't it?"

She nodded, still unsure of her voice.

"Then why no sounds of revelry? The place is quiet as a catacomb. Where are the other guests?"

"I don't know."

Rogan dropped his oilskins on the floor of the vestibule and stepped into the great living room. In the uncertain light of the candles there was an almost tangible malevolence about the place. He walked forward to meet it, his hard eyes moving from side to side like those of a wary fighter sizing up an antagonist.

Frant's talk of the place had prepared him for one of the white- columned Palladian mansions that dot the Carolinas, but this vast pile belonged to an earlier civilization. Built in a time when buccaneers and hostile Indians were realities, it had copied the sturdy lines of its Tudor forebears in stone quarried to make space for its own cellars.

Then, too, Rogan's host had promised a houseful of guests, yet Nancy Garwood denied knowledge of their whereabouts. The whole thing began to smell very like a trap, and Mr. Kincaid did not intend to be caught inside it. He turned and found that the girl had followed him.

She was pretty, there was no denying it. Even in that dimly lighted room her hair glowed with the buttercup yellow that had fascinated him in New York because it was as authentic as it was unusual. Her figure also deserved, and received, attention. She suggested a streamlined Boucher nymph and matched his own personal taste to a nicety. Nevertheless, he reminded himself, Nancy's charms might have a purpose. One does not bait a trap with thick ankles. Besides, Frant had said she was an actress, and his words were borne out by that touch of theatricality in her clothes which is the hallmark of show people. Perhaps she was acting now.

He put a finger under her chin and raised it until she was looking straight into his eyes.

"I'm beginning to believe"—Rogan watched her closely while he spoke—"that this house-party business was just a gag to get me down here and that the rest of the guests are products of Jackson B.'s over-fertile brain."

"Oh, no," Nancy gasped. "They were here all right, only . . . they've disappeared."

"Disappeared!"

"Well, maybe not really," she admitted. "I suppose I just got frightened at being alone, but I couldn't find anybody and it is only ten o'clock. That must be pretty early for people to go to bed— even 'way down here."

"How did you get separated from the others?"

"I don't know. It was . . . queer. We were in the dining room having dinner, and the next thing I remember I was upstairs lying across my bed. I hadn't even undressed." Nancy glanced ruefully down at the rumpled chiffon of her skirt. "I felt a little weak when I woke up, but I wasn't sick or anything, and I only had one cocktail before dinner. It doesn't make sense."

Mr. Kincaid stroked his long chin for a moment, looking down at the thin evening frock that was nearly her only garment.

"Standing here doesn't make sense either." He pulled the girl's arm through his and marched her across to the fireplace. "You'll catch cold in that gossamer gewgaw you're wearing if we don't wrap a little heat around you—to say nothing of the fact that I myself am a saturated solution of rain-water and brine."

As Rogan stooped to build up the fire, Nancy sat on the sofa watching him. When Frant had introduced them three days before in a New York night club, she had taken to this man at once. His easy smile, his tall, well-tailored figure, and his lean, unsymmetrical face that was such a curious blend of good looks and downright ugliness—all these formed a combination that she had found irresistible. Afterward she had danced with Sam Grace, the gossip writer, and Sam had told her Kincaid was a professional gambler.

"Falling for him?"

"Some," she had confessed.

"Better forget it. Kincaid bats around all over the world. You'd be lucky if you saw him two days in two years."

Nancy had made a little mouth. "I could go with him."

"Not with that guy."

"Sort of lone wolf?"

"Kincaid hasn't enough warm human feelings to make a wolf—'lone shark' would be more like it." He had gone on to recount anecdotes in which the gambler's ruthlessness was matched only by his prowess.

Seated across the table from Rogan in Fifty-second Street, it was easy to take Sam's stories for the customary exaggerations of his profession. Now, alone with the gambler in this gloomy room— alone with him on the whole island, for all she knew—those stories were more disquieting.

Still, she reasoned, Rogan had no cause to be at odds with her. Maybe if she were nice to him . . .

Nancy had just reached this tentative decision when Kincaid said, "There," and stood erect, dusting his hands. The new wood had begun to catch, and the room seemed brighter. He took off his sodden coat and held it to the flame.

"Let's get this business straight. Frant owns this house. You drove down from New York with him and arrived on the island this afternoon. Then for some reason you fainted during dinner. When you woke up, Frant, his guests, and his servants were all gone."

"That's right."

"What were the other guests like?"

"I don't know exactly," Nancy admitted. "Not that they were queer or anything, just that I never met anyone like them before. The servants treated them as if they were royalty, and Jack said some of them were rich, but they were kind of quiet somehow and they didn't have hardly any jewelry."

"I see." Mr. Kincaid hung his coat on the fire screen. "They don't sound like the type of people you'd expect Jackson B. to invite on a house party."

"I was sort of surprised, myself, when I saw them," the girl agreed. "But I think they were Evan's friends mostly. He's Jack's half brother, you know."

"The one Frant claims is an English lord?"

"Yes. I'm not sure he really is a lord. That may be just one of Jack's lies. To tell you the truth, I'm not even certain he's an Englishman. He talks like one, but Miss Makepeace says he's Welsh, and anyway his mother must have been American, because she was Jack's mother, too."

"Miss Makepeace is one of the missing guests, I take it."

"Uh-huh. Her brother's here with her. They used to own this house. Then there's another girl, Sue Braxton. I think Evan wants to marry her. She likes him, too."

"Is that the crop?"

"Sue's grandfather was here."

There was silence after that. Mr. Kincaid stood with his back to the fire while he considered the situation. Even if he discounted Nancy's story of the vanished guests, the puzzle of the house itself still remained. Try as he would, he could not make the place match with any reasonable estimate of his host's character. The thick stone walls, the hammer beams, huge as ships' timbers, that disappeared into the darkness near the great roof, the quiet, well- chosen furniture—all were at variance with the blatant little man whose breezy boasts had brought Kincaid south. He looked down at the girl.

"After mature deliberation I've decided the best way to find our fellow guests is to hunt for them. Where do we start?"

"The dining room, I guess. That's where they were last time I saw them."

Nancy rose unsteadily. Rogan put an arm around her for support. She looked up at him with a little smile of apology.

"Sorry. I'm still sort of wobbly."

"Would you rather stay here?"

"Oh, no. I'll be all right as long as I don't make any sudden moves. Anyway, I'd rather walk around than wait here wondering what's become of the others. Jack kept talking about ghosts and things all through dinner. If I sit still I may start thinking about them."

"He didn't mention the *Mary Celeste,* did he?"

"Mary Celeste?"

"She was a ship. Another boat found her batting about in the middle of the Atlantic with her sails set, every stick and rope in place, a half-eaten meal on the table—and not a soul on board."

Nancy's eyes were round. "What do you suppose happened?"

"That's something no one has ever figured out. The point is that Frant may be pulling some sort of practical joke with an idea based on the *Mary Celeste* story."

"That would be just like Jack," Nancy agreed, "but the others wouldn't have helped him, and they're gone, too."

She led the way to a door on the left of the fireplace. They passed through a library walled with books and into the dining room. Rogan had made no guess as to what his candle might reveal. Yet he found himself curiously unprepared for the actuality. The place was in perfect order. The chairs were ranged neatly against the walls, silverware gleamed on the buffet, and in the center the great table of mahogany had been cleared and polished. Even the hearth had been swept and the fire extinguished with water.

Nancy dropped on the nearest chair and looked about her. "There's nothing here at all."

"What did you expect?"

"Oh, things lying around—a torn letter—a rouge-stained cigarette butt—you know, clues."

Rogan put down his candle.

"The clues we need are all in your mind, and we have to get them out."

"But nothing happened before I fainted," she protested.

"Something must have made you faint. Whatever it was, the shock might have driven the events that led up to it out of your mind. That sounds queer, but it's really quite common. The doctors have a couple of words for it. As a matter of fact, the answer must be something like that, or you'd know more about what went on. Perhaps if you keep trying you can bring some of it back."

Nancy smiled wryly.

"If it hit me so hard I forgot backwards, maybe I'd rather not remember." She shrugged and continued, "How do we start?"

"Didn't anything out of the ordinary take place during dinner?"

"You mean like the empty chairs?"

"Empty chairs?"

"Yes. You see, there were only eight of us for dinner, but the table was set for thirteen."

"Is that Frant's lucky number?"

"No, he'd invited the other five all right—you, and four people named West. But, of course, you didn't come. Mrs. West found out about the storm from the weather bureau, and that scared her and her whole family off. I didn't like the idea of sitting down with thirteen chairs at the table myself, but I couldn't talk Jack into taking the extra ones away. I think he wanted to spite Evan."

"Don't tell me his lordship descends to such plebeian superstitions."

"Sure he does. He's superstitious about everything. Jack kept kidding about it. He hardly let up for a minute. That's what the paper was about, too."

"What paper?"

She gave a little gasp.

"You know, things *are* coming back to me. I'd forgotten that paper. Jack had it in his pocket and he read it to us while we were having our coffee. It was something a fellow in England had copied for him out of a bunch of old books."

"What was in it?"

"I don't know exactly. Some sort of scandal about Evan's side of the family, I think. It was all mixed up, anyhow, and full of long words I never heard before."

"Don't you remember any of it?"

"Well, it told how somebody got himself killed three or four hundred years ago. And there was a priest in it, and witches, and devils, and a lot of talk about water."

"How did Evan take that?"

"He was pretty sore, I guess. Anyway, he grabbed the paper out of Jack's hand and threw it in the fire."

Rogan stared down at the wet ashes.

"Hmm. Wonder if that's why they put the fire out."

"To save the paper, you mean? I don't think so, because right after that we all went out into the big room."

Kincaid picked up the tongs and began turning over the ashes and charred wood in the fireplace.

"You certainly were right about remembering things," the girl went on excitedly. "It's all clearing up now. We went into the living room, and . . ." She jumped up. "That's it. Listen! I know how I got upstairs . . . nobody carried me . . . I walked up myself—*after Jack died!*"

Rogan spun around on his toes, but Nancy was still fumbling for memories.

"That's it . . . that's what happened. Jack's dead! He died because of what Evan said! *And it's true!* I went into his room, and . . ."

Rogan was just in time to catch her as she fell forward in a dead faint.

2

The Curse That Worked Backwards

KINCAID LIFTED the girl in his arms and carried her back to the great hall, where he placed her upon the sofa before the fire. If Nancy's unconsciousness were assumed, she deserved a higher rating in her profession than he had been inclined to grant her. On the other hand, her faint was suspiciously becoming. Her yellow hair lay on the dark upholstery like spilled paint, and one strap of her bodice had broken, disclosing the upper halves of round white breasts.

Rogan's quick ears caught the click of a latch, and he looked up to see a line of light illuminate the corridor that led from the far side of the room. Evidently the house was not so empty as Nancy had led him to think. The light came from an opened door. Rogan watched a man step into the corridor and move toward him. As the newcomer entered the living room he spoke.

"Is that you, Stirling?"

"Sorry, I'm Rogan Kincaid."

"Mr. Kincaid!" The speaker moved closer. He was tall and gaunt, and his long nose jutted out between black brows that shaded small, keen eyes. "How long have you been here?"

"Only a minute or two."

"You don't mean you left Bailey's Point in this storm!"

"Oh, no, we left before dark, but the motor failed. The wind caught us just as we got started again."

"But good heavens, man, how did you ever manage to bring a boat ashore through this surf?"

"We didn't. The boat's still out in it. I tripped on a coil of rope and went overboard."

"But . . ."

"It was even more of a miracle than it sounds. I'd put my life belt on over my oilskins and got so tangled up in them I had all I could do to keep afloat. The storm, of course, kept blowing the boat southward, and I expected the waves to take me along with her. They didn't. Instead some queer undertow caught me and dragged me *upwind.*"

The other nodded. "That was our local current. It sweeps up this coast to a place called 'Gallow's Cove.' Drowned bodies are sometimes carried there by it."

Rogan laughed. "No doubt fate is reserving me for a hanging."

"Let us hope not." The tone suggested a belief that the hope might prove futile. "I'm Arnold Makepeace." He held out his hand. "If The Kraken seems primitive and desolate, Mr. Kincaid, you must blame that on the storm. The light plant hasn't been used for years, and the first flash of lightning put it out of commission."

"We do seem to be under the weather rather literally tonight. Unfortunately"—Rogan pointed down at Nancy—"Miss Garwood is under it figuratively as well. Perhaps—"

"Miss Garwood?" Makepeace stepped around the end of the couch and stared at the girl. "What's wrong with her?"

"She was alone when I arrived, and I'm afraid I frightened her."

Arnold Makepeace eyed Rogan suspiciously. "Are you sure that was all?"

"Not really. Perhaps Frant's death had something to do with it."

"What do you know about Frant's death?" The other's voice was sharp.

"Only the bare fact. Miss Garwood muttered a word or two as she toppled over. Why? Was there something queer about the way he died?"

"Nothing"—Makepeace spoke too loudly for conviction—"except that it was very sudden. Dr. Braxton has not made a definite diagnosis as yet, but I feel sure he will agree with me that apoplexy was responsible."

Kincaid wondered whether Dr. Braxton would do anything of the kind. Makepeace, however, had no intention of allowing further questions. He gestured toward Nancy.

"Perhaps we'd best get this young woman to bed. Her room's upstairs. Do you think you can carry her?"

"It'll be fun to try." Rogan lifted the girl's lovely figure in his arms.

Makepeace, candle in hand, led the way up the steps that mounted the seaward wall of the great room. As they reached the gallery at the top, Rogan saw a woman emerge from a corridor paralleling the one below. She turned toward them and waited until they came up to her.

By the light of the candle she carried, Rogan saw that she was an angular gentlewoman of all-too-certain age, with features so absurdly like Makepeace's that the latter's introduction was not needed to establish her as his sister. The eyes behind her gold- rimmed spectacles were bright as she looked at Nancy.

"She fainted," Rogan explained. "We are about to put her to bed, but you'd probably be better at that than we would."

Julia Makepeace's eyes flickered to her brother's face.

"Are you certain it's *only* a faint?"

He snapped at her, "What else could it be?"

"Anyway, she's still breathing." Miss Makepeace touched the girl's cold cheek. "We'd better get her to bed at once, but I hate putting her in her own room." She glanced at Rogan. "It's next to Mr. Frant's."

Kincaid wondered why that seemed a complete explanation. "I'll change with her, if you like," he offered.

"That would be kind." Miss Makepeace turned to her brother. "See if you can find Stirling, Arnold."

"Yes, of course. And by the way, Julia, Mr. Kincaid already knows of Frant's apoplexy."

Miss Makepeace eyed him for a moment but made no answer. Instead she turned and led the way along the gallery to a bedroom that had been built over the great hall below. Rogan followed her into the room and laid his burden on the bed.

The older woman sat beside Nancy and felt her wrist.

"Her pulse seems fairly strong, but I hope my brother finds Stirling without any trouble. Stirling," she explained, "is Dr. Braxton. We're lucky to have him."

Miss Makepeace stood up. "There's nothing I can do here till the doctor arrives. I'd better get one of this girl's nightgowns, or whatever she wears, so I can put her to bed when Stirling has seen her."

When the door closed behind Miss Makepeace, Nancy opened her eyes. "Hello."

"Hello. When did you come to?"

"While you were carrying me along that sort of balcony thing."

"Why the possum act? Don't you like our Miss Makepeace?"

"She kind of scares me." Nancy's fingers plucked at the bedspread. "What happened?"

"Nothing. You overdid the walking around and fainted again. I brought you upstairs."

The girl looked at Rogan for a minute and then said, "Jack's dead, isn't he?"

"Yes. Were you very fond of him?"

"Not really, I guess. Jack was a funny sort of a little fellow, but he treated me all right. I wish I could remember how he died, though. There was something funny about it. Oh, I remember—spilled salt!"

"Spilled salt?"

"You know, what you said—superstitions. Evan has 'em. Jack kept kidding him about it. From the minute he got here, all he did was make lousy jokes about the way his brother felt. Evan knocked my compact out of my hand and broke the mirror. Jack was awfully nasty about it—told Sue she couldn't marry Evan for seven years without sharing his bad luck—that kind of thing. A couple of minutes later Evan spilled a little salt. You should have heard Jack then."

"His lordship answered back, I take it?"

"Not till after—" She broke off, remembered horror in her eyes, and then asked, "What do you think killed Jack?"

"Makepeace says apoplexy."

"It wasn't the curse, then? I suppose I never did believe it was really . . . only . . . the way he died—" Nancy shuddered. "It was awful."

There was a pause. Then, "Rogan . . . did you ever hear of a curse that worked backwards?"

"I never heard of a curse that worked."

"This one seemed to. I wish you'd been here. Then maybe—"

A latch clicked behind Kincaid, and Miss Makepeace came into the room. "Stirling not here yet?"

"No."

"I wonder where he could have gone?" She looked at the girl for a moment, then turned back to Rogan. "I'm afraid your introduction to The Kraken hasn't been too pleasant, Mr. Kincaid. I was born on this island and love it, but in weather like this it must seem forbidding to a stranger."

"I assure you I found it a haven of refuge, and the house is wonderful."

"One of my ancestors built it over two hundred years ago. He was wrecked here, which explains why he called it The Kraken."

"Not to me, I'm afraid. What is it—Indian?"

"Norse. There is an old legend of a monster, big as an island, that used to swallow whole ships and carry them down to its lair, where it could mumble the sailors' bones at its leisure."

Nancy stirred uneasily. The older woman was instantly contrite.

"I'm sorry. I'm so used to the legend I forget how gruesome it sounds."

Rogan smiled down at the girl.

"This kraken has more growl than bite. I swam right into its jaws and it didn't even lick its chops."

"Swam?" Miss Makepeace's voice rose with the question.

Kincaid told how he had reached the island. "If luck hadn't been with me," he finished, "I'd never have made it."

"Luck certainly was with you," she agreed, "but you can thank your stars the Handyman was with you, too."

"Handyman?"

"The Hangman's Handyman. It . . ."

The door to the cross-gallery opened, and a stranger appeared, followed by Makepeace. Rogan looked at the newcomer with interest. His hair was white and there was a scholar's stoop to his wide shoulders, but his face was strong and he carried his years well. Miss Makepeace spoke.

"Mr. Kincaid managed to get here in spite of the storm, Stirling." She gestured toward the older man. "This is Dr. Braxton."

Rogan stepped forward and held out his hand.

"It's a privilege to meet you, doctor. I've heard something of your work."

"Thank you."

While the other's troubled eyes examined his face, Rogan waited for some sign of recognition. None came. Dr. Braxton put his black medical bag on the foot of Nancy's bed and shook hands.

"Mr. Makepeace told me you were here. I brought some dry clothes." He took a bundle from under his arm, handed it to Rogan, and then sat on the edge of Nancy's bed to feel her pulse. The girl's breathing was deeper now and the blood was beginning to creep back under her rouge.

"There's nothing to worry about." Dr. Braxton spoke without looking up. "I'll give her something to help her sleep, and she'll be all right by morning."

"The rest of us won't," said Miss Makepeace, "if we don't get some food into us and go to bed. Arnold, suppose you show Mr. Kincaid to his room and then start some sandwiches. I'll join you in the kitchen as soon as I've finished with Miss Garwood."

As they passed through the door, Rogan saw the gleam of a hypodermic in the doctor's fingers.

Arnold Makepeace led the way along the gallery that skirted the shadowy abyss of the room below. They turned down the corridor, and Rogan, always quick to notice the layout of any place in which he found himself, saw that it contained two doors on each side and a fifth at the far end. His guide pointed to the last and said, "Frant's."

Kincaid's room was on the left, next to that of their dead host. Makepeace waited until the other had started to strip off his sodden clothes and then said, "I'll bring you some supper. Is there anything I can do before I go?"

"You can tell me something about Frant. Was he a particular friend of yours?"

"Hardly. I'd never met him before."

Rogan chuckled. " 'The people in this simple tale are total strangers to each other.' "

Makepeace seemed insulted. "Not at all. We've known Frant's half brother, Lord Tethryn, for some time. Our invitation came through him. And, of course, Dr. Braxton has been friendly with Frant for years." The dry voice carried disapproval.

"Is Lord Tethryn the elder brother?"

"Oh, no. He's quite young. Thirty or so. The relationship was on the mother's side. She married a Welshman, Sir Humphrey Faulkland, after Frant's father died. Sir Humphrey made munitions during the war. No doubt he had political pull, too. At least they gave him an earldom. I understand there was a good deal of that sort of thing in the early twenties. The young fellow has good stuff in him, though."

"Is he engaged to Miss Braxton?"

"Not that I've heard of. No doubt an engagement is contemplated, but I'm sure there's nothing official as yet."

"Frant's death must have been a shock to his brother. Miss Garwood tells me they quarreled just before Frant was stricken."

"Miss Garwood exaggerates." Makepeace moved to the door. "Well, if there's nothing more . . . ?"

"Nothing, thanks. You don't think the dispute brought on our host's apoplexy, then?"

"What? No. Of course not. Impossible. I'll see that you get some supper." And Makepeace was gone.

Now what, Mr. Kincaid asked himself, did that mean? Had Frant really died of a stroke caused by a quarrel with his brother? Hardly. If so, Makepeace would not have insisted so loudly on apoplexy. On the other hand, what was to be made of the words Nancy had spoken before she fainted, "He died because of what Evan said," and her cryptic remark about "the curse that worked backwards"?

He began to dress in the clothes Dr. Braxton had brought— pajamas of wine silk with robe and morocco slippers to match. Rogan smiled wryly as he noted the excellence of their fit. He picked up the candle Makepeace had left him and stepped into the corridor.

When he came out onto the gallery, the room below was empty. Rapidly he ran over in his mind the location of the other guests. The doctor and Miss Makepeace would still be with Nancy. Makepeace was supposedly in the kitchen. Frant was dead in his own bedroom. His half brother and Dr. Braxton's granddaughter were still to be met. That made seven. Rogan frowned. Nancy had spoken of thirteen places at table, including the five vacant chairs. There must be one more guest on the island—a guest whom no one had mentioned.

Mulling this thought in his mind, Kincaid turned to his right and descended the stairs. By the time he reached the main floor, however, he had decided to put his new problems aside and continue the search in the dining-room fireplace that had been interrupted by Nancy's faint. What the actress with her theatrical background had called 'the paper' was probably unimportant, but if it still existed, this would almost certainly be his only chance to get it. Rogan disliked leaving stones unturned. They usually proved to be stumbling blocks.

He entered the library and paused for a moment to run his eye over the books that lined its shelves with an almost Prussian neatness. If Makepeace had been compelled to let his personal collection go with the house, he must have been hard hit. Spenser and *Euphues,* Hakluyt's *Voyages,* and Dekker's plays stood in calf bindings old when the house was built. Sets of Poe,

Dickens, and other standard authors stood beside a much-read collection of works on spiritualism which ranged from Sir Oliver Lodge's *Raymond* to *Leaves from a Psychist's Casebook* by Harry Price. Farther along his eye caught Lévi's *The History of Magic, Le Dragon Rouge,* Blavatsky's *Isis Unveiled,* Roger Bacon's *Mirror of Alchemy,* and Swedenborg's *Of Heaven and Hell.* Poe, Price, and Paracelsus. He chuckled. A gap in the black-bound set of the Virginian's works caught his eye, and Rogan wondered who had chosen such macabre reading on a day of death. He glanced around the room in search of the missing volume.

He found it, dropped face downward beside a chair. It fell open to the last page of *The Facts in the Case of M. Valdemar,* and the title brought back vague memories of the Frenchman whose existence had been so curiously prolonged by mesmerism. Before Kincaid could read more than a few words, however, footsteps sounded in the next room. He slipped the Poe volume back on its shelf and turned to face the newcomer.

3

What the Fire Had Not Burned

AS SHE MOVED into the doorway, the pale yellow of her long housecoat brought warmth and color to the gloomy room. Brown-haired, brown-eyed, slim-bodied, this girl turned Nancy Garwood's beauty to tinsel merely by being in the same world with her.

"I'm Sue Braxton."

Rogan introduced himself. The girl moved closer, peering up at him and liking what she saw. The dark, level eyes looked honest. It was part of his stock-in-trade, but Sue could not know that and his direct gaze gave her comfort. She approved also of the firm line of his jaw and of the wide, humorous mouth that seemed on the point of laughing at things which made other people afraid.

The girl lowered her candle. "It's lucky for us you came," she said. "I think we needed somebody from outside. Have you seen the others?"

"Most of them."

"Lord Tethryn?"

Rogan shook his head, and she continued. "I'm worried about him. He ought not to be left alone after what happened, but Aunt Julia gave me alanol and put me to bed. I couldn't sleep so I came down here."

"I didn't know Miss Makepeace was your aunt."

"She isn't really, but I've known her since I was born. I practically lived on The Kraken until the Makepeaces sold it to Mr. Frant."

"What in the world did a man of Frant's tastes want with a place so far from the bright lights?"

"It's only eight miles to town. That's nothing if you have a telephone."

"Don't tell me the phones here are connected to the mainland?"

"Oh, yes. That's how Mr. Frant got your telegram saying you'd changed your mind and were coming. Uncle Arnold had a private cable laid when he owned this island."

"Perhaps that's why he went broke and had to sell it. Still, I can't picture Frant here. I spent Tuesday evening with him and he kept four waiters busy saying, 'Yes, Mr. Frant,' and 'Right away, Mr. Frant.' A fellow like that wouldn't be happy on any island but Manhattan."

"Oh, he didn't intend to live here himself. He never even came here until yesterday, and none of us had met him before—except Grandfather. Mr. Frant bought The Kraken as a speculation. He expected to make a big profit, only the recession kept up and he couldn't sell. He's had it for several years now."

"Was Frant on bad terms with his brother?"

"Evan was only his half brother," she corrected. "That was at the bottom of everything, I think . . . the fact that Mr. Frant was connected with the Faulkland family without actually being part of it."

Sue broke off suddenly and sat down, holding the tall candlestick on her knees.

"When Mr. Frant got here this afternoon he was afraid. He talked all the time so the rest of us would keep our eyes on him. Besides, he seemed to feel he had to show how brave he was, and people don't do that unless they're really afraid 'way down deep, do they?"

Rogan slipped his long body into a chair that faced the girl's. Her words were bringing the picture of Frant's actions into focus with what he knew of the man himself. The idea that their diminutive host had deliberately picked a pointless quarrel with his half brother had been difficult to swallow. Now it began to make sense. As Sue went on to recount the incidents of the broken mirror and the spilled salt, the little man's feverish attempt to cover his own inward nervousness became as vivid as the candle flame that flickered as she breathed.

"Do you mean Frant was afraid of his half brother?" Rogan asked.

"Oh, no. He was afraid of the curse. He's been brought up on the story, you see. Mr. Frant lived in England after his own father died and his mother married again. I guess his nurse told him the story. He must have believed it then. Probably when he got older he tried not to believe, but couldn't help himself."

"Exactly what was this curse?" Rogan asked. "I met Frant only twice, but both times he mentioned something of the sort. Unfortunately, I gave it little attention. All I remember is that it isn't the usual sort of tale where some old crone curses the family and the eldest son never lives to inherit the title."

"It's the other way round."

"What other way is there? Miss Garwood said something about the curse 'working backwards,' but—"

"It does. The Faulklands weren't cursed themselves, you see. They inherit the power to curse others."

Sue seemed to feel she had made the point clear, for she went back to her narrative.

"Mr. Frant kept hinting about the curse all through dinner, but he didn't actually mention it until we were having coffee. Evan had stood things till then without showing much, but that got under his self-control and he mumbled something about the story being only a pack of lies. Of course Mr. Frant had been waiting for some opening like that and he jumped at it."

"You think Frant was worked up because he took stock in the curse and Lord Tethryn didn't?"

"Oh, no. Evan really believed in it even then. It's not just a legend. We were alone for a few minutes right after dinner and he told me a story. . . . Only, you see, he kept what he thought to himself before the others, while Mr. Frant couldn't help showing things. That was the reason for this house party, I think—to get Evan in front of a lot of his friends and make him admit he believed in the curse."

This threw a new light on the matter, and Rogan asked, "What makes you think so?"

"Because Mr. Frant had gone to the trouble of having the records searched for the original account of the story. He had a copy of it in his pocket. Didn't you know?"

Rogan shook his head, and she went on.

"I think that's what Mr. Frant had been building up to all along. When Evan claimed the story was a lie, Mr. Frant laughed at him and said he was prepared to produce 'the documents in the case.' Then he pulled a thick wad of paper out of his pocket and showed us the seals on it where somebody in England had sworn that it was a true copy of the records and where the parish clerk had sworn that he'd sworn. You could tell that Mr. Frant had taken pains to have it all very official."

"What was in it?"

"I wish I could remember the exact phrasing. It was written in funny, old-fashioned language and it was hard to understand because Mr. Frant read very fast for fear someone would stop him before he got through. Besides he didn't know how to pronounce all the words, so you couldn't be sure just what he was talking about."

"That was the paper Evan burned?"

"Yes. I don't blame him, of course, but I wish he hadn't. We might know a whole lot more about things if we had time to study what it said."

"Wait a minute." Rogan rose. "How long were you in the dining room after the paper went in the fire?"

"Not over a minute or two. Why?"

"And would the servants start cleaning up right away?"

Sue's eyes gleamed.

"Oh, I see what you mean. Jub put the fire out. He used to work for the Makepeaces, you know, and he always poured water on the fire before he cleared the table even. Do you suppose there's any of the paper left?"

"Depends on the way it was folded."

The girl caught up both candles and ran ahead of him into the dining room. Rogan took the fire tongs and began clearing away the larger chunks of half-burned wood. His previous search had been perfunctory. Now he proceeded with care, moving each section of ash to one side with the shovel before starting on the next.

"Can you make it out even if it's charred black?" Sue asked.

"I'm hoping it won't be. You said the paper was folded. When a man reads something like that he usually puts each page in back of the rest as he finishes it. The creases make the sheets stick closer together and the middle might not have . . . easy now, what's this?"

"That's it! That's it!"

"Evidently, but don't get excited. If this comes to pieces in our hands, where will be we?"

Gingerly he brushed off the ashes and then lifted the blackened wad of paper in his finger tips. It still presented a solid bulk which promised well for the legibility of the inner pages.

Sue brought a huge Sheffield tray from the sideboard and set it on the table.

"Here, use this to work on and you won't get things messy."

"Thanks, and could I have a couple of table knives? These sheets are stuck together. I'll need something to separate them."

While the girl rummaged in a drawer, Rogan examined his find. It was in better condition than he had dared hope. An inch had been burned from the top and bottom of each page, and the first and last sheets were damaged past saving by any means at their command. The rest, however, was quite legible even by candlelight and needed nothing but an occasional guess at the letters that formed the end of any unusually long line.

"Can you read it?" Sue asked.

"Yes, but it begins in the middle, so we can't tell who wrote it."

"I remember that. It was a Roman Catholic priest named Father Zachary. He lived near the old Faulkland place in Wales, right after James the Second got kicked out of England. I don't think priests were very popular in those days, but nobody seems to have bothered him. What's the first part you can make out?"

She looked over Rogan's shoulder and read a few words.

"There isn't much missing. Just something about how he heard rumors that some ancestor of Evan's was experimenting in alchemy."

With their heads almost touching, they bent over the charred script.

. . . nor could any one be perswaded to suspect the said Humphrey Faulkland, for he, as magistrate of the island of Penarn, had himself been instrumental in hunting down and destroying no less than seven of these wretches. However, as I learned later, he had fallen into this temptation through mischance, for when the men returned from the taking of the warlok Ullworthy, they brought back with them his books dealing with art magicall and also his instruments, thinking they might serve as evidence against him. Now the night after Ullworthy was burned, the magistrate took the warloks papers into his closet, thinking to destroy them in the hearth fire, and so rid the world of such pestilent writings. Yet it chanced that the first volume he chose was one he had not before examined, and as he started to cast it into the flame it did fall open at a certain page revealing somewhat of the secrets of the damnable art called alchimie. Now this Humphrey Faulkland, the magistrate, was a great miser, and the thought tempted him that here in his fingers lay the means whereby he might inrich himself, nor did he give thought to his immortal soul, but on a sudden began to read the said book . . .

"I don't think what's missing there is important," Sue remarked as Rogan gently freed the top page from the rest and moved it to one side. "Just something about the early experiments."

. . . his fell unlawfull purpose, so that he sank ever deeper into the mire, passing from alchimie to witchcraft, and from thence to things still more foul until at last he did not scruple to stoop to the awful depths of necromancy it self and call back the souls of the dead, yet never could his thirst for gold be appeased.

All this I learned from the baylife Levan who did tell me of it in the very chamber where I write these words. Yet altho' in his Relation the said Levan did admit to commerce with things Infernal, yet could he not be perswaded to make his confession to me in due form, being an heretick Calvinist, and was only brought to seek me out through the extremity of his terror.

Now the manner of my participation fell about in this wise. Shortly before dawn on the morning of Jun. 30th, being Saturday, I was roused by an huge noise as of one pounding on my door and crying aloud, and there was a great storm of rain without, so that I was sorely wondered that I had not been before awakened by the noise of the water. And as I did approach the door I heard the voice of a man calling on me for Christs sake to unbar it as he was in terror of his soul. So I opened the door and to my great surprize beheld that Levan that was Baylife to Sir Humphrey. Albeit I was hard put to recognize the man, for he had come on foot and his cloaths were so ruined with the mud and the water and his face so distorted . . .

. . . for that I was the only Priest on the island either Catholick or Heretick. For although I have not been permitted to practice the rituals of the Faith publiquely since his Majesty the King fled the country, nevertheless here in this remote place I am unmolested. And when I asked the baylife Levan why he had not sought the viccar on the mainland, he did reply that he would not cross water, no, not though his soul were damned through consorting with a Priest and a Papist. For such strange phancies has Heresie bred up in these people that they believe a True Priest to be a worse thing than the Fiend himself. So . . .

The beginning of the next page was so badly charred that Rogan had to spell it out letter by letter.

. . . affrighted of a spirit Elementary of the sort called Undens, such as do inhabit watery places . . .

He looked up at Sue. "Any idea what an unden is?"

"That's just an old way of spelling 'undine.' "

"It couldn't mean he was afraid of a water fairy!"

"Undines aren't fairies. They're 'elementals'—what he calls 'spirits elementary.' They are supposed to be subhuman and some of them are pretty horrible."

"Don't tell me you're an authority on this sort of thing?"

"Oh, no, but Uncle Arnold is, and he had a lot of books about it." Sue gestured toward the close-packed shelves. "I got interested in them one summer when I was about fourteen. All I can remember is snatches. Go on reading. I think this is where he tells about elementals."

. . . And when I did reproach him saying that spirits submundane have no existence, being but phancy and fable, nor are they to be found mentioned in Holy Writ, he did answer me that with his own eyes he had seen not one but two such spirits, a male and a female, and that not five nights since, only he did add that these daemons, for such I believe them truly to have been, were not Undens but were rather Sylphs of the air, and of these he said he was not too greatly affraide having been born near Helvellyn and being accustomed to the crags of that Mountain, for it was his belief that no one who could stand on great heights without giddiness need fear the Elementaries of the air, as indeed he claimed to have proved in his own person. But it is well that you should have this part of his Relation in his own words:

"I, Jonas Levan, being Baylife to Sir Humphrey Faulkland . . ."

"Apparently," Rogan remarked, "Father Zachary wasn't taking any chances of having Levan go back on his story."

"You can't blame him. Wait till you read it."

". . . and when my Master had explained these things to me I said him yea, never the less was I sore affraide and would only consent that he might evoke the Sylphs of the air, for it seemed to me that as a cragsman I might stand some chance with them although none at all with the Others. So my having agreed, albeit unwillingly, my Master did bid me accompany him into his closet and did disclose to me a trap-door cleverly contrived in the floor which I had hitherto took to be entirely of well-mortared stone. And on raising this trap-door he did disclose a chamber subterraneal some five ells in bigness, but whether it had aforetime been a priests hole or a dungeon he did not say. Then he had me to descend and I saw that the walls of the chamber were lined with shelves and benches, having upon them magicall instruments and globes of glass of divers curious shapes, and there were likewise furnaces for heating these things, but there were no windows in that room . . .

". . . and dipping it in the blood did draw upon the floor squares of some nine feet bigness, one within the other, and did make crosses and other holy signs between them. And within these squares he mark't two circles and within these yet two more squares and did write the whole all over with crosses and with Holy Words, and in the eight corners did put the names of God. Then did he light candles, the tallow of which was (as he told me) made from human fat and scented with church incense, and he let put one of these candles in each of the corners and bad me stand beside him in the innermost square. This was I loath to do, yet he exhorted me saying that the figure was to be our fortress, for no thing unchristened could pass by the lines and the crosses nor by the holy words which he had written. And when I had joyned him therein he took a little whip or besom which he called an aspergillum, and it was made in this manner that the ends thereof were twigs of vervain, basil, and other plants tied to a handle piece of hazel wood with a thread drawn from the shroud of a man hanged. This he did use by dipping it in . . ."

Instead of going on with the next page, Kincaid turned to the girl.

"It seems to me that we may be attaching too much importance to this story. I didn't know Frant well, but even in the short time I was with him he showed a really remarkable talent for drawing the long bow. I've met my share of home-grown Munchausens, but Jackson B. was way ahead of the field."

Sue touched the manuscript.

"You think he made this up?"

"It would be right in his line. I met Frant on shipboard and he regaled the smoking room with a collection of tall tales I've never heard bettered. One of them was a rather vague description of the Faulkland curse. It sounded then as if he invented the story as he went along. Maybe he did, and this is just a fancy version."

The girl shook her head.

"I don't believe Mr. Frant could have gotten this up, even without the clerk's signature and the seals and things. Whoever wrote this knew what he was talking about, and Mr. Frant . . . wasn't very well educated. There are lots of things here he wouldn't have even heard of . . . the way the diagram on the floor was laid out, for instance, with its squares and circles."

"That's orthodox, is it?"

"I think so. I'm certain I've read about it. Besides, later on Father Zachary talks about some pieces of apparatus that must have been used in alchemy. Most of the names were words I never heard."

"Maybe Frant made them up, too."

"Not words like these. They wouldn't have sounded right. Go on reading. You'll see."

". . . and when he had repeated this Invocation the third time and used the rest of the consecrated salt in the damnable manner I have mentioned I heard a noise like to the rushing of a great wind, which was a marvel seeing we were below the earth and there were no windows in the chamber. And with the wind came a voice as it were of silver bells tinkling, and immediately there stood before us a lady of the most singular beautie I have ever beheld, and on her left wrist she carried a pigeon or other white bird, but save for that she was naked.

"And in spite of the beautie of this vision I was sore affrighted at seeing her, knowing her to be a thing damned and unnatural, and in my affrightment I did step backward until I was like to move completely out of the figure my Master had traced on the floor, and would have done so had he not caught me and pointed over my shoulder. And when I turned and look't, I felt the palms of my hands go clammy and my tongue grew cold in my mouth, for behind me within an ells distance was another of these daemons, save that it was a male of them and as horrid to behold as the female was beautiful, and it was about the bigness of a yoke of oxen. And when I saw how near my steps had carried me to the edge of the barrier, and that one more would have brought me within reach of the male daemon, I fell down in a swound from sheer terror so that my Master had much ado to drag me back into the centre square again. And when I awoke . . .

". . . blaming his failure to do so on my swounding. But afterward he did admit to me that he had controlled these spirits as he would but could get no gold of them, such not being in their power which holds only over airs and things vaporous. The same was, as he said, true of the fire spirits which some call Salamanders and others Aetneans which are igneous and unsubstantial in their nature. Nor was there any hope that he could command the Gnomes (which are spirits of earth) in this matter, sithence they detest of all things in men covetousness and greed, for that these qualities are very common among themselves. Remained only the Undens or Water Daemons, which have treasure in plenty from ships sunken and the like. However the Sylphs which he had conjured did warn him that if he were timid in water or of a cold irresolute nature, he would never master the Undens, the which was of especial import since these watery beings are the most dangerous of all their kind . . .

". . . did flatly refuse to assist him for I have all my life had a great terror of water, so much so that I cannot abide to pass over it (be it ever so little) without fear and sickness. Furthermore I did remind him of the warning he had received, how no one of cold nature dared meddle with these beings lest they engulf him.

"And for four days my Master seemed to have given over his diabolick practices, yet yester eve when he saw the great rain there was (for such weathers are auspicious to these things) his covetousness did so get the better of him that he did descend alone into his laboratory, thinking the risk light when set against the great plenty of treasure he did hope to gain.

"Now this was at 11 h. P.M. and shortly after midnight I heard a noise as it were of water lapping about the piles of a wharf, and this although the manor house is from the sea a furlong and more in distance. And all the while the sound grew greater and the whole house trembled and shook until at last it pitched like a ship on an angry sea. Then on a sudden I heard Sir Humphrey cry once and once only, yet the terror of that cry was such as to bring the cold sweat out on my body so that my cloaths were wet through tho' I was at that time well covered from the rain, and . . .

". . . stench as of carrion and of decaying fish so that I dared not go into the closet."

And when the said Baylife, Levan, had finished telling me these things he did beg me with many and piteous cries to return with him to the manor house and exorcize this daemon, lest after battening on Sir Humphrey (as he made no doubt it had) it should ravage the countryside.

And I have determined to yield to his entreaty for altho' I am forbidden by their Majesties' law to carry out the offices of the True Faith yet it seemeth best to me that I should suffer in my own person rather than that the people of this island should be left at the mercy of woeful monsters. And I have written this in my chamber before accompanying the said Baylife to the Manor, sithence the business I go upon is mischancy. For altho' I bear about me the Holy Crucifix and Blessed Relics yet no man knoweth his end, and if it should chance . . .

Rogan lifted the page and placed it with the others he had read.

"There was nothing wrong with Father Zachary's courage, anyway. Did he write the rest of this after he came back?"

"Yes. Go on."

. . . thereafter. Nor could we in any way endure that the trap-door should be opened but were forced to give over all that day. But on the next day, being the Feast of the Most Prescious Blood, we did open the trap and I did descend by a little ladder so strait that I was hard put to it to maintain myself and to carry the Holy Candles and the other things needful.

Now I could see by the light of the Holy Candles the fashion of that chamber. And it was filled with unlawful instruments such as alembicks, matraces, athanors, and the like, but all much ruined and destroyed by the visitation, for they were tumbled about and broken and moreover covered with a thick silvery slime as if sea slugs had been in the place. And there was markt on the floor a diagram or pentacle so besmeared and trampled upon that I could not discover the shape thereof nor read the signs that were written in its corners. Neither could I at first, in the meager light of the candles (for there were no windows in the place) make out the body of him who had brought this horror on himself, yet at last I did see in a corner, nigh hidden by one of the overturned benches, a great mugger of bones and slime, like a cast from an owl's stomach. But when I would approach nearer a spider ran out at me, having already built her nest in the skull. Yet did . . .

. . . exorcism was finished and I would have sought the ladder again my foot slipt on something soft so that I fell, having all I could do to keep the Holy Candles alight. And it was in this manner that I did come to see what was written on the floor of that chamber, eaten into the stone as if by sea worms:

"Od claims the Sire and shall repaye the Sonne
And thy Sonne's Sonne until thy Race be runne."

And altho' I looked a long time in hope to discover some trace of the letter 'G' before the first word of this inscription yet could I never do so, wherefore I am convinced that the said word is not 'God' but 'Od' only and is the name of this daemon, which is . . .

Rogan took a deep breath.

"That seems to be all that's left of Father Zachary's story," he said. "The next page is copied from a letter by someone else, and I still don't see where the curse comes in."

"Don't you understand? That's what the verses mean. Od was some sort of undine. He killed Sir Humphrey and then promised to repay his descendants. I think the letter tells about it."

Rogan read:

. . . copied out of a letter written in 1793 by one Samuel Ilverston of Ruthin which is within twenty miles of the island of Penarn where the Faulklands had their seat. Ilverston, after a long dissertation on the curse, holds its hereditary character to be abundantly proved and cites the following instances:

"It is well known and attested by many witnesses then living that Evan, the son born to the said Humphrey after his death, did curse one Wat Yenning a tanner who did thereupon fall down and was found to be dead. Whereupon the said Evan being a magistrate and the sole law in Penarn did cause him to be placed in a coffin quickly, and buried that same day for fear (as he pretended) of the plague. Yet in spite of such unseemly haste the pallbearers could scarce perform their duties being overcome with sickness by reason of . . ."

". . . also, and this is attested by divers respectable witnesses whom I have myself known and talked with, there can be no doubt that Humphrey, grandson of the said Evan and great-grandson of the first Humphrey did blasphemously and impiously curse one Home Tarver a carter saying 'Od rot you,' whereupon . . ."

The rest of the page was so damaged by both fire and water that Rogan could make nothing of it, and the two remaining sheets were mere charred fragments.

He sat back in his chair. So that was the full story of the Faulkland curse. It was easy to see how the thing had gripped Frant's imagination, and the imagination of everyone else in the house apparently, since they all seemed bent on talking about it. In their case, the story must have gained an added force from the fact that the little man had read it to them shortly before his death. The eerie atmosphere of that ancient, stone-walled house might even have persuaded them that there was some far-fetched relationship between the curse and the death itself. That would explain this girl's strange attitude and the hesitancy with which the others spoke of their late host. It even explained Nancy's faint. Well, the quicker that nonsense got straightened out the better. There were other things to worry about. He looked up at Sue.

"I think you are wrong to trace a connection between this legend and Frant's death. He wasn't descended from old Humphrey Faulkland, so he could hardly have inherited the curse. In fact"—Rogan was to remember afterward that he had laughed a little—"even if the story is true, it couldn't have affected Frant unless his half brother cursed him and he dropped down dead."

The last heat from the long-extinguished fire had gone now and the room was cold. Outside the storm howled itself away to the southward. A voice spoke from the doorway.

"You didn't know then, did you? That's exactly the way it happened."

4

The Conjuration of the Four

"EVAN!"

Sue moved swiftly to the man in the doorway.

"Thanks." He took her hand for a moment. "Don't worry about me. I'm going outside—just couldn't stick it in my room any longer."

"I'll come with you."

"Right. The rain's stopped." He seemed suddenly to remember Rogan's presence and walked forward. "You're Kincaid, aren't you?"

Evan had changed from the formal attire he must have worn at dinner, and his big body was clad in gray flannels. In the glow of the candles his face looked like a badly made waxwork.

"I'm glad you managed to live through the storm. Let us hope you find The Kraken equally harmless."

Rogan shrugged. " 'From ghosts, and bogies, and things that go bump in the night—good Lord deliver us.' "

"Quite. I don't blame you for being skeptical. You didn't see my brother die."

"I haven't even found out *how* he died. No one here talks about anything else, but when they come to the point they all sidestep."

"That's because the thing was so damned impossible they don't believe it themselves, even though they watched it with their own eyes. All the same, you have a right to know." Evan turned to the girl. "Tell him, Sue."

"But you—"

"Don't worry about me. I want to hear your story, too. Do you think it does me any good to keep wondering if I'm crazy, because what I saw couldn't have happened?"

"I told you how Mr. Frant acted during dinner," Sue began hesitantly to Rogan. "Afterward we went into the living room. I made Evan go over to the piano with me, and Aunt Julia tried to keep Mr. Frant away from us by persuading him to play bridge. It didn't work. Pretty soon he left the card table and came over to where we were. He started right in talking about the curse again. I told him to stop making so much fuss about a stupid legend. Mr. Frant said he hoped it was *only* a legend, because if it wasn't, Evan had a taint in his blood and shouldn't get married."

Sue colored and glanced at Tethryn, who had picked up the charred manuscript and started to read it. He gave no sign of having heard her, and she continued.

"Evan flared up then and asked Mr. Frant if he wanted the curse tried on him. I could see Mr. Frant didn't like that, but he'd gotten too far into the argument to draw back. He pretended to laugh and said he'd be glad to offer himself in the cause of science. I don't remember what Evan's answer was—something with 'bloody' in it, because Mr. Frant laughed again and said, 'The real curse, my boy, not just silly British swear words.' "

She broke off and glanced at Evan. This time he spoke.

"Tell Kincaid all of it."

"He said . . ." Sue gulped. " 'By God, you've asked for it and here it is. *Od rot you, Jack! Od rot you!* ' "

The girl took a deep breath and shuddered. She was silent for so long that Rogan asked, "What happened then?"

"Mr. Frant died."

Kincaid stared at her. "But surely there must have been something else?"

Evan laughed harshly. "There wasn't anything else. My brother"—he looked down at the manuscript—" 'did thereupon fall down and was found to be dead.' "

Rogan had no answer for that. There was none.

A flare of light caught his eye, and he looked up to see that Evan had crumpled one of the pages of the manuscript and touched it to the candle flame.

"Don't do that."

"Why not? Everyone on the island has seen this thing, and nobody else has a right to. Do you think I like having it around?" Evan tossed the burning paper to the hearth and began dropping the other sheets on the flame one by one. He glanced at Sue.

"If we're going outside, you'd best get a coat."

"I won't take a minute." She smiled at him for encouragement and was gone.

Evan stood watching the fire that grew as each added bit of paper caught. Finally he spoke.

"It's hard for us to realize what a curse really is. We get all mixed up with profanity and oaths and just plain bad language, until we can't even think of a curse in its original meaning—as a prayer, or a command, to some stronger power for evil."

Rogan nodded. "I see what you mean, but that part is over. Yet you seem to feel there is still danger here. Why?"

"Once a force is set free it may be impossible to control."

"Come now. I can understand why your brother's death leads you to believe in the efficacy of the curse, but why attribute the working of that curse to the power of some evil spirit called Od?"

Evan shivered. "I wouldn't name it if I were you."

The Welsh undertones in his voice had grown stronger. He fed the last sheets of the manuscript to the flame and straightened up, wiping his fingers on his handkerchief.

"You don't believe in elementals?"

"There is a storm outside," Rogan said. "We are shut off from the rest of the world, and the candles people this house with shadows. Under such conditions it is easy to believe anything."

"It's not only that. Come, I'll show you." Evan swung on his heel and walked into the library. Rogan followed. The earl stopped before a section of the book-lined walls and held his candle high.

"Look. There must be two hundred volumes here on transcendentalism. They were written over a period of three centuries, and the newer works are as numerous as the old. The authors are French, English, German, Russian, American—yet they all treat elementals as an established fact. There *must* be more to it than storm and lonely houses and shadow."

Evan handed his candle to Rogan. Then he chose a thin blue volume from the shelves and flicked over its pages.

"This is Waite's *The Occult Sciences.*"

He began to read:

Amidst the superstition, the stupidity, the malice, and perversity of goetic experiments, we may recognize the existence of one central truth, which is of great importance in rational mysticism, the existence of a class of intelligences in the extramundane spheres, whose natures are gross, formless, and undeveloped, or have been developed along the lines of that intense spiritual malice which is commonly identified with the essential nature of devils.

Rogan shrugged. "Do you remember your Shakespeare? 'I can call spirits from the vasty deep.' 'Why, so can I, or so can any man; but will they come?' "

"The question is: will they go?"

"But surely, man, even if elementals exist, even if you have called one up, it must be possible to exorcise it."

"Possible, yes." Evan slid the Waite volume back in its place and selected a translation of Eliphas Lévi's *Dogme et Rituel de la Haute Magie.* "But the ceremonial is elaborate and very difficult—listen."

When an elementary spirit torments the inhabitants of this world, it must be conjured by air, water, fire, and earth; by breathing, sprinkling, burning of perfumes; and by tracing on the ground the Star of Solomon and the Sacred Pentagram. These figures must be perfectly correct and drawn either with the charcoal of consecrated fire or with a reed dipped in various colors, mixed with powdered loadstone. Then, holding the Pantacle of Solomon in one hand and taking up successively the sword, rod and cup, the Conjuration of the Four should be recited with a loud voice, after the following manner:

Caput mortuum, the Lord command thee by the living and votive serpent!
Cherub, the Lord command thee by Adam Jotchavah!
Wandering Eagle, the Lord command thee by the wings of the Bull!
Serpent, the Lord Tetragrammaton command thee by the angel and the lion!
Michael, Gabriel, Raphael and Anael!
Flow, Moisture, by the spirit of Eloïm.
Earth, be established by Adam Jotchavah.
Spread, Firmament, by Jahuvehu, Zebaoth.
Fulfil, Judgment, by fire in the virtue of Michael.
Angel of the blind eyes, obey, or pass away with this holy water! . . .

The sound of Sue's return interrupted the reading. Evan slipped the book back on its shelf and turned to greet her. She had changed to a sports dress of soft blue and thrown a light coat around her shoulders. Her clothes were of a deceptive simplicity that spoke of fine materials and perfect fashioning. Kincaid made a mental note that the Braxtons had escaped the financial reverses which had come to Makepeace.

He waited until the sound of the heavy outer door told him they had left the house, and then sauntered into the living room. As he did so, a door situated on the far side of the fireplace, and evidently leading to the kitchen, opened. Miss Makepeace entered, bearing a tray with cups and a steaming urn of coffee.

"I'm glad to see you alone," Rogan greeted her. "Maybe you'll tell why you've been holding out on me."

She proffered the tray.

"I'm not holding out. Have some?"

"Thanks. Does Od take his black?"

Miss Makepeace looked at him sharply and asked, "Who told you—Sue?"

"And Lord Tethryn."

"I'm glad. The silence idea was my brother's. He's a lawyer and it sometimes goes to his head. The situation is . . . difficult, and I believe he wanted to clear up where we stood before talking to a stranger."

"What was I supposed to think in the meanwhile?"

"Nothing as bad as the reality, I assure you. What happened here tonight didn't leave much scope for exaggeration."

Julia Makepeace set her tray on a low table before the sofa and began to pour the coffee.

"I'm glad you know," she repeated. "We were all too upset to think clearly, and I welcome a chance to talk to an outsider."

"You'll never have better chance or cleaner straw," Rogan assured her. "I'm just the outsider you've been looking for. What's your explanation of Frant's death?"

"I haven't one. I keep telling myself the whole thing was only a horrible coincidence, and I try to keep away from the shadows." She shuddered. "I'm not usually imaginative, believe me, but none of us are normal tonight. There's my brother, for example. He's interested in spiritualism. He calls it psychical research, but that's what it amounts to. I expected him to claim what happened tonight as final proof of a spirit world. I almost wish he had. Arnold's ghosts have a sort of back-parlor smell about them that makes skepticism easy, but this Od thing terrifies you whether you believe in it or not. Even its name is horrid. I keep wanting to make puns on it, but somehow I'm afraid to."

Rogan picked up his coffee cup.

"What's Mr. Makepeace's explanation?"

"He seems bent on making it natural death—why, I can't guess. I thought at first he was trying to comfort the rest of us, but he's quite serious."

Makepeace came in from the kitchen. He stiffened slightly as his eyes fell on Rogan. "I thought you'd want to go to bed after your involuntary swim, Mr. Kincaid," he began, glancing down at the tray of sandwiches he carried, "and I was about to take your supper to your room."

"There's no use keeping it up, Arnold," his sister cut in dryly. "Evan told him."

The lawyer frowned.

"Lord Tethryn is part Welsh, Mr. Kincaid. His brother's death has brought a strain of native mysticism to the surface, so you must not take his theories too seriously."

"I'm surprised to hear you say that. Your sister gave me the impression you were a believer in the spirit world."

"I am convinced of human survival. That is a scientifically established fact, but this transcendental drivel about elementals is another matter entirely."

"Perhaps. But if Frant's friend Od didn't crawl out of somewhere and smother him, how did he die?"

Makepeace turned to his sister.

"You see? There it is again. Everyone seems bent on making a mystery of the thing." He swung back to Rogan. "My dear sir, Frant's death was, as I told you, apoplexy—or perhaps heart failure —brought on by shock. Such instances are common. Even the dramatic elements of this one were duplicated in New York some years ago."

Rogan nodded. "I remember that. It was in the *Times*. Some crazy fellow thought he was God. He picked on a perfect stranger and launched a curse at him. The man had a weak heart and died on the spot."

"Exactly. The case was on all fours with what happened here," the lawyer continued. "If it had not been for the storm no one would have questioned it. The storm set the mood. It put the electrical system out of commission and forced us to use candles. Ordinarily The Kraken is a very pleasant place. Tonight it looks like the Castle of Otranto, simply because of the weather. That turned a perfectly ordinary death into a howling melodrama and made us all behave like lunatics. There was nothing mysterious about the way Frant died. His heart gave out. You can take my word for it."

"Thanks," replied his sister. "I'd rather have Stirling's. Here he comes now."

Makepeace looked up and saw the old doctor descend the stairs from the gallery above.

"Ah, Stirling, we've been waiting for you. Please tell Julia that Frant's death was perfectly natural."

Dr. Braxton looked into the faces around the fire—Makepeace precise and self-confident, his sister tense under her surface calm, Rogan dark and enigmatic. The old doctor answered:

"I can't do that."

Makepeace's poise slipped.

"'Come now, Stirling," he protested, "don't tell me I'm going to have to argue with you, too."

"I'm not the one you'll have to argue with. There are others."

Dead silence followed that. It was as if a moving-picture film had caught in its track, leaving each shadow figure stopped in the chance position of the moment.

From somewhere in back of Rogan a voice said:

"Maybe he was poisoned."

The group around the fire jumped. The film had suddenly started again. Mr. Kincaid turned more slowly than the others and saw behind him the missing member of the party.

It would have been impossible to imagine anything more at variance with an atmosphere of black magic than the figure that met his eyes. The newcomer was a youth who might have been over twenty but who certainly did not look it. He was clad in a white mess-jacket the tailoring of which was a poem in pure mathematics, and a varnish of taffy-colored hair topped his cherubic face. His upper lip sported what was probably a mustache.

Makepeace was violently annoyed.

"You must forgive my nephew, Mr. Kincaid. His name is Bobby Chatterton, and I'm afraid he is rather given to startling people."

The boy was overcome with embarrassment.

"I'm sorry," he stammered. "I didn't think . . ."

"Don't let that stop you from making suggestions," his aunt encouraged him. "The rest of us don't."

"Speak for yourself," Makepeace retorted. "Do you realize that what Bobby said was tantamount to a statement that Frant was murdered?"

"Of course," she answered cheerfully. "And speaking for myself, I admit I'd rather have a nice sane murder than this ghost talk we've been indulging in. What is your diagnosis, Stirling?"

It was a long time before the doctor answered.

"I wish I could share Arnold's belief that Mr. Frant's death was natural. I'm afraid it wasn't."

Makepeace threw up his hands.

"You're the last man on earth I expected that from! Good God, Stirling, you might as well throw away your science and take to exorcism."

Dr. Braxton raised troubled eyes to his friend's face.

"I'm afraid," he said, "that no exorcism will help us now."

With that the talk died. The flickering candles peopled the room with twisting shadows that seemed more alive than the figures huddled in front of the fireplace. The old doctor was the first to break the silence.

"Please don't think I have reached any conclusions. I haven't . . . except that I feel sure Arnold's hypothesis of natural death is untenable."

"But, Stirling," the lawyer protested, "a man doesn't die from a curse!"

"You're forgetting Bobby's theory," the doctor reminded him. "I'm not an expert, and it's been years since I saw a case, but our host's symptoms were not inconsistent with cyanide poisoning."

"So that's what you've been getting at!" Makepeace accused. "Murder! That's as wild as this curse nonsense. I grant you no one here was attracted to Frant, but we'd hardly have poisoned him. We'd have had no motive. Most of us never saw the man before today! Your diagnosis must be faulty."

"I hope it is. Unfortunately, I'm not the one you have to convince. Murchison, the coroner's physician, may be a drunkard but he's no fool. I'm very much afraid that when I describe the symptoms to him, he'll put the death down to one of the cyanides."

"Preposterous."

"I'm no lexicologist," the doctor shrugged, "but there are other poisons almost as fast as cyanide—oxalic acid, for instance . . . or nicotine. I believe pure nicotine has been known to kill in less than a minute."

"My point does not rest on the nature of the poison," Makepeace persisted. "Frant could not have been poisoned at all. A slow poison would have shown preliminary symptoms and a fast one is completely out of the question. There was no possible way in which Frant could have gotten any foreign substance whatever into his system in the five or ten minutes before he died. He didn't eat or drink in that time and he wasn't smoking. He didn't touch anything. He didn't come within six feet of any of us. The poison idea is simply untenable."

As the lawyer's voice went on in the intricacies of detailed argument, Kincaid's attention wandered to Bobby. The boy had filled a cup with coffee and seemed to be engaged in dipping a half dollar into the liquid.

Rogan leaned over and asked in a low voice what he was doing. Bobby seemed pleased to be noticed. He held the silver disk horizontally between the ends of his fingers and lowered it carefully to the surface of the coffee. He whispered back:

"I'm just . . . that is, I'm trying to make it float."

Mr. Kincaid's limited capacity for surprise was exhausted.

"Think you can?"

"If the coffee's hot enough."

Rogan could not decide how heat was supposed to affect the buoyancy of the coin, but he continued to watch.

"It's hot enough," Bobby announced. He took his hand away carefully. The silver seemed to rest on the liquid.

"It'll float," he explained, "as long as the coffee's hotter than the money." The half dollar began to sink slowly, and he added: "But silver doesn't stay cool long, and then . . ." He pointed to the coin which settled sidewise like a foundering ship and disappeared from sight.

The boy looked up and saw that Makepeace had stopped talking and that the eyes of the whole group now followed the demonstration.

The lawyer, annoyed at having his audience distracted, apologized again.

"You mustn't pay any attention to Bobby, Mr. Kincaid. He'll bore you to death with his parlor tricks if you let him."

"Sorry." His nephew fished the half dollar out of the cup with his spoon and wiped it on his handkerchief. "I was just trying to work out something."

The phrase puzzled Rogan. Then an explanation of the boy's meaning occurred to him and he hinted at it.

"Lots of us need things like that to help our brains work. I know one man who juggles Indian clubs when he's thinking."

Bobby fingered his mustache.

"It's not like that exactly." He looked up, saw that his uncle had started talking again, and continued in a whisper. "It's more like a . . . sort of . . . diagram." He dipped the spoon into the coffee again and brought up a crumb of sugar. "You see"—Bobby reddened guiltily—"that part about the temperature wasn't true. I stood a lump of sugar on the bottom of the cup when you weren't looking. The coffee hid it. Then all I had to do was to balance the half dollar on the sugar . . ."

He paused, evidently flustered at having made such a long speech. Rogan finished it for him.

"And when the sugar dissolved, the money sank. What's that a diagram of—ghosts floating around?"

"Well, no . . . I wasn't thinking about the floating. I was . . . well, that is, it was the sinking. I mean the sugar didn't make the money float. It just kept it from sinking as soon as it would without it. Like the poison Uncle Arnold's talking about."

Bobby's words were vague, but Rogan thought he saw the idea behind them. He waited until Makepeace, who was still arguing the impossibility of poison, paused for effect, and then asked a question.

"What happened to Frant after he died?"

"Eh? What's that?"

"I mean, was the curse fulfilled literally? My information was not very specific, but I certainly gathered that the words called less for death than for dissolution."

Miss Makepeace caught her breath, but only Rogan noticed it, perhaps because her brother's crow of triumph followed so quickly.

"Thanks, Mr. Kincaid. That point quashes the curse theory, anyway. The body was all right when Evan carried it upstairs . . ." Suddenly his jaw dropped, and he turned to stare at the doctor. "Good God, Stirling! It *was* all right, wasn't it?"

5

The Case of M. Valdemar

DR. BRAXTON looked at his friend's startled face for a moment and then smiled gently. "You needn't worry about that, Arnold. There's nothing wrong with the body."

"Still," Miss Makepeace remarked, "we mustn't expect a curse to be carried out to the letter. After all, if a man is dead he's as good as . . ."

"For heaven's sake, Julia," her brother interrupted, "must you talk like that?"

"You're quite right, Arnold. I'm sorry. Nerves."

"Mr. Chatterton"—Rogan indicated Bobby—"has an interesting suggestion . . ."

"Nonsense!" The lawyer grasped at normalcy. "The boy never had an idea in his life."

"He has just pointed out," Kincaid went on smoothly, "how Mr. Frant could have been poisoned."

"What's that?" Makepeace sputtered.

"Simply this. You say that in the ten minutes before he died, Frant couldn't have taken a poison strong enough to account for his rapid death."

"Don't tell me Bobby thinks he did."

"Oh, no, but he suggests that the action of the poison might have been delayed by some timing device. Suppose the poison were disguised as medicine, say in a gelatin capsule. If Frant took one ten minutes before his death, the poison would not become effective until the gelatin dissolved in his stomach. Then it would hit him all at once."

"Mr. Frant went upstairs right after dinner," Bobby added diffidently. "I mean, he might have taken some medicine then. People sometimes do . . . take medicine after dinner."

"As a matter of fact, Frant did just that," Rogan confirmed. "I had supper with him in New York three days ago. He carried a box of capsules in his pocket and took one a few minutes after he'd finished eating."

Miss Makepeace turned to the doctor. "Is there anything in the idea, Stirling? Would it work that way?"

"Not with an ordinary gelatin capsule, certainly. The gelatin would dissolve almost instantly in the stomach, which is why many physicians prefer such capsules to the tablets druggists like to sell us these days."

"But isn't there some sort of preparation," Rogan insisted, "that will keep the gelatin from dissolving so fast?"

"I was coming to that. There are several, of which salol is perhaps the best known. Such a coating would probably pass unnoticed."

"Oh come, Stirling," the lawyer interrupted, "can't you see you are giving Mr. Kincaid a false impression by discussing the details of a suggestion which is inherently impossible." He frowned at Rogan. "You seem to have formed the idea that Frant was cursed and that some time later he died. Even that would have been a sufficiently remarkable coincidence, but actually he was stricken immediately. I doubt if as much as a single second elapsed between the time the curse left Tethryn's lips and the beginning of the agony that killed his brother. It was as if the words had been bullets."

Makepeace sipped his coffee and then continued.

"You must understand that the unlikelihood of Frant's death from poison coinciding with the curse increases enormously as the time element is shortened. If he had died an hour afterward it would have been striking enough. If the time interval had been only five minutes it would have been almost a miracle. But that any device, such as the poison capsule you mention, could have taken effect at the exact moment of the curse is beyond belief."

"I doubt if that line of reasoning applies here," Dr. Braxton objected. "God knows I don't want this to turn out to be a murder case any more than the rest of you do, but it never does any good to dodge facts. The idea that Frant was stricken with an attack of some sort at the precise moment of the curse involves exactly the same coincidence as the poison theory, with the additional disadvantage that the symptoms indicate poison rather than heart failure."

Makepeace found a flaw in the old doctor's argument.

"I submit that if Frant died of shock there is no need to consider coincidence at all. The curse itself would have operated psychologically to bring on an attack. Mr. Kincaid just cited a case where that very thing happened."

"If you're looking for likely explanations," Julia Makepeace contributed, "why not consider suicide?"

"Nonsense. No one would kill himself like that."

"Nonsense, yourself," his sister retorted. "Suicides do the most frightful things to themselves. Look at Portia."

"What did she do?" asked Bobby. "That is, I didn't know Portia killed herself."

"She didn't—not the one you mean," snapped his aunt. "I'm talking about the Portia who married Brutus."

"The *et tu* Brutus?"

"Exactly. She died from swallowing red-hot coals one after the other."

"I know how that's done," said the boy.

"How what's done?"

"Swallowing hot coals, like they do in the circus."

"The suicide theory solves the timing problem," put in Rogan hastily. "It's not hard to think of a method by which he could have controlled the exact moment of his death. For instance, he might have smeared his lips with poison and licked them right after he was cursed. But you'll have difficulty finding a motive. Frant was rich . . ."

"Rich?" snorted Miss Makepeace. "The man was bankrupt."

Mr. Kincaid permitted himself to display surprise.

"But he owned this house . . ."

"Which," she interrupted dryly, "will hardly bring enough to clear the mortgage."

"Julia is right," her brother agreed. "I need scarcely add that the news of Frant's insolvency was as startling to us as to you."

"How did you find out?" Rogan asked.

"He told us himself at dinner. Oh, he was quite blatant about it, said this party was not costing him a cent. It was all coming out of his creditors."

"It occurs to me," Dr. Braxton remarked, "that nervous bad temper induced by his financial troubles may account for Frant's treatment of Evan tonight. There must be some such explanation, for I remember him as a rather genial person. The same thing might have led him to suicide."

"Possibly," the lawyer conceded, "but even if we accept the bankruptcy motive and Julia's generalization about the indifference of suicides to pain, I can't make out why he should have gone to so much trouble to arrange matters so his death would reflect on his brother. If we can't prove disease or suicide, the thing will hang over the boy as long as he lives."

"I can answer that," said Miss Makepeace. "He was jealous of Evan."

"Nonsense. Frant never saw Sue until yesterday."

His sister smiled dryly.

"Much as I hate to admit it, there are other motives for jealousy besides sex."

"You mean he resented the fact that his younger half brother was a lord?"

"I don't think the title itself had much to do with it, but Mr. Frant must have known in his heart that Evan was the better man. They were both sons of the same mother, yet while Evan inherited his father's characteristics and became a gentleman, Mr. Frant inherited *his* father's characteristics and became a loud-mouthed boor. As long as he was rich and successful he could pretend he didn't mind, but when he no longer had the advantage of wealth he decided to kill himself. There's a Chinese custom of commiting suicide on an enemy's doorstep, so that your ghost will haunt him through life. Something of the sort may have caused Mr. Frant to provide such an elaborate stage setting in the hope that he could work off his spite against his half brother."

Dr. Braxton stared moodily at the coffee in his cup.

"It's a ghastly idea, Julia, but you may be right. If Frant wanted to hurt Evan he could not have found better chance or cleaner straw. The boy believes in the family curse, and we will need real evidence to talk him out of it."

Miss Makepeace nudged the doctor. Rogan looked up to see Sue enter the room with Evan. The walk in the wind had brought a hint of color to the girl's cheeks and Tethryn had lost his waxlike pallor.

Before they could find chairs, Miss Makepeace rose.

"I think," she said, "that we'll all be better for a night's sleep."

"Miss Makepeace is right." Evan looked down at Sue. "You ought to get to bed. You'll need all your strength tomorrow, I'm afraid."

Sue smiled and touched his hand. "What about you?"

"I'll be in my bed almost as soon as you are in yours. I want a drink first, that's all."

They exchanged good-nights. As Evan started for the dining room, Dr. Braxton spoke to Sue in a low voice.

"Miss Garwood isn't feeling well, and Mr. Kincaid gave her his room. He'll have to sleep in her old one. You'd better move her things."

"I'll help, if you like," Rogan offered.

"Thanks. You can carry the bags. I'll call you when they're ready."

Miss Makepeace watched her mount the stairs and then turned to the others. "I'll say good-night, too." She held out her hand. "Don't judge The Kraken till you see it in daylight, Mr. Kincaid, and in the meanwhile I hope you won't be troubled by specters."

He smiled. "As a matter of fact, I welcome the chance to add an ectoplasm to my collection. I already have a splendid assortment of pink elephants, preserved in alcohol."

After Miss Makepeace had gone, the four men waited before the fire for Evan's return. He came carrying a bottle-laden tray.

"I thought the rest of you might want one."

Dr. Braxton shook his head. "Finish yours and let's get to bed. You were right about our needing our strength in the morning."

"I'm not going to bed. The wind has blown itself out and in another hour the sea will be calm enough to risk a crossing to the mainland. I am going back to town and report to the police."

The old doctor shook his head. "I was afraid something of that sort was in your mind. In your place I should want to do the same thing. However, you could not a make a bigger mistake than by walking into a police station tonight and giving your version of what happened here. The desk sergeant would certainly not believe you, but he might lock you in a cell and turn the newspapermen loose on you."

Evan bit his lips.

"I don't expect it to be pleasant."

"It won't be pleasant for Sue, either," Makepeace informed him.

"This has nothing to do with Sue."

"My dear boy," the lawyer insisted, "nothing under heaven can keep her out of it. You are in no danger whatever of being convicted of killing your half brother, but everyone on the island is in real danger of the press. They will print stories about all of us. They will dig open our family graves, and what they cannot find out they will invent."

"I don't want to drag Sue and the rest of you into this mess," replied Evan, "but what can I do? The police have to be told, and sooner or later everything will come out. If I go to the station, I may draw their fire."

"That simply would not work. Our only hope is to have the story break with a minimum of spectacular detail. If you go to the police now, that in itself would be a sensational story."

Dr. Braxton said, "Have you any suggestions, Arnold?"

The lawyer nodded. "Fortunately for us, McArdle, the District Attorney, is out of town on some political business and won't be back until tomorrow afternoon. The assistant in charge is Wade Yeager. Wade used to be in my office and owes me a great many favors. I think I should call him at his home and tell him nothing except that Frant is dead under circumstances which make it impossible for you to give a certificate. I shall ask him to get in touch with the proper police officials tonight and have them come here straight from their homes tomorrow. Whatever official solution they decide on, we may be sure it will not include black magic. In any case, the coroner's physician can give a certificate and we may keep the more spectacular details from reaching the press at all."

"That is a good plan," the doctor agreed. "I'm only afraid the phone isn't connected. The instrument in my room is dead, I know."

"The phones in the bedrooms don't work," said Bobby, "but the one at the switchboard in the pantry is all right."

"So is the one in the library," Makepeace added. "I'll call Wade from there." He turned to Evan. "You'd better come with me in case he wants to talk to you. You too, Stirling."

They left. Rogan leaned back on the sofa and looked at Bobby.

"Are you acquainted with the Hangman's Handyman, by any chance?"

"Who's he?"

"That's what I'd like to find out. He seems to be one of our delightful island fauna—protégé of Miss Makepeace's, I gather."

"Of Aunt Julia's?"

"At least she mentioned him favorably. She was chary of details, but his title is suggestive. I like to imagine him as an amiable and hulking half-wit, with an idiot smile wandering in and out among greenish freckles—and a mouthful of mossy tombstones for teeth."

Bobby shook his head.

"I never heard of him."

Makepeace came back, much pleased with himself.

"Everything is arranged." He rubbed his hands. "Yeager will have the police leave Bailey's Point at daybreak without reporting to headquarters. That will get them here around seven and put us a day ahead of the news-papers."

Rogan stood up. "Where are the others?"

"Lord Tethryn felt he should notify Frant's only other relative, a cousin, I believe. At least his name is Frant, too."

Evan returned with the old doctor, and Makepeace asked, "Did you get him?"

"Yes. John's not coming to the funeral. He's had some offer that will take him to South America. He used to travel for my brother's firm, you know, and the bankruptcy leaves him out of a job. Naturally he feels he should accept this new position. It means he'll have to sail at once."

Mr. Kincaid was annoyed. There were several questions that an employé of Jackson Frant's firm could answer and which he did not care to put to Lord Tethryn.

Sue came out on the gallery and called softly.

"Your room's ready now."

"Thanks. I'll be right up."

He climbed the stairs. The girl walked down the corridor with him. Nancy's bags lay on the bed. Rogan closed them, talking as he did so.

"You people here were a big surprise to me," he confessed. "I didn't be-lieve Frant when he told me about you. He boasted about this place, and his money, and his titled brother. I took him for the non-Irish champion free-style liar and didn't pay any attention. Now I get here and find it's all true."

"The money isn't."

"It was true once, apparently. Besides, he made up for it by several statements of unquestionable veracity."

Sue nodded. "The curse, too."

"Not the curse." Very gently he explained the suicide theory and the suggestion of Frant's motive for involving Lord Tethryn. The girl shud-dered.

"That can't be right. Mr. Frant wasn't like that, even if he did behave terribly tonight. He's done a lot for Evan. You see, Evan's father spent so much of his fortune for England during the war, he didn't have enough left to tide him over the depression there in '22. He only lived a few years after that and died in debt. By then Mr. Frant had come back to this country and started to make money manufacturing chemicals. He took care of Evan after the old earl died and gave him a job when he was old enough."

"Is Lord Tethryn a chemist?"

"It wasn't that kind of job. Mr. Frant had a lot of outside interests—a yacht, race horses, things like that. Grandfather mentioned this house in one of his letters, and Mr. Frant sent Evan down here to buy it."

"Lord Tethryn knew about the bankruptcy, then?"

"Oh, no. Mr. Frant didn't say a thing about that when he sent Evan down here to open this house and invite some of the local families for a week end. As a matter of fact, we were rather thrilled, because Evan thought his brother intended to retire from business and become a sort of country squire."

"Somehow," said Rogan, "I can't picture him as a country-squire type. He gives meaning to Hamlet's phrase. Frant simply wasn't born to occupy a manor."

"I guess you're right," she admitted, "but I don't suppose Evan ever thought of his brother in that light. It's hard to see your relatives the way other people do."

"I wouldn't know about that," Rogan told her. "I never had any."

She thought that was sad, but did not like to say so to a stranger.

Kincaid picked up two of Nancy's bags. Sue walked with him into the hall and stopped at the door of the adjoining room.

"This is mine," she informed him. "If there's nothing more I can do I think I'll go to bed. I'm very tired."

Rogan entered Nancy's bedroom without knocking. She opened her eyes and smiled up at him.

"Hello."

"Hello. I thought you were supposed to be asleep."

"I was, I guess, but I keep waking up. Things are sort of confused. How did I get here?"

"I carried you."

"Oh, yes," she nodded. "I remember. Did you undress me, too?"

"I gather Miss Makepeace did that, but if you're looking for a maid . . . ?"

She smiled again.

"I'll think it over. I'm glad you came, anyway. I've been lying here wondering about Jack . . . ." Her voice trailed off.

Rogan sat down on the edge of the bed.

"Worrying about Frant won't help any."

"I know it won't. 'Specially as I've got plenty of worrying to do about me. We came down in Jack's car, and I haven't enough money to get me back to New York."

Mr. Kincaid found himself in a similar position, but scarcely felt the news would cheer her. He asked: "How are you feeling?"

"Better, thanks. The question is, how do I look?"

"Succulent."

"I suppose I am pretty pale. Dr. Braxton made old Miss Makepeace take my make-up off."

Rogan looked at her critically.

"Personally," he told her, "I prefer my women with nothing on at all."

Nancy rolled her eyes at him.

"I wish I knew what made me faint, though—the first time, I mean. It wasn't on account of the way Jack died, I know, because I remember that now. I remember being upstairs afterward, too, so it must have been something that happened later."

"Maybe it will come to you in the morning."

"Something had better come to me in the morning. They ought to have New York consuls on islands, so when you get deported you could be sent back home. Maybe the doc would help me. You think? Jack said he was a sort of silent partner in the patent-medicine business."

"As there isn't any business left, Dr. Braxton will probably be more silent than ever. I'll speak to him, though, if you like, and see what can be done."

"Would you? That'd be swell. I don't guess I'm at my best with the people here. They make me feel sort of cheap. And that's funny, because they're not a bit like Jack said they would be. I mean they're not smart or swank or anything."

" 'Good wine,' " said Rogan, " 'needs no bush.' "

She puzzled over that, and he left her. When he returned with the other bags she was asleep. He closed the door gently and went downstairs.

The huge room was empty but for the shadows. He heard voices off to his right and, following them, came to the library. No one was there, but the sound of conversation drifted in through the dining-room door.

Rogan listened long enough to learn that Makepeace was expounding the suicide theory to Evan. Then, seeing no occasion for hurry, he slipped the Poe volume from its shelf. Vaguely his memory connected some reference in the charred manuscript with an incident in the Valdemar tale. Yet as he skimmed through the story of the moribund Frenchman who, when hypnotized, had managed so strangely to survive his own death, the connection escaped him—until he came to the last page.

. . . at length the . . . hideous voice . . . broke forth: "For God's sake! Quick! . . . Quick! . . . Put me to sleep or quick! . . . waken me! Quick! *I say to you that I am dead!*"

I was thoroughly unnerved, and . . . struggled to awaken him. In this attempt I soon . . . fancied that my success would be complete . . . and I am sure that all in the room were prepared to see the patient awaken.

For what really occurred, however, it is quite impossible that any human being could have been prepared. As I rapidly made the mesmeric passes, amid ejaculations of "dead! dead!" absolutely bursting from the tongue of the sufferer, his whole frame, at once . . . within the space of a minute, shrunk, crumbled . . . absolutely *rotted* away beneath my hands. Upon the bed before the whole company, there lay a nearly liquid mass of loathsome—of detestable putrescence.

Rogan shoved the book back into its place and walked into the next room.

The men grouped at the end of the long mahogany table looked up as he entered, but they were too engrossed in their conversation to give any further sign of recognition. Rogan slid into a chair from which he could watch Dr. Braxton's face.

"It's no use," Evan was saying. "I realize you mean to be kind, and I'd rather think Jackson killed himself than know I murdered him. But he didn't kill himself. I killed him." Suddenly he flared out. "I don't want to talk about it."

Dr. Braxton rose and laid a hand on the younger man's arm.

"We can't let you go on thinking you caused your brother's death. Believe me, the only way to exorcise devils is to talk about them."

There was a moment of silence. Rogan glanced at Bobby. The blond youth was engaged in making a turtle out of a raisin and bits of clove.

Evan flung himself into the chair from which the doctor had risen. "All right," he said. "Talk!"

Makepeace began. "If we wish to know truth we must seek it through logic. All real knowledge is based upon that. What we call thinking is merely arranging the evidence of our senses in some logical pattern. The same logic holds whether we discuss God or mathematics, because the supernatural is not a denial of the natural. It is a continuation of it."

He picked up a walnut and crushed it between his fingers as he talked.

"No matter what you may think yourself, your belief in the curse is based upon the legend. But the legend itself implies the existence of elementals, beings whose reality is supported by no evidence whatever."

Evan shrugged. "The elementals aren't important. Father Zachary only heard about them secondhand, anyway."

"He claimed to have seen the pentacle on the floor—"

"Which might have been used for necromancy. You believe in *that*, you know, even if you call it spiritualism."

"My dear boy," Makepeace retorted, "I am not denying the paranormal. My point is that the other world is no more subject to chance than this one. Its laws can no more be broken than this table can break away from the law of gravitation and float up to the ceiling."

Tethryn threw up his hands. "What difference does it make? I killed Jackson. I cursed him, and he died. Don't you see that's the one fact you can't get away from? That happened. Maybe that damned couplet had nothing to do with the curse. Maybe the first word of it is not 'Od' but 'God.' Maybe the whole thing is pure legend and never happened at all. I don't know. I don't know anything about the story for certain. I only know one thing about the curse—it works."

Dr. Braxton put his hand on Tethryn's arm.

"But, my dear boy, that is the very thing you cannot know. It is not a subject upon which proof is obtainable."

"Yes, it is," Evan insisted. "There's plenty of proof. Go up and look at Jackson's body if you don't believe me."

"Even if there is no evidence of poison," the doctor persisted, "that can hardly be taken as a sign that he died of a curse."

"It isn't that . . . it's . . . Oh, my God! Let me alone!" He was on his feet again. "Do you think this is the first time I've killed something with the curse? It isn't . . . do you hear me? It isn't the first time!"

Someone knocked over a glass. There was no sound after that until the spilled whisky crawled to the edge of the table and began falling to the floor in slow drops. Bobby, who had created a dozen raisin turtles, took an orange from the fruit bowl and began tossing it in the air and picking the turtles up one at a time like jacks.

"Bobby's right." Tethryn dropped back into his chair. "Don't pay any attention to me. I'm a fool. I shouldn't have said anything."

"No doubt." Makepeace's voice was dry as a breaking stick. "But you've said too much not to say more."

The old doctor nodded. "What Arnold says is true, Evan. You'd better explain."

It was a long moment before the younger man looked up. When he did, both the wildness and the tense calm that had preceded it were gone.

"It's . . . it's so bloody anticlimactic after . . . what happened to Jackson. It wasn't a man I killed before. It was a kitten. That sounds funny, doesn't it? Just a kitten. But it was the most terrible thing that ever happened to me . . . until tonight. I was only a little chap, you see . . . not more than eight, anyway, and I was frightfully fond of the kitten. She was a jolly little thing, gray with one black ear. I never saw another quite like her. You know what horrid little beasts boys are. I pulled her tail one day and she scratched me. Even after I let her go, she just stood there with her back all arched and spat at me. I was furious, but I was afraid of her too, and I didn't dare hit her. I don't know what made me think of the curse then, but I did. I was so angry that I used it, though I realized it was wrong. I don't know exactly what I expected to happen. Nothing much did. Midge just mewed a little and crawled off in the bushes. I even remember thinking that the nasty old curse wasn't any good."

He paused, and again there was no sound save for the soft drip of the spilled whisky as it fell from the edge of the table. Evan took a deep breath like a swimmer about to plunge into icy water.

"The next day I found her. There was no doubt about what killed her. It wasn't just the flies, I'll swear to that. She looked as if she had been dead a week."

Dr. Braxton cleared his throat. "I understand how you feel about the kitten," he said. "It was a terrifying experience for a boy. But don't you see, you must have made a mistake? The kitten you found wasn't yours. You couldn't have recognized it after it was decayed. Kittens are very much alike."

Evan smiled at him, but there was no mirth in his smile.

"Midge was all gray with one black ear," he repeated. "Did you ever see a kitten marked that way? I never did—but once." He turned to the lawyer. "I don't know why I've argued with you. It's all so plain. If you won't believe me, go up and look at poor Jackson's body. He's been dead over an hour now." He rose and started toward the door.

Dr. Braxton put out a hand to stop him.

"Don't go out, Evan," he begged. "Stay here with us."

"I want to see how the storm is. I'll be back in a minute. You needn't be afraid. I killed one man tonight. I'm not going to kill another."

The doctor dropped his hand to let him pass.

Rogan waited until the Englishman had gone. Then he picked up a candle and rose to his feet.

"I think," he said, "we'd better have a look at Frant."

The doctor led the way up the stairs, with Makepeace at his heels. Bobby trailed behind his uncle, leaving Rogan—cautious when there was no profit in audacity—a discreet last.

No one spoke. If the room at the end of the dark hall held the carrion at which Tethryn had hinted, it would be time to seek an explanation of the impossible.

Dr. Braxton put his hand on the knob and opened the door. The flames of the candles, sheltered behind protecting hands, gave little light, but none was needed to tell them what lay on the white counterpane like a slug on a marble tile.

6

Night Prowler

THE FOUR MEN stood staring down at the horror that had been Jackson Frant. In that dim room, the tropical white of his clothing—still neatly pressed—was almost invisible against the bedspread, so that his hands and face appeared as dark splotches. There was a long pause.

"I won't believe Evan was right." The lawyer's voice was a brittle whisper. "There must be some other answer. What is it, Stirling? Poison? Disease? There must be something."

"There may be, but I am not the one to find it. I'm an old man, Arnold, and I have seen many medical miracles. I have seen men given up for dead rise and walk. Once, in Africa, I saw a leper cured by a witch doctor. I had a case myself in which a man was killed by spontaneous combustion. His very flesh burst into flame and he died in greater agony even than this poor devil. You can read about that in your books on medical jurisprudence if you like. But I never saw anything to match this. Dead two hours, lying in this cool, wind-swept room, and he has rotted past recognition."

"Past recognition!" Makepeace caught at that. "Past recognition . . . It isn't Frant's body. It can't be."

"Whose then?"

"What difference does that make? Surely it's better to believe . . ."

"It isn't better to believe anything than the truth."

Bobby said, "It's *his* ring."

Dr. Braxton bent over the bed for a long minute while the wax from his guttering candle splashed on the dead hand.

"Bobby's right," he said, pointing to the initials "JBF" cut into the soft gold of the signet. "He's had that for years, and tonight he had it on when Evan carried him upstairs. I remember. His arm hung down and the ring clicked against the banisters."

Makepeace protested. "It's easy to slip a ring on the finger of a corpse."

"And leave no traces? See for yourself."

Makepeace bent in his turn.

"It doesn't look as if that ring had been put on tonight," he admitted. "Still, when you consider the appalling alternative . . ."

They avoided each other's eyes.

"There are no degrees of the impossible," the doctor said brusquely. He turned and passed into the corridor. As Rogan followed, his glance caught the door leading to the bedroom that had once been Nancy's and he remembered her broken phrase, "I went into his room . . ." The reason for her faint was no longer a puzzle.

Makepeace closed Frant's door behind them.

"What are we going to tell Evan?" he asked.

"What can we tell him? He knows." Dr. Braxton led the way toward the great hall. The shadows closed in behind them as they passed.

Evan was waiting before the dead fire. Evidence of what they had seen was written in their faces, and he read it.

"It's true then! Oh my God, I didn't really believe it. Deep down in my heart I knew it *couldn't* be true—and now it is."

He slumped into the nearest chair and sat staring at the ashes as if the miracle of flame which could reduce solid logs to an impalpable gray powder might explain what lay in the room upstairs.

Dr. Braxton opened his medical bag. He took out a glass vial and offered it to Evan.

"Two or three of these tablets will help you sleep."

"I hope something will. I know how Macbeth felt. 'Faulkland hath murdered sleep, and therefore Tethryn shall sleep no more.' "

"Steady, boy." The doctor put a hand on his shoulder.

Evan stood up. "You're right. It's no good funking anything, is it? No matter what."

He moved toward the stairs. Rogan and Bobby followed. They reached the gallery and turned down the corridor. Evan stopped in front of the door opposite Sue's.

"This is as far as I go." He saw Bobby's glance go to the vial of sleeping tablets and added, "Don't worry. I won't take too many of these. Not that it would do any harm if I did. The doctor wouldn't have trusted me with them else."

"My room's across from yours," Bobby told Rogan. They moved down the corridor and stopped, their eyes on Frant's door.

"Got any tricks that will explain that one?" Rogan asked.

Bobby shook his head.

"I've known Sue for a long time."

"What has she got to do with it?"

"Nothing." Bobby pushed open his door. "I think I'll go to bed now. Good-night."

Alone in his room Rogan felt in the pockets of his coat. Sea water had ruined his tobacco past hope, but his pipe was safe. He thrust it between his teeth and threw himself on the bed. There would be at least an hour to kill before he could make the move he planned.

That incredible corpse in the next room was only one of a dozen unsolved problems. Neither Kincaid himself nor Nancy Garwood fitted into the normal atmosphere on The Kraken any better than their host, yet he must have had some reason for inviting them. Why had his boasts, such obvious lies in New York, come true here? Or conversely, why had the truth sounded false before? Who had been reading the Poe story? And what had Bobby meant when he had spoken of Sue?

Such questions could not be answered without more information than Rogan possessed. He brushed them aside and let his fancy play with Od and with the vaguer but somehow more imminent phantom—the Hangman's Handyman. The figure of the Handyman fascinated Kincaid. Miss Makepeace's reference suggested some character of local legend, and certainly this old house seemed an appropriate haunting place for such a specter. The great hall with its timbered roof was a glorified gibbet in itself. One could easily imagine a dozen dark figures dangling, each from its own hammer beam, while the Handyman—simple soul—toasted his shins before the fire in anticipation of—

It was an unfortunate moment for Mr. Kincaid to notice the iron ring in the ceiling of his own bedroom. Its original use as a support for an oil lamp was obvious, yet it might also have served a darker purpose.

He shrugged and stood up. Around him the old house groaned in its sleep, and malignant shadows strove to enter the pentacle of light thrown by his candle.

Sue Braxton's room was next to Rogan's. She had gone to bed, but a succession of small noises kept her nerves taut—the creak of boards, footfalls, the soft closing of doors. She tried to interpret these sounds, but her tired brain brought no answer—only fear.

Even the long intervals when no sound came were filled with worry about Evan. She had tried to talk to him after his brother's death, to assure him against all evidence that he had been in no way responsible. She knew that she had failed.

The girl rose from her bed and moved to the window. The storm had nearly blown itself out, and she could see a faint glow where one corner of the crescent moon broke through the thinning clouds.

Sue leaned against the window and reviewed in her mind all that had passed. She had been spared the knowledge of the literal fulfillment of the curse and so was free to hope that somewhere there was a point she had overlooked, a fact missed that would persuade Evan of his innocence.

Sue forced her mind to focus on the moment when Evan had uttered the curse. She had been by his side at the time, facing as he faced. She had felt his body stiffen, had seen the smug grin on Frant's face change first to surprise and then to terror as each word struck home like a hammer blow.

She shivered and turned back to her bed.

It was then that she heard the sound in the hall. It was not loud, but the very furtiveness of it cut across the remembered horror in her mind and pulled her to her feet. It came again. The girl caught up her robe and tiptoed to the door. Cautiously she peered out into the hall.

Silhouetted against the moonlight that filtered in from the huge living room was a dark figure.

Sue did not scream, but she did gasp. The figure turned and moved slowly back along the corridor. Her fear was so great that she lacked the power to move. The faint light gave her no clue as to what it might be, even when it stopped. It was then so close that she could have put out her hand and touched it had she dared.

For a long moment it remained motionless. Suddenly it spoke.

"Sue?"

Relief flooded her.

"Bobby, you fool!"

"Ssh," the boy hissed. "Somebody just went downstairs."

"Well, what of it, you idiot? It was probably one of the men after a drink. Go to bed."

A tiny tinkle drifted up from the floor below. Sue stiffened.

"It's somebody after the spoons."

"No, it isn't. That was the telephone. It makes a noise like that sometimes when you hang up. I'm going down."

"Let me get my slippers and I'll come along." Sue stepped back into the room.

"Sue."

"What's the matter?"

"I don't think you'd better go."

"For heaven's sake, why not?"

"Well, whatever it is downstairs may be dangerous, and I probably wouldn't be able to protect you."

"You goose!"

The boy put out his hand in the dark and found hers.

"Come on," he said.

As they tiptoed down the stairs, Sue found herself wondering what had led her to embark on this harebrained hunt for a night prowler. At best they would be made ridiculous by having their quarry turn out to be some harmless member of the house party, while if they should find something else . . . Suddenly she realized that her feeling of childish adventure came from Bobby. It is woman's favorite jest that men are only grown-up children, but in Bobby's case the joke could be taken quite literally. He existed in a world where everyone was stronger and wiser than he—a world, moreover, in which nothing really serious could happen. Somehow his conviction of safety was contagious.

After a whispered conference at the foot of the stairs, they decided that the pantry phone was the most likely source of the noise they had heard. Gingerly they pushed open the kitchen door and slipped in. The moon had gone now and the room was dark as a robber's cave. Sue stood on tiptoe, poised for flight at the first sound. None came. Simultaneously they both decided they were on a wild-goose chase. Bobby squeezed Sue's hand and, reassured by the answering pressure of her fingers, groped his way to the table, where he found matches and a candle.

Almost before she heard the scrape of the match head, Sue realized something was wrong. As the flame grew she looked past Bobby and saw a man—a man with a gun.

From somewhere on her left a calm voice said, "Better light the candle, Chatterton. He'll shoot if the match goes out."

The words brought Sue's head around, and she recognized Rogan. His lean height filled the pantry doorway. For a moment the expression on his face puzzled her. Then the candle flared, and she saw that he was grinning! Again the feeling of unreality swept over her. It was like a play she had once seen, a burlesque in which all the characters had gotten the wrong rôles.

There was a bowl of crackers on the table. Mr. Kincaid strolled over and took a handful. He put one in his mouth and began munching it slowly. Sue looked from him to Bobby. Her heart began to climb back down her throat. What a great team they'd make—Rogan to give you confidence when there really was danger, and Bobby when there really wasn't.

The man with the gun said, "Put up your hands!"

"Do what he tells you," Rogan advised. He lifted his own hands and at the same time threw one leg over the corner of the kitchen table and sat down.

As Sue's hands rose, the stranger stepped forward into the pool of light where she could see him clearly. He was of medium height, but he somehow conveyed the impression of being undersized. His blue eyes were red-rimmed as if he had been drinking—or crying. He said, "Where is he?"

"He?"

Sue was behind Rogan, but she could almost see his eyebrows go up with the question. It came to her with a shock that the tall man was enjoying himself. For an instant she suspected a hoax. Then the stranger's voice answered, and she knew he spoke in deadly earnest.

"Where's Frant?"

"Which Frant?"

The red-rimmed eyes narrowed. "Are there two?"

"There were two."

"It's Jackson Frant I want, president of the Swave Company, damn him!"

"Jackson B.?"

"Yeah."

"You're too late. He's already damned." Mr. Kincaid looked up at his right hand, which still held a cracker. He dropped it into his mouth and chewed. "By professionals," he finished thickly.

The gun muzzle wavered and then came to rest on a line with Mr. Kincaid's stomach.

"If you don't tell me where he is before I count three I'll start shooting."

Rogan finished his cracker. "My name's Kincaid," he said. "What's yours?"

"What's that to you?"

"Makes things cozier. You know," he added sadly, "you're going about this the wrong way. Why don't you tell us what you want with Frant? Maybe we'll help you."

"Fat chance of his friends helping me."

"What makes you think we're his friends?"

"You're in his house, aren't you?"

"You're in his house, too. That makes us all friends together. Have a drink?"

The stranger started forward and then drew back again.

"I'm not taking chances," he told Rogan. "I don't know much about gun play, but I know enough not to get near the other fellow."

"Then why are you trying to get near Frant?"

"He killed my wife, damn him!"

"Killed your wife?" Sue's surprise was so great that she hardly realized she had spoken.

"He poisoned her, I tell you! Poisoned her with that fat cure of his. He's worse than a gunman. Killing a woman just so he could sell a dollar bottle."

"But . . . but . . ." Sue stumbled over her words. "Mr. Frant didn't sell a fat cure."

"Didn't he, though? Ask him about dinitrophenol! That's what he poisoned her with. Same as if he'd shoved it down her throat."

"I don't believe you!"

"And why not? Because he's got a lot of money, I suppose. You rich people always stick together."

Rogan laughed at him. "Behave yourself. Frant hasn't got a dime."

"Yeah? Don't let that bankruptcy fool you. Frant's got plenty the court won't ever find out about. He's the kind that would."

"How did you know he was bankrupt?"

"Why shouldn't I? The papers were filed two weeks ago."

"Oh," Sue broke in. "What does that matter? It's this other story I don't understand. It can't be true." She turned troubled eyes to Kincaid. "Why, it was Grandfather who told Mr. Frant about dinitrophenol. He wanted him—Mr. Frant, that is—to experiment with it. He thought it might prove a useful drug."

"Useful to poisoners!" The stranger spat the words out.

Bobby's voice popped up, as usual, from nowhere.

"But if Dr. Braxton thought it was good . . . that is . . . well, I don't see how it can be poison."

"It is poison, I tell you!" The man was beside himself now. "Have you ever seen a person die of fever? Not kid stuff, but real fever—a hundred and six or seven with no letup at all. That's what Frant's poison did to Mary. It killed her, I tell you, and I'm going to kill him!"

"Oh, no, you're not." Rogan's voice cut through the room like a thrown knife. "You're too late. He's dead!"

"Dead!"

The tall man nodded.

"Dead as a used herring."

The stranger screamed at him. "You're lying!"

Mr. Kincaid's lazy smile returned.

"There's more than my word for it, you know. Mr. Chatterton here can take you upstairs and let you look at the body."

"Maybe." The other's eyes were points of blue fire. "But if you're lying to me . . . !"

"It's all right really," Bobby told him. "He's dead. I'll show you."

The man with the gun started forward. Rogan's right foot rose in a swift arc, catching the revolver and knocking it up. At the same time he threw his body backward on the table and kicked the man in the face with his left heel. The stranger reeled across the room, struck the wall with a crash, and fell to the floor—still holding the revolver. Rogan dove forward and landed squarely on top of the other man. He wrenched the gun free and rolled to his knees.

Bobby said, "Oh, neat!"

"Thanks." Rogan slipped the revolver into his pocket and grasped his captive's wrists. "See if you can find some rope."

"What are you afraid of?" Sue's voice was scornful. "You're twice his size."

"Just an old Kincaid custom. I like to have all the odds I can on my side."

"It isn't your fault he's alive. Did you have to be so brutal about it?"

Rogan shrugged. "This fellow was frightened, and he didn't know how to handle a gun. He'd have shot first and thought afterward. That's why I made Chatterton light the candle."

The girl was not mollified.

"And I suppose you learned all that in the second after Bobby's match lit?"

"I'd learned most of it before. I was stalking him when you came."

"In the dark, when you knew he had a pistol? You'll have a hard time now convincing me you're a hero, Mr. Kincaid. Remember," she flared, "I saw you kick him in the face. He wasn't going to hurt any of us. It was Mr. Frant he wanted. He'd have been easy enough to handle after you showed him the body."

"But," Bobby broke in, "we couldn't show him the body."

"I'll bet you couldn't!" Kincaid's prisoner struggled wildly. "You ain't fooling me a bit. Frant's not dead."

"Yes he is," said Bobby. "Really. Only—I mean—he's so dead you couldn't recognize him."

"I'd recognize him all right—dead or alive."

Sue grabbed the boy's arm. "What are you talking about? Why shouldn't he recognize Mr. Frant?"

"If I were you," Rogan suggested, "I'd let that question wait until morning."

"I'll do nothing of the kind. I want to know what you and Bobby are talking about."

"Very well, but remember you asked for it. No one can recognize Frant's body, because the curse seems to have worked literally."

"You mean . . ."

Rogan nodded. " 'Od rot you.' He looks as if he had been dead a month."

"Then . . . Evan was right." Sue caught hold of a chair and lowered herself into it. "It's true."

Rogan's captive was less easily convinced. "Don't believe 'em, lady. I saw Frant this afternoon, myself!"

"He's changed since," Kincaid said dryly, and added an explanation.

"You're crazy. What could do that to a guy?"

"Nobody knows. But something was prowling around The Kraken that didn't do Frant any good."

"What sort of something?" The stranger's voice was derisive. Suddenly his eyes widened and he repeated the question in a frightened whisper. "What sort of something?"

Rogan put his head on one side and looked down at the speaker. "What do you know about it?"

"I touched some kind of thing on the path coming up here. It was slimy, but you couldn't quite feel it—like a dead jellyfish. My God, let me out of here!"

7

A New Use for Vinegar

WITH SURPRISING AGILITY the captive wriggled free and broke for the door. Rogan lunged at his ankles and tripped him. The man fell sidewise, struck his head against the sink, and landed on the floor in a heap. Sue ran toward them.

"Good heavens, you've killed him!"

"Hope not. Be a mess if I have."

Kincaid's fingers moved over his captive's body, ostensibly to feel for signs of life. Without letting the others realize he was searching, he learned much about the contents of the man's pockets: letters, a watch, a wallet, a few coins, a knife, and in the selvage pocket of the coat—a capsule.

"He'll be around in a minute." Rogan rose to his feet. "Did you get that rope, Chatterton?"

Bobby tendered a hank of clothesline. The tall man placed his prisoner's limp body in a chair and began to truss it expertly.

When he finished, Sue asked: "Do you think he really did touch it?"

"Od, you mean?"

She nodded.

"When I saw Frant's body I stopped thinking," Rogan told her. "Perhaps it was Od, perhaps it was the Hangman's Handyman, perhaps—"

"Don't be silly. How could he have touched the Handyman?"

"How could he have touched Od, for that matter?" Mr. Kincaid looked down at her white face. When his voice came again it was unexpectedly gentle. "I seem to remember that you missed supper. Sit tight while Chatterton and I raid the larder."

Sue grasped the edge of her chair with both hands and tried not to think, while the two men looted the refrigerator. Rogan kept up a running commentary of small talk as he transferred the contents of the icebox to the table, but Sue heard none of it. Dully she watched their hands—the man's brown and muscular, the boy's soft and white, but there was about them a kinship of swift efficiency. She had never noticed Bobby's hands before. It was difficult to reconcile their purposeful movements with his shy personality, their crisp dexterity with his halting speech.

Sue heard Rogan's voice say "and deep-dish apple pie." She came to herself to find him grinning at her across a table piled with food. As she smiled back automatically, he pointed to a plate of sandwiches.

"For the inner man," he announced, and poured her a glass of milk.

She was surprised to find herself quite hungry and accepted the food gratefully. Kincaid watched until she bit into her sandwich. Then he straddled a chair and sat, long legs thrust out in front of him.

"Frant's death is unpleasant enough at best," he began, "but this business about spirits and goblins makes it worse. Until we can find a rational solution of what happened, we'll all feel uncomfortable in the shadows."

"But how can there be a 'rational' solution," the girl protested, "if what you say about the body is true? Trying to be scientific about everything is just as absurd as being credulous about everything."

"Perhaps, but whether our 'rational solution' is true or not, we still have to find it, if only for Lord Tethryn's sake. The police—"

"Police!"

He nodded. "They'll be here in the morning. If they're looking for notoriety, they can have it for the asking—at Lord Tethryn's expense. Given the curse theory they have a first-degree murder charge against him."

"That's fantastic!"

"No doubt. Unfortunately, it is also technically complete. You said Lord Tethryn told you a story before Frant was killed. Was it the one about the kitten?"

"Yes, but—"

"The police can use that as proof he knew the curse was deadly. They can claim premeditation, too."

"How could they? We all saw the quarrel start."

Rogan shook his head. "It may have started years ago, for all you know. My point is that Frant has been bankrupt for two weeks. The police may claim that Lord Tethryn must have known about it, yet when his brother announced his insolvency tonight Tethryn pretended to be surprised. The police will argue that he was lying and, if so, must have been playing some deep game. Under the circumstances they'll automatically assume the game involved murder."

"But I told you how much Mr. Frant had done for Evan. Why should he kill him?"

"If their relationship was what I think it was, Lord Tethryn had more cause for resentment than gratitude. And don't forget Frant had just committed a new crime by going broke and leaving Tethryn without support—just when he wanted to get married, too! Perhaps the rich Miss Braxton would think twice before marrying the traditional bankrupt lord."

"As if it would make any difference to me whether Evan had money or not!"

"He might think it would. Besides, the bankruptcy meant a lot of notoriety for the company, and I gather from our friend here that its dealings were none too savory."

The girl's brow wrinkled.

"I don't understand about that." She looked at the unconscious captive. "He must have made some dreadful mistake. Mr. Frant was a manufacturing chemist. Grandfather wouldn't have had anything to do with him if he'd really sold quack medicines. Anyway, how could Evan hope to cut down notoriety by such a murder? The papers will be full of it."

"But such romantic notoriety. Old family curse. Quite in the best British tradition. In the midst of so much glamour, vulgar details like the patent-medicine business might be ignored."

"I don't believe there was anything to be ashamed of about Mr. Frant's business. Even if there were, Evan didn't have anything to do with it. He wasn't a chemist and didn't have any direct dealings with his brother's firm."

"Perhaps not, but he must have known what that firm dealt in."

"Not necessarily. Even Grandfather thought Mr. Frant was a fine chemist. If Mr. Frant was a fake and was good enough to fool him on a thing like that, then you can't accuse Evan just because he was fooled, too. Why, you might as well suspect Grandfather!"

Rogan pointed to the bound man.

"Our friend here does."

"But that's just the trouble," Sue protested. "If you find this 'rational explanation' of yours, where are we? It's *really* murder then, not a lot of far-fetched theories—but who could have done it? Evan certainly didn't, and Grandfather is out of the question. The rest of us never saw Mr. Frant before."

Suddenly her eyes filled with suspicion.

"Unless you killed him."

Rogan laughed. "Frant was dead when I reached the island."

"There's that Garwood girl. She knew him well."

"Intimately, perhaps, but not well. Besides, killing Frant involved a good deal of ingenuity and imagination. I doubt if she has much of either."

"Evan's imagination isn't the practical kind, and goodness knows he's not ingenious."

Bobby, who had been engaged in a lone-hand attack on the apple pie, got up and wandered about the kitchen, poking in cupboards. There was an unexpectedness about the blond youth that made Mr. Kincaid wary. He asked the object of the boy's search and was told "lump sugar." Sue spoke again.

"Anyway if . . . if Mr. Frant's body is . . . like you said . . . what could have done that except the curse?"

"I don't know," Rogan admitted. "Almost anything would seem likely, if Od is the only alternative."

A match flared on his right and he turned to see Bobby holding the flame under a lump of sugar. The older man's eyebrows rose in inquiry, and Bobby, embarrassed as usual at being noticed, stammered an explanation.

"You see . . . that is . . . it won't catch fire, but . . ." He dropped ashes from his cigarette on the other end of the lump and rubbed them in with a deft thumb. "If I put ashes on it, it burns." Here he struck a new match and held it to the sugar. The ash-smeared crystals lit and glowed with a dull blue flame. Bobby blew out sugar and match and looked up, like a dog which has performed a trick and waits uncertainly for its master's approval.

Sue stared at him. "What's that for?"

"Well, you wanted to know what might have killed Mr. Frant . . . and I thought maybe poison . . ."

"But no poison on earth . . . !"

Rogan put his hand on her arm.

"Wait a minute. He has an idea. If someone asked you to set sugar afire with a match, you'd have thought it couldn't be done, wouldn't you? And if you had to guess what would make it inflammable, the last thing you'd have thought of would have been ashes."

Sue's eyes lit up with interest. She turned to Bobby.

"You mean there might have been a sort of—what's the word—catalytic? A catalytic agent?"

Bobby nodded.

"It wouldn't even have had to be something rare. I mean just so that nobody ever heard of the poison and the what-you-may-call-it working together before."

The girl's face fell.

"But how could we find out what it was or prove it if we did?"

"We wouldn't have to," Rogan pointed out. "The police won't really like the case against Lord Tethryn. It would put their names in the papers, but they'd never get an indictment on it—and, after all, that's their job."

"You think the police will accept Bobby's idea?"

"Or something like it. For instance, there may have been two poisons. The first might have been something like prussic acid. A small amount of that would kill quickly, and it could have been given in a coated capsule as Chatterton pointed out earlier this evening. Later, whoever killed Frant could have gone to his room and injected a large quantity, even several pints, of a second poison in a vein."

Bobby asked, "You mean like embalming fluid?"

"Whatever it was, it wasn't embalming fluid, quite the reverse." Rogan smiled. "Though it might have been injected that way."

"But," Sue persisted, "what could it have been?"

"That I can't say. It offers a line to work on, and that may be enough for the police as long as they don't have to swallow the curse theory. In an affair as curious as this one, you can hardly expect a simple answer."

The bound man stirred in his chair. Bobby pointed to his fingers.

"Look!"

Kincaid bent and examined the roped hands.

"What is it?" Sue asked.

"His fingers are stained."

"From which," she chided, "the great detective is about to deduce that he smokes too much."

"All deductions are false," Rogan retorted, "including this one."

"It's some sort of chemical," Bobby added.

Sue caught at that. "Poison! Maybe he killed Mr. Frant."

"But . . . ." Bobby stammered, "if he did . . . I mean . . . why should he want to shoot him?"

"He didn't, silly. That could have been just a bluff. Perhaps he couldn't get off the island."

"If the police found him here, he'd be a sure suspect," Rogan agreed. "He may have some kind of evidence on him. We'd better look through his pockets."

All three of them joined in the search. Rogan found two letters and read them. Both were addressed to: Mr. Alfred V. Hoyt, 617 Mulberry St., Des Moines, Iowa, and both were in envelopes engraved with the style of a firm of Hartford attorneys. The first was a mere note:

DEAR SIR: We regret to inform you that we have no present information regarding the whereabouts of our client. Very truly yours, Jeffries, O'Brien, and Jeffries, per J.C. JEFFRIES, JR.

"Junior didn't waste words." Rogan handed the letter to Sue, adding, "It's dated August 10th. Our friend's been on the trail nearly a month."

Sue's excitement grew. "That proves premeditation."

The second letter was longer and signed by the senior Jeffries. The Swave Company which, it appeared, was not a corporation but a private enterprise, was entirely owned by Jackson B. Frant. The widespread sale of the firm's product had resulted in a score of damage suits totaling nearly half a million dollars. The firm of Jeffries, O'Brien, and Jeffries regretted to inform their correspondents that Mr. Frant had instructed them to withdraw from the entire case since the company had almost no tangible assets. Mr. Frant had recently suffered losses in various personal ventures, and his real property was already mortgaged beyond what it would bring at a forced sale. The letter closed with the statement that although formal bankruptcy proceedings were hardly worth while, creditors could please themselves on that point.

The remaining loot proved less interesting. The wallet contained six one-dollar bills, a driver's license, and a membership card in the Loyal Order of Moose, both made out in the name of Alfred V. Hoyt. The watch was a shabby gold-filled affair. Rogan pried open the back of it with Hoyt's knife and found a yellowed photograph of a girl in a bathing suit. "Runner-up for Miss Des Moines: 1929," he guessed, and turned back, waiting for the others to run across the capsule.

Sue found it, announcing her discovery with a barely suppressed shout of triumph.

"Look . . . he's still got some of the poison!" She started to take the top off. Rogan's strong fingers on her wrist stopped her.

"There are several things that look like that," he warned, "that nobody tastes but once. If the thing that killed Frant is one of them, you wouldn't be very good company after you'd tried it."

"I wasn't going to taste it—just to smell."

"Even smelling's not safe. Frankly I'd prefer to test that stuff on someone less pleasantly contoured."

"But don't you see? This is dinitrophenol! It all fits in."

"Perhaps," Rogan conceded. "Though I gathered that dying from dinitrophenol was a lengthy business."

"He could have mixed something else with it, couldn't he? You said yourself there must have been two poisons. This isn't medicine or anything like that." She dropped the capsule in Rogan's hand. "Look at it."

Certainly it did not appear to be the sort of thing one buys in a drugstore. It was large, and instead of tightly packed powder it contained crystalline lumps of some dirty-white substance.

Bobby interrupted again.

"Look! He's coming to."

Rogan pushed away the plates and sat on the table facing his prisoner. There was nothing in the least threatening in his attitude. He had a sandwich in one hand and a glass of milk in the other. His long legs swung rhythmically. He smiled.

Hoyt took some time to regain consciousness and at first did not seem to realize where he was or why he was bound.

"Who are you? Why have you got me tied up? You can't do this sort of thing. Let me loose!"

Rogan continued to smile.

"You'll have to answer a few questions first. How long have you been on the island?"

"I don't know. I came after the storm died."

"Guess again. You got here this afternoon."

"The hell I did. I had to make sure Frant was coming, didn't I? I wasn't taking any chances. I've been hunting him for a month . . . ever since Mary died. I went to his place in Hartford, but they said he wasn't there. He wasn't, either. I waited around for a week. Then I wrote his lawyers. They pretended they didn't know where he was. They were lying, but I found out from them he had some houses in different parts of the country. This is the third one I've tried. I've been in this neighborhood four days now. They told me at Bailey's Point he was opening up this place and coming here himself. I saw him get out of his car and take a motorboat—him and that yellow-headed girl."

"How did you get here?"

"I found a boat. It didn't belong to anybody. It was sunk in a salt marsh just this side of the point. The name was sort of chipped off, but"—he gave a sickly grin—"I figured it said 'Empty,' so I took it. And look—all that business about touching a spook—I didn't mean it. You had me going for a minute. It must have been some of the moss stuff they have on the trees down here. That's nasty-feeling when it's wet."

"No doubt. How did you get in the house?"

"The back door was open."

An exclamation from Bobby brought Rogan's head around.

"What's wrong?"

"Well . . . you see . . . I saw Uncle Arnold when he locked up last night."

"Did he lock the back door?"

"He locked all of them, and the windows, too. Evan opened the front door afterward, of course. But . . . you see . . . we were watching that most of the time."

The tall man swung back to Hoyt. He continued to smile.

"Now let's rub all this out and start over. You couldn't have gotten in after the storm stopped because the back door was locked. That means you came before the storm and hid somewhere in the house. While everyone was at dinner you poisoned Frant's medicine."

"You're crazy!"

"You hated Frant enough to poison him."

"What would I need to poison him for? I had a gun."

"Not for Frant. Frant killed your wife with poison and you killed him with poison—poison like this."

With the swiftness of a conjuror's trick Rogan whipped the capsule from the table and held it up. New fear leaped into the red-rimmed eyes.

"I wasn't going to poison Frant, I tell you. I was going to shoot him." His gaze turned to the capsule. "That . . . I was going to take that myself . . . afterward."

Rogan gestured toward Hoyt's mouth.

"Here's your chance."

The avenger of beauty shrank back in his chair.

"I don't want it. I didn't kill him. I don't have to take it now."

Mr. Kincaid's smile twisted into the conscienceless grin of a hunting shark.

"You wanted revenge, didn't you? You meant this for Frant. It's the same stuff he sold your wife."

"That's what I ought to have done—filled him full of his own medicine and made him cook himself to death, like Mary." He relaxed. "But I didn't. That's cyanide. Anyway, where'd I get dinitrophenol? They stopped selling Frant's stuff after Mary died."

"You're a chemist, aren't you?"

"Of course not."

"Then how did you stain your fingers? How did you get hold of cyanide?"

"I'm a photofinisher. I use it in my work."

"In capsules?" Mr. Kincaid's voice underlined incredulity.

"No. I filled that myself . . . to use after I shot Frant."

Sue crossed to Hoyt and stood looking down at him.

"Tell me the truth," she demanded. "Did your wife really die of dinitro-phenol?"

"Of course she did. Her doctor couldn't do anything for her. He told me all about the stuff and why real doctors don't use it because a dose that's safe for one person will cook another to death."

"That's true," Sue acknowledged, "and with some people even small doses cause blindness. But chemists can often overcome difficulties like that. Mr. Frant promised Grandfather his laboratories would—"

"He never had any laboratories, just a business office, and a room where girls made pills and put them in boxes."

"But he'd promised he'd do research. Grandfather warned him the stuff was dangerous."

"Your grandfather's in it, too," Hoyt exploded. "If he was a regular doctor he wouldn't be telling people about beauty treatments."

"It isn't only a beauty treatment." Sue's eyes flashed dangerously. "When overweight people are too sick to diet or exercise—"

"Oh," said Bobby suddenly. "That boat!"

"What about it?"

"He said it was marked 'Empty.' Don't you see . . , I mean, it must have been one of Uncle Arnold's."

"I believe you're right!"

"Would you mind letting me in on the secret?" Rogan asked.

"Uncle Arnold had two boats," Sue explained, "besides the speedboat, that is. He thought he bought them at a bargain, but the motors went bad, so he named one of them *Caveat* and one *Emptor*. That's Latin for 'Let the buyer beware'."

"Uncle Arnold has a whimsical sense of humor. The boat marked 'Empty' is, I take it, your old friend the *Emptor.*"

"Yes. Don't you see that proves this man must have been here before, or how would he have gotten the boat? It was locked in the boathouse."

Rogan looked at Hoyt. "The beans are spilled all over the place now, my friend. Will you confess quietly, or do I display my talents for persuasion?"

The bound man struggled against his ropes.

"I don't know what you're talking about. I didn't steal the boat, I found it. And I didn't get here till after the storm, either."

"And I suppose you didn't poison Frant."

"Of course I didn't."

"All-right." Rogan slid off the table. "This is going to hurt you more than it does me—much more."

In his raid on the pantry he had discovered a jug of vinegar. He walked over and picked it up.

"What's that for?" Sue asked.

"Ever hear of the water torture?"

"You mean drop by drop, like they do in China?" said Bobby.

Kincaid shook his head.

"I mean the kind they used in the Inquisition. They strapped you on your back, held your nose, and poured water in your mouth. Great fun really."

He set the jug on the floor. Then with no apparent effort he lifted Hoyt, chair and all, and laid him on his back on the table. Bobby looked on with interest.

"Where does the vinegar come in?"

" 'It's my own invention.' Use it instead of water. It works faster, though I admit they're *very* sick afterward."

Sue slipped in front of Rogan.

"You aren't going to mistreat him!"

"You'll never get the truth any other way." Kincaid pushed the cork out of the vinegar jug with his thumb. He looked down at Hoyt. "Last call. Did you poison Frant, or do you like vinegar?"

The girl grabbed Rogan's wrist. "There's no need to torture him. We know he was here before. We know he had poison, and we know he wanted to kill Mr. Frant."

"We also know that a confession in the hand is worth two in the future. If we let him get away with a lie now, he'll think up some new ones by morning and be so cocky no one can break him."

"I won't have him hurt!"

"Vinegar won't hurt him, just sour his disposition."

Sue smiled. "I'm sorry. I should have realized you didn't mean to torture him."

"How well you know me." He slipped past Sue, gripped Hoyt's nose with his left hand, and said, "Say 'Ah.' " The other gasped for breath, and Mr. Kincaid splashed vinegar into his mouth.

"Strange," Rogan remarked. "You can preserve a man in vinegar, but you can't preserve vinegar in a—"

Sue grabbed the jug out of his hand.

"I told you . . . I won't let you hurt him!"

"This is only funnin'. You ought to see some pretties I picked up in Japan."

"I won't let you!"

The gayety faded from Kincaid's eyes.

"You want to keep Lord Tethryn out of this mess, don't you?"

"Yes, but torture isn't going to help any. You said yourself the police wouldn't believe in the curse if they had any other theory. Well, we have a theory for them. Let's lock this man in the storeroom. Then the police can have him in the morning."

"It's nothing to me either way." Rogan shrugged. "Get some cushions from one of the living-room sofas while I untie him."

Sue looked at him suspiciously.

"What are the cushions for?"

"The storeroom floor is stone. Hoyt looks like the kind that would rather sleep on cushions."

"You really mean that?"

Rogan crossed his heart.

"You don't make sense." She shook her head. "First you want to torture him, and then you worry about what he sleeps on."

"I make the only kind of sense there is. As long as we could get something out of Al the Avenger by pickling him, I'd have dilled him to death, but there's no point in making him sleep on a stone floor."

"That sounds like logic," Sue admitted, "but I still don't think it makes sense. I'm in favor of the cushions, though. Come on, Bobby."

"What'll we do with this?" Bobby pointed to the pile of Hoyt's possessions on the table.

For answer Kincaid stepped into the pantry and returned with a tin cracker box. He dumped the crackers on the drain board of the sink, blew out the crumbs, and placed the box on the table. While Sue and Bobby put the little photofinisher's things inside, Rogan took the gun out of his pocket with a hand wrapped in one corner of his robe.

"Fingerprints," he said in answer to the question in Sue's eyes. "Some of mine are on it already, so a few more probably don't matter, but we may as well play safe." He broke the gun and spilled bullets on the table. Then he deposited the revolver in the box. "I'll keep the cartridges myself. Better not leave them with the gun. Everything?"

"Where's the poison?" Bobby found it and dropped it into the box, which Rogan closed with a snap.

"That's that." He picked Hoyt up and set his chair on the floor. "I'll untie him while you get the cushions."

"Sure," Bobby assented. "Come on, Sue."

Rogan's swift fingers worked at Hoyt's bonds.

"You're in a tight spot, my friend," he said. "But you wanted Frant dead, and you got what you wanted whether you killed him yourself or not. Now, take my advice and stick to your story that you didn't reach the island till about two-thirty. *Don't go making up accusations yourself.* There are some influential people here, and they'll have the police on their side. Shoot off your mouth about Frant and the doctor, and the first thing you know you'll be holding down a slab in the state medical school."

Bobby pushed through the door, his arms full of cushions. One hand held a bottle of whisky. He extended it.

"Evan left this in there. I thought . . ."

"That our friend might like a nightcap. Good boy."

Rogan passed the bottle to Hoyt and pulled him to his feet. The little photofinisher was cramped by his long bondage, but with Kincaid's help he managed to walk to the storeroom. The tall man glanced at the pillows Bobby had dropped on the floor.

"These will be enough," he remarked. "Where's Miss Braxton?"

"Gosh!" said Bobby. "She was with me." He turned back toward the living room. Rogan paused long enough to lock the door and then followed him. Just as Bobby's hand turned the knob of the living-room door, they heard Sue scream.

8

The Tale of the Black Sheep

THEY FOUND HER standing in the center of the great room, dropped cushions around her feet. Her face was white in the light of the candle Rogan had caught up as he passed through the kitchen. When they reached her she whispered:

"There's someone else in the room!"

"Where?"

"Behind me, I think. I heard him breathing!"

"Not right behind you, anyway." Rogan lifted his candle.

"But"—there was still panic in her eyes—"it was so close I didn't dare turn around. I even felt its breath on my neck."

"Gee, I'm sorry," Bobby apologized. "I shouldn't have left you alone in the dark."

"It wasn't your fault." She looked at Rogan. "He poked up the fire when we came in, so that we could hunt for pillows. Anyway, I'm not afraid of the dark. Only . . . there *was* someone here. Really there was." Suddenly she sank into a chair. "I'm sorry to be such a fool."

"Dark houses make shaky nerves." The tall man pulled a candle from the pocket of his robe. He lit it.

"I put this out when I started stalking Al the Assassin," he explained to Bobby. "Take it and see Miss Braxton upstairs. I'll clean up in the kitchen."

Sue smiled at him. "Thanks." She rose and smoothed out her housecoat. Bobby kept his eyes on her even as he took the candle.

Rogan watched them climb the stairs hand in hand. It was not until they reached the gallery that he permitted his eyes to flicker downward to the floor where they had caught a gleam reflected from Bobby's candle.

He did not stoop to examine it. Instead he crossed swiftly to the kitchen door, turned to answer Sue's soft good-night, and then passed into the kitchen.

Once there, Rogan made no effort to clear away the remains of the supper, but went directly to the box on the cupboard shelf. He opened it and stirred up its contents with an exploring finger. The capsule fascinated him and he picked it up. He had no strong convictions as to its contents, nor had he any idea of what use he could make of it. That, however, was for the future. He dropped it into his pocket and put the box back on the shelf, feeling that he had an ace in the hole. Silently he crossed to the living-room door and opened it.

In the center of the great room Miss Makepeace, candle in hand, bent over the spot on the floor where he had noticed the glitter. He gave a discreet butler's cough.

She rose to her feet and turned. Her thin hand flew to her throat.

"You frightened me."

"Fear seems to be endemic in this house. Something here frightened Miss Braxton a few moments ago." He put his head on one side. "You weren't by any chance that something?"

"Sue . . . where is she?" Miss Makepeace seemed scarcely to hear his question.

"She's all right now. She's gone to bed. Didn't you know?"

Miss Makepeace shook her head.

"I'd been lying awake. I heard someone scream, and then there were footsteps. I decided I had better investigate."

"Do you think that was safe?"

"No. But I'm not sure lying in bed is safe either."

Rogan grinned.

"Lots of girls have doubts on that score." Suddenly his face grew serious. "You'd better get back to bed before something really frightens *you.* "

"Something has."

She pointed to the floor. Rogan looked down. The glitter that had caught his eye was a line of water drops, such as might be left on the floor between two rugs by a person wearing a wet bathing suit.

"Taste it," she commanded.

Mr. Kincaid dipped the end of a finger into the largest drop and touched it to his tongue.

"It's salt!"

"Sea water," she amended.

"How did it get here? I tracked some in, of course, but that must have dried long ago."

"Look and make sure."

Rogan took the candle and crossed to the hearth. By bending low he was able to make out salt stains on the flags, but there were no signs of moisture.

"It's dry all right." He returned to the wet patch in the center of the room. "This is fresh. Still, after all the strange things that have happened in this house, what's a little salt water?"

"Nothing, if we can explain how it got there. Everything if we can't."

"Are you implying that whatever frightened Miss Braxton left this wet trail on the floor?"

Julia Makepeace seemed not to hear him . . . as if her mind were traveling down some strange path of its own. She said, "Mr. Frant described them as monsters, things translucent and bloated, like huge sea toads."

" 'Yea, slimy things did crawl with legs, upon the slimy sea.' " Rogan smiled. "Perhaps, but I doubt it." He bent and took both her long, blue-veined hands in his. "In any event, a full stomach is the master exorcist. Come out in the kitchen and have a sandwich."

She smiled wanly. "Thanks."

In the kitchen Rogan found a box of candles and managed to achieve quite a festive air by lighting ten of them. While she ate he busied himself straightening the room. Halfway through her sandwich Miss Makepeace suddenly cocked her head on one side and spoke.

"In a way I'm glad Sue woke me, Mr. Kincaid, because it gives me a chance to talk to you. Do you mind if I tell you a story?"

"Is it a ghost story?"

"In a sense. It's a story about a dead man who came back to life."

"I shall pay strict attention, though I warn you my capacity for shudders is a little threadbare."

"Dr. Braxton once went to a camp meeting," she began. "He arrived just as the people were getting religion and wallowing around on some straw that had been placed on the ground to make wallowing a pleasure. The revivalist took one look at him and yelled: 'My friend, come to Jesus!' Dr. Braxton said, 'Not tonight.' The preacher shouted back: 'Now is the time, brother! Now is the time! You'll never have better chance or cleaner straw.' "

She stopped.

"I've had a hard day," Rogan told her, "and am not at my best, which perhaps accounts for my failure to see your point."

"I am telling you about one of the funniest things that ever happened to Dr. Braxton."

"The old boy must have led a singularly dull life."

"Not at all. The incident was screamingly funny when it happened, but it's dull as ditchwater when you tell about it."

"Please don't think me rude if I agree with you."

She smiled. " 'Better chance or cleaner straw' isn't the point of an anecdote. It's a sort of catch phrase that reminds one of a humorous experience. In other words, it's part of one of those dreadful family jokes no one outside the family understands. A thing like that never spreads, but it sometimes sticks in the family for a long time. Even Sue uses the phrase, though the incident took place long before she was born. I've heard the doctor use it often." Miss Makepeace paused. "You used it tonight."

"I'm sorry," Rogan answered, "but I still don't understand. The Braxtons and the Kincaids have a family joke in common. What does that make us—kissing cousins?"

Miss Makepeace picked up a candle and held it before his face. She was sure now. This man's eyes looked out below dark level brows, Dr. Braxton's from under white bushy ones; but they were the same eyes. Then the lines beneath them—not deep, but setting off the top part of the face as if it were a mask—the doctor, when he was tired, had lines like that.

"You are Dr. Braxton's son and Sue's uncle," she said. "You're Mike Braxton." The man's face grew wary.

"I admit I could use a large slice of fatted calf right now, but what do you expect to get out of it?"

"Out of what?"

"Palming me off on the old doc as his long lost son."

"Young man . . ." Julia Makepeace began. Then she stopped suddenly and laughed. "Good. Very good. If anything in the world could have made me doubt your identity, that would. However, I'm beyond doubting—I know. It isn't just that 'better chance' business. That started me thinking, but once I did—why, your whole body gives you away. Look at your hands. They're exactly like Stirling's. And that trick of smiling with only half your mouth. I've seen your grandfather Dundas do that a thousand times. You're Michael Dundas Braxton. It's past questioning."

"And Dr. Braxton, do you suppose he'll find a way to question it?"

"Of course not . . . his own son?"

"He didn't recognize me tonight."

"His memory for faces is another family joke. I suppose you counted on that. Besides, it takes a clue. Superficially there's no resemblance. After all, you were only nine when you were kidnaped."

He returned her gaze for a moment and then answered: "I wasn't kidnaped. I ran away."

"Ran away! For goodness' sake, why?"

"Did you know me when I was young?"

The woman nodded. "You were quite a handful."

"I was more than that. I was a misfit. I don't mean I was unhappy. It was simply that I saw everything from a different point of view than the people around me. White children brought up in China feel the same way, only they have their families to tie to. I was all alone."

"You never struck me as being a lonely child. I remember you as the ringleader in every sort of deviltry you could think up."

"Being alone is different from being lonely. I've never been lonely in my life. There are a lot of people like me in the world. People like you don't often meet us."

"And you thought all this out at the age of nine?"

"Hardly. I just felt it. Then one day I chucked a rock at a boy named Elmer. I missed and broke a window in Grime's drugstore and one of the big colored jars behind it. I had visions of jail and I didn't like the idea. I knew my family wouldn't like it either. There seemed only one way to solve both problems. I lit out."

"But your father had the police search everywhere. How did they miss you?"

"I hopped a train and lived off hobos for two days. Then I met an old Swiss named Anton Schwartz. He gave me a job as a shillaber. In a way I've been at it ever since."

"What's a shillaber?"

"Somebody who always wins. Schwartz ran a shell game. I'd come up to his pitch and plank down a dime. Sure enough the pea was under the shell I picked. Old Schwartz would yell out: 'So simple a child can do it!' and then he'd clean out the suckers. Sometimes I did female impersonations."

She looked up at the lean, hard-bitten face.

"I can imagine you in a pink hair ribbon."

"I was charming, and did the suckers fall for it!"

Miss Makepeace finished her meal and rose to help clear away the remains. She was silent so long that the man asked:

"You aren't thinking of bugaboos again, are you?"

"I'm thinking of the best way to tell your father. It will be something of a shock at best."

"Why tell him?"

"Surely you intend to."

"I don't know. I envy people who can conduct their lives by a set of rules. 'He's my father, therefore he has a right to know who I am.' My life doesn't seem to work that way. Standing up for my rights has gotten me in as much trouble as most wrongs. A man has a right to commit suicide, but no one lets him if they can help it."

"Why did you come if you didn't mean to tell your father who you are? Don't expect me to believe it was a coincidence."

"No. I met Frant eight months ago. Last Wednesday I ran into him by accident in New York. He was a little drunk and boasted about his titled brother and his important acquaintances. I didn't pay any attention until he mentioned his relations with a Dr. Braxton. Even then I didn't accept when he insisted I join the party here. Later I thought it over and decided to come down and see for myself whether my father had turned out to be the sort of man Frant said he was."

Miss Makepeace looked at him sharply.

"What do you mean by that?"

"Answer a question for me first. How much do you know about my father's dealings with Jackson Frant?"

"Only that they were friends. Why?"

"Then you didn't know that Frant's real business was the sale of a known poison as a reducing medicine?"

"Fiddlesticks!"

"Oh, it's quite true. That's why Jackson B. went bankrupt. Several people were injured by his stuff. They sued him. One woman was inconsiderate enough to die. Her husband blamed it on Frant."

"Even if you're right, that has nothing to do with your father."

The man shrugged.

"Oh, yes, it has, and there's no point in keeping it a secret. The Victorian idea that a woman's fair name must be kept pure long after her body has always struck me as ridiculous. I suppose the same thing applies to a man's honor. In any event, it will all come out tomorrow since Miss Garwood knows. Put briefly, my father, the celebrated Stirling Braxton, was a silent partner in Frant's racket."

"I don't believe it!"

"No? Neither did I—at first. I'd always thought of my father as a combination of Bayard, Solon, and Aesculapius. I knew that was too much to expect of any man, but I honestly believed he tended toward some such combination of virtues. I forgot, you see, that the saying 'like father, like son' might work both ways."

"But what evidence could you possibly have to make you lose faith in your father?"

"Enough. Frant himself told me about the partnership."

"Mr. Frant was a congenital liar. Surely you wouldn't believe a word he said."

"I didn't when he told me, but I couldn't be sure. That's why I came here. And what do I find? Frant said his brother was a belted earl, no less. That was an improbability that makes Munchausen sound like Cassandra. Yet when I get here it turns out to be true. At least everyone believes it."

"It's true, all right. I looked it up in Burke. Evan's father was made a baronet in '15 and an earl a few years after the war."

"To hear Frant tell it, it sounded like the blackest lie in history. On top of that he mentioned the Faulkland curse. That was so wildly improbable I didn't feel he expected me to believe it, even as a legend. Yet that's true too, or true enough. After those experiences with Jackson Frant's veracity, can you wonder if I believe his statement that my father is a part-time quack?"

"But surely, on a matter like that, you wouldn't take any one man's word."

"There's a woman's word as well. Miss Braxton (or should I say my niece) informs me that the active ingredient in Frant's nostrum was suggested to him by her grandfather."

"Sue said that?"

The man nodded.

"You must be wrong," Miss Makepeace pronounced stiffly. Then when he made no reply she went on. "But . . . but . . . don't you see, even if your father did make such a suggestion, it was perfectly innocent. He thought highly of Mr. Frant's ability as a chemist. Surely the mere fact that he discussed a dangerous drug with the man doesn't prove they were in business together."

"There's only one flaw in that argument. My father did *not* think highly of Frant's chemical ability. On the contrary, he must have known Frant was a charlatan."

"That's simply incredible."

"Perhaps, but it's also the one thing in this whole crazy business that's absolutely certain."

Rogan took a handful of matches from a box and began making patterns with them on the table.

"I told you I'd seen Frant swallow some medicine in New York," he went on. "Miss Garwood was with us and made the remark that she had been afraid to take pills of any kind since a friend of hers had gotten chloride of mercury by mistake."

"That's just the kind of foolishness I'd expect from her."

"Apparently Frant felt the same way. He pointed out that his medicine wasn't chloride of mercury, but only calomel."

Rogan was silent at that and went on with his match figures for so long that Miss Makepeace prompted him.

"Well?"

"Well, it so happens that chloride of mercury *is* calomel. It's the *bichloride* that is poisonous. Every high-school chemistry student knows that, but Frant didn't. Do you suppose he could have talked chemistry to my father for a minute without giving himself away? If Dr. Braxton said Frant was a chemist, he must have been lying. There's only one conclusion to be drawn from that."

Miss Makepeace leaned forward and put her hand on his.

"No," she said. "There's another conclusion—the correct one. I don't know what it is, but I do know your father. He'd rather cut off his right arm than be mixed up in the sale of a patent medicine, even a useful one. No man ever lived with a higher regard for the ethics of his profession."

Rogan swept his matches into a pile.

"I'm afraid 'professional ethics' is just a high-sounding expression for trade-union rules. Did you ever read the Hippocratic oath? I did—two days ago. The first half of it deals with the duty of doctors to each other, and the rest is pretty obviously intended to prevent things that would give the profession a bad name." He quoted: " 'Whatever house I enter, there will I go in for the benefit of the sick, refraining from all wrongdoing or corruption, and especially from any act of seduction of male or female.' There's not a word in the whole oath, except the trade-union part, that a decent profession wouldn't take for granted."

"It isn't fair to judge modern doctors by Hippocrates."

"It wouldn't be if they didn't boast about the oath, presumably on the ground that no layman will take the trouble to read it."

"I don't know about that, but it seems to me you ought to stick by your father whatever happens. You owe him that much anyway."

"That," Rogan answered, "is propaganda the parents' protective league has been trying to put across for a hundred centuries. Sometimes there may be a point to it, but not in my case. I've been supporting myself ever since I was able to, and you'll hardly ask me to believe that my parents gave me birth as a personal favor. Besides, I've grown out of belonging to a family. A runaway child does that just as much as an adopted child grows into one. I didn't know Sue was born until Frant told me Tethryn wanted to marry her. I don't even know how many brothers and sisters I have."

"Three brothers and a sister," Miss Makepeace informed him.

"Quite a crowd. I can hardly have been missed."

"That's not true, and if you tell your father who you are you'll realize it." He shook his head.

"If my father is the kind of man I think he is, I prefer not to have him back. If he's the kind of man you think he is, he won't want me back."

"Any father would want his son."

"That," Rogan answered judicially, "depends on the son."

"Surely . . ."

"You'll think me a queer one to criticize my father when you hear what I am, but we all have our codes, and we all think the other fellow's is lower than our own. To me the unforgivable sin is hypocrisy. If my father were an honest quack advertising *Dr. Braxton's Best Prescription* in the newspapers I wouldn't mind, but hiding that sort of thing behind a great medical repu-tation is a little too much even for me. Probably that's not logical, but who is, when he finds that his idol is clay to the waist!"

"You may feel that about your father, but I'm sure he wouldn't about you."

"He wouldn't, not if he's in the jam I think he is; but if he's the man you claim, he'll be happier if I keep out of the picture. Do you know how I earn my living? Poker. You learn a lot of things on a carnival lot, but honesty isn't one of them."

"Whatever you are, your father—"

"What about the rest of my family? I've spent two years in prison—Sing Sing—for a confidence game. Should I wear my old school tie to the family reunion?"

Miss Makepeace's eyes filled with tears. "You're bitter."

"Not in the least." He chuckled. "I've had a good life and I expect to keep right on having it. I've lived three times as much as everyone else in this house put together. I've appreciated it, too, thanks to old Schwartz. He was crooked as a barrel of worms, but he spoke four languages and had a string of European degrees as long as a June day. However, Dr. Braxton and the rest of my family won't see it that way, and I don't blame them. From their point of view I'm too black a sheep to be worth my wool."

"Your father would give everything in the world to have his son again."

"Permit me to doubt it. What a man really wants is an heir. It's a sort of immortality. He wants to leave his name, his thoughts, his work, his money, and feel they'll be in safe hands. The Dr. Stirling Braxton you believe in hasn't one single thing he can trust to Rogan Kincaid."

In the pause that followed, the clock in the library struck five. Rogan caught Julia Makepeace by the hands and pulled her to her feet.

"Come on," he said. "I've talked too much. The sun will be up before we're in bed."

She ran her thumbs over his finger tips and then looked straight into his eyes.

"Why have you told me these lies about yourself? I've never met a professional gambler, but I know they keep their hands soft, because Bobby does for his card tricks. And besides, no one ever got sunburned sitting at a card table."

The man laughed.

"Those things are my stock-in-trade. People who reason as you do aren't afraid to play with me. I've worked the boats a good deal, and an hour a day on the sun deck gives anyone an honest complexion." He began blowing out the candles. "As for my hands, I gave up fancy card work long ago in favor of smart poker. The man whose brains are in his fingers is a sucker for any wise one that comes along. I know. Last year I took five thousand dollars off the bottom-of-the-pack boys alone."

He had left one candle lit. He picked it up now, and Miss Makepeace was too interested to notice that he was edging her through the door.

"I might believe you," she admitted, "if you hadn't said you were raised on a carnival lot. You're an educated man."

"An education is free to anyone who takes the trouble to go to a public library often enough. Schwartz saw that I got the habit. He taught me his languages, too."

Her room was on the lower corridor, under his own. Rogan walked with her to the door. Miss Makepeace put her hand on the knob and turned.

"You have an answer for everything, Mike Braxton. But then, as I recall it, you always did. Don't believe ill of your father. You'll never convince me that he isn't all you used to dream him."

Rogan made a little bow and handed her the candle.

"Good-night," he said. "And you might consider the implications in the idea that Frant did not die last night."

Without another word he wheeled and walked away from her along the corridor. Miss Makepeace stood staring after him until he turned toward the stairs. Then she suddenly realized that she held the only light and that he had gone off into the dark.

A quarter of a century of living on the edge of disaster sharpens the senses. As Rogan closed the door of his room behind him, he heard the sound. It was not loud, no louder than the slither a snake might make crossing a rock. At first he was not sure he heard it at all. When it came again he was puzzled. The soft footfall of some nocturnal prowler he would have recognized and been prepared to deal with, but this was strangely different from anything he could remember hearing before.

He stepped noiselessly to one side and listened for the sound. It came again. There was something of the sea about it—an almost noiseless swishing drip, at once purposeful and unhuman. He thought of the sea water in the hall below and of Miss Makepeace's talk of undines. There were matches in his pocket, and he reached for one. Then he dropped it. The scratch of the match would give him away before there was light enough to disclose his adversary. Mr. Kincaid stretched out his hands and stepped soundlessly forward in the dark.

The game of hoodman-blind that followed was a test of nerves. He had no way of telling whether the thing was hunting him or fleeing from him. For the most part it moved silently like some spirit of the fog, but occasionally he heard a wet slobbering hiss, like a sea beast breathing. Once something slid against his fingers—something smooth, slimy, impalpable. As he closed his hand on it, it was gone.

Then suddenly—without warning—it was upon him, wet and horrible. It enveloped him like a fog, covering his head, stifling him. When he struck out with his arms it gave like water, but at the same time offered a yielding resistance that robbed his blows of power. For the first time in his life he knew panic. The wild unreason of fear engulfed him. He tried to cry out, but the words were crushed back against his mouth. Then a part of the clammy blackness turned rigid, as if his adversary could materialize bone and muscle to serve its need. He redoubled his struggles, but the thing tightened about his throat like a rope. The yielding horror that clung to him prevented his reaching that part of itself which was choking him, but he did manage to swing one hand in a wide circle before his chest. His arm met no resistance. Only the pressure at his throat seemed tangible and real. The blood pounded in his ears until it drowned out the roar of the surf below. Weight, at once substance-less and overpowering, forced him to his knees. Consciousness slipped away from him. The struggle was over.

9

Sea Water

TOBEY CHATTERTON awoke from a nightmare in which formless mon-sters had pursued him screaming. As he fought his way back to conscious-ness he realized that the screams were real. He leaped out of bed and fum-bled for matches. By the time he managed to light the candle the cries had stopped. Cautiously he opened his door and peered out. A dim glow came from the living room. Bobby crept toward it. Then he heard footsteps that he recognized as his aunt's. He stepped out onto the gallery. Miss Makepeace was breathlessly climbing the stairs. The boy ran toward her.

"What's the matter?" he asked. "I heard someone yell and—"

"I know. I did the yelling." She sank on the top step. "I can't go any far-ther—till I get—breath. Something happened—Mr. Kincaid's room—go see."

The boy darted off, and a moment later she heard him pound on Rogan's door.

A voice called from below. Miss Makepeace looked through the banister to see her brother and Dr. Braxton approach the foot of the stairs.

"Arnold."

"Good heavens, Julia! What's the trouble?" Makepeace ran up the steps.

"I'm all right. Just winded. It's Mr. Kincaid. Something's happened to him. His room's over mine. I heard the sound of a struggle and then the thud of a falling body. Now Bobby can't get into his room. There must be something dreadfully wrong."

"Come on, Stirling."

As the two men turned down the corridor, Evan opened his door.

"What's going on?" he asked sleepily.

"That's what we're trying to find out," Makepeace replied.

Bobby left off pounding. "The door's locked, and Mr. Kincaid doesn't answer."

"So I see," his uncle responded dryly. He knelt and peered into the key-hole. "The key's on the inside. I can just see the tip of it by the light of my candle."

As Makepeace rose to his feet, Sue came into the hall.

"What's the matter?"

"We don't know yet," the lawyer told her. "Mr. Kincaid seems to have locked himself in."

"Well, good heavens, if all the noise you're making doesn't wake him, he must be dead."

She looked up to see Evan staring at her. The expression on his face brought memory of the past night's events back with a rush. She leaned weakly against the wall.

Tethryn seized Makepeace by the shoulders. "She's right. He *is* dead! That damned thing is loose now *and it means to go on killing.*"

"Steady, boy." The lawyer caught him by the elbows and shook him gently. "No good thinking things till we get inside and find out what's happened."

Miss Makepeace came into the hall then. Her brother started to explain the situation, but she waved him aside.

"I heard you from out there. What's Bobby doing?"

"Eh?" Makepeace turned and saw that his nephew was kneeling in front of the door. He had a sheet of newspaper in his hands and seemed to be trying to slip it over the sill.

"What in the world . . . ?"

"I got this paper from my room," Bobby explained. "I thought maybe I could push it under Mr. Kincaid's door. Then if we could knock the key out with something . . ."

"It would fall on the paper and you could pull it into the hall," finished the lawyer. "Good idea. Now if we can just find—"

Miss Makepeace offered a hairpin.

"Here," she said, "and hurry."

But Bobby was having trouble with his paper. Wherever he tried to force it through, it stuck and wrinkled.

"It's no use," he complained. "The door fits so tight I can't even get the paper under."

The strain of waiting had told on Evan. His face was drawn and gray. At Bobby's announcement of failure he could stand it no longer. "I'll get in, key or no key. Stand clear."

He turned on his heel and walked into Bobby's room, going all the way to the far wall to obtain the greatest possible run. His body hit Rogan's door with tremendous force. There was a crash of tearing wood, but the oak panels still held.

"No use, Evan," said Dr. Braxton. "It's too solid to break, and you can't get it open without driving the bolt through an inch of the jamb. Bobby can go for an ax."

"The jamb cracked," Evan replied. "Maybe it'll split this time."

Miss Makepeace flared. "Men are such fools. Why don't you try a key from one of the other rooms?"

But Evan was already back in Bobby's room, bracing himself for a second run. This time he hit lower, his shoulder hardly above the level of the knob.

The door gave with a crash, and Evan shot through it to land on hands and knees less than three feet from the still body of Rogan Kincaid.

As the others crowded into the room, Sue stayed in the doorway, clutching her candle. The picture of Frant's death still burned in her memory, and the sight of Rogan's limp body, as it was lifted from the floor and placed on the bed, robbed her of courage.

Evan stood looking at Kincaid. He kept saying "Why a stranger? Why not me? If it had to kill again—why not me?"

Makepeace put a hand on his shoulder. "Steady, boy, there's nothing supernatural about this. Kincaid was strangled."

"You're sure?"

Makepeace pointed down at the bruised throat. "As a matter of fact, this will probably help us clear up your brother's death as well. It's ridiculous to suppose there are two murderers on The Kraken." He turned to his nephew. "Bobby, go down to the servant's quarters and have Jub organize a search of the island. If they find a man, have them bring him to me."

The lawyer's word reminded Sue of the prisoner in the storeroom. She was about to speak of him when Bobby answered his uncle.

"Yes, but . . ."

"But what?"

"How did he get out?"

"How did who get out?"

"Whoever . . . that is . . . the murderer."

Mr. Makepeace was annoyed. "Through the door, I suppose."

"Yes, sir." But Bobby continued to look puzzled. His aunt came to his defense.

"Bobby's right, Arnold. You said yourself it was locked on the inside."

The lawyer was tempted to sarcasm.

"Surely, Julia, even in your cloistered life . . ."

"Besides," put in Bobby, "it was bolted."

"I don't believe it."

Makepeace walked to the door and bent to examine it. There was no doubt about the bolt. It was large and old and rusty. It was bent now so that it could not be moved, but in any case it must have worked stiffly. Nor was the evidence of the hasp less impressive. It had been torn from the jamb and lay on the floor. The wood from which the screws had been pulled was raw and new.

Julia Makepeace was still looking at the door.

"Where's the key?" she asked.

"It was in the lock."

"Well, it's not there now."

Before her brother could answer, Bobby pointed to the floor. When the door had burst open, the key had been thrown out and now lay in the center of the room. Makepeace crossed to it and knelt.

"I can't see any scratches on it," he admitted, as he rose to his feet, "but the light is bad and we probably couldn't make them out without a glass, anyway. We'll have to leave the key where it is for the police. Don't let's make an unnecessary mystery about this thing. A key can be turned from the outside with nippers, and a bolt can be shot with a piece of string."

"Not if the door fits as tightly as this one," his sister reminded him. "Bobby couldn't get a piece of paper under it."

Makepeace thought a minute and then began to laugh.

"We are," he said, "giving a first-class exhibition of how ordinarily sensible people can believe the wildest fairy tales when they are wrought up. There is no need to be puzzled by a locked and bolted door when there are three windows in the room, one of them half open."

"I did that," said Bobby.

His uncle smiled benignly. "I think we may assume that what you could do was not beyond the powers of the murderer."

"Sure . . . only . . . well, that is, I wanted to look at the screens."

"Screens can be opened, too."

Bobby took a deep breath and spoke very low.

"But . . . you see . . . they're stuck."

Makepeace went to the half-opened window and tried to raise the screen. He strained with all his might but it did not move. Silently and with the beginning of awe in his face he went to the second window, then to the third, and finally he examined the window in the bathroom. The screens were old, but the bronze in them was still good. They were screwed in place. There was old paint over the screw heads. The lawyer walked over to Sue.

"Have you been standing in the door ever since we came in?" he asked.

"Yes, but . . ."

"And nobody went past you?"

"Of course not. What are you getting at?"

Makepeace turned and faced the others.

"I don't want to alarm you," he said, "but the man who throttled Kincaid is hidden in this room."

"I looked," said Bobby.

That simple statement put an end to the lawyer's self-assurance. The native incredulity which, for all his avowed spiritualism, was strong in him, snapped. In that moment he would have believed anything.

His sister gave way less easily. In spite of her willingness to believe the night before, or perhaps because of it, she felt she must cling fast to reality. The fact that Rogan had been strangled did not trouble her as much as it might. He was a changeling, come out of nowhere and gone again before she had time to fix him in her mind. As long as Dr. Braxton did not know, perhaps it was better so.

But the idea of the phantom murderer clutched at her heart. It was not so much bodily fear as fear for her reason. She had given way once. She determined she would not do so again.

Candle in hand, she searched the room. She climbed on a chair in the closet and peered into the half-darkness above the shelves. She examined the bathroom and pulled aside the shower curtains. For the first time in her life she looked under the bed.

There was nothing there, but on the bare floor beside the rug lay a drop of water, ringed with salt crystals.

She wondered dully whether she were going to scream or faint and knew she would never forgive herself for doing either. Instead, quite as if she had nothing to do with the matter, she saw her finger point to the floor and heard her voice say calmly, "Water."

Her brother looked down at it.

"You know, that's queer. I hardly thought of it when we picked him up, but Kincaid's clothes are damp. What do you make of it?"

Still in the same calm tone and still without her volition, Miss Makepeace's voice said, "Undine."

Evan clutched at her shoulder. "You mean it's sea water?"

"Look for yourself."

He dropped on his knees and bent over the stains on the floor.

"Evan, don't!" Sue moved to his side. "What difference do a few drops of water make when there's a whole ocean of it right outside?"

"Right outside"—Tethryn rose to his feet—"outside a sealed room with no hole in it big enough for a mouse to crawl through." He dropped an arm around the girl's shoulders. "Thanks, dear, but it's no use. I raised a devil last night . . . a blind devil that kills anything it meets. Maybe it will find me next. God knows, I hope so." He turned to Makepeace. "You laughed at it last night . . . said it didn't exist. Well, here's your undine, straight from the sea. Get down on your knees, man, and pray it didn't hear you when you laughed."

The lawyer's gaunt face was dark with trouble as he answered.

"I can't believe you're right. Granted that Kincaid's death is somehow connected with your brother's, how do you account for the differences between them? As I told you last night, the other world is no more purposeless than this one. Then why should a power, that could strike one man down like an invisible plague, need to attack another in the dark, crush his throat, and leave a trail of sea water to mark its passage?"

Sue turned on him.

"You're making it perfectly beastly," she flared. "You're like a savage seeing a god in every thunderstorm. Suppose the door *was* bolted and locked. Suppose you can't get the windows open. What of it? Do you know all the tricks? Does anyone? If you want to spend your money letting a lot of crooked mediums make a fool of you, go ahead! But I won't have you worrying Evan with this talk about undines and ghosts. Besides, Mr. Kincaid's not dead. If you had eyes in your head you'd see that Grandfather's still working over him. He wouldn't do that if he were dead. There'd be no sense to it!"

The lawyer opened his mouth to speak and then closed it again. He walked across the room and touched Dr. Braxton on the shoulder.

"Is that true?" he asked.

The old doctor straightened up. "Eh? Is what true? Sorry. I was so busy I haven't been paying attention to you people."

"Is Kincaid alive?"

"He's alive all right and I think he's going to keep right on living. If he does, though, it won't be because of me. The man has the constitution of a Scotts terrier. Look at him." The doctor pointed down at the lean torso from which he had stripped the soggy jacket. "I doubt if you could stick a knife in him."

"When is he going to wake up, Stirling?" asked Makepeace. "It is important for us to hear his story of what happened, before the police come."

"Well, you're not going to. I think his unconsciousness is passing into natural sleep. That's the best thing in the world for him. I can't do anything more until I get an X-ray of his throat. I'm not even certain that's necessary. He's been swallowing saliva at regular intervals without much difficulty."

"But . . ."

"You'll have to let me handle my patient my own way, Arnold. The police are your affair and they'll probably keep you busy. I suggest we all go and dress, so as to be ready for them."

The breaking in of Rogan's door had roused Nancy Garwood. With her, waking up was a lengthy process, so that when she found herself staring at the fog wraiths outside her window she had no recollection of the noise that had brought her out of her slumber.

The gloomy dawn accorded so exactly with her own outlook that instead of going back to sleep she lay there thinking over the predicament in which she found herself. Her last show had run just long enough for her to pay off her debts and acquire some new clothes. She had counted on the present invitation to serve as a meal ticket until fall, when she had been promised another part. Now here she was, broke and stranded. Furthermore, Miss Garwood realized that the police were going to be most unpleasant about

Frant's death. That sort of thing didn't do a girl's professional standing any good, either. Obviously it was up to her to find a friend before the police got there.

She slipped out of her rumpled nightdress and contemplated her body in the long mirror. She had no reason to be dissatisfied. While she took a shower and did things—delicately—with lipstick and powder, she thought over the surviving male members of the house party. The Chatterton kid was too young and Dr. Braxton too old. Makepeace looked like a New England conscience. That left Lord Tethryn and Rogan Kincaid. Ordinarily, she decided, inspecting herself in the mirror, a girl could have the earl for a kind word, but he was in worse trouble now than she was. Rogan, then, was her only choice. She rummaged through the bags he had brought until she found a nightgown that was a sin in itself and put it on. The thought of Rogan frightened her a little. If even half the things she had heard of him in New York were true . . .

Still, what could she lose? There was no doubt that it would be a big help to get him on her side. Besides, the police might come any minute, now it was light, and she couldn't afford to wait. Rogan was probably the only man on the island who would admit to being pleased if she went into his room at seven in the morning.

A few minutes with a hairbrush, a pair of high-heeled mules, and a negligee designed for emphasis rather than concealment completed her preparations. She stepped into the hall.

She had no means of knowing which room was Rogan's, but it was a safe guess that he had switched with her. Nancy tiptoed down the hall, found the door partly open, and peeped through. She stepped in and closed the door behind her.

Dr. Braxton had been mistaken in thinking that Rogan would pass from coma into natural sleep. Actually the gambler had awakened while the doctor and Bobby were dressing him in dry pajamas, but he had given no sign of returning consciousness. He wanted to think, but there was barely time to recall the events of the night before when he heard soft footsteps approach the side of his bed, and a feminine voice said, "Hello." He opened his eyes and looked at Nancy.

The girl smiled. "Like me?"

His throat hurt, but he didn't care.

"If this is heaven, how did I get here, and how do I happen to be a Mohammedan?"

Nancy had never heard of the delights promised Moslems in paradise, but she recognized a compliment when she heard one.

"Like to talk?" she asked.

"You talk. I'll look."

The girl favored him with another of her quick smiles and dropped on the edge of his bed.

"Did they tell you what happened to Jack?"

"Can't talk. Busy looking."

"This is important. I'm still pretty hazy about what happened last night after Jack died."

"You haven't remembered what made you faint then?"

She shook her head. "I wish I could."

"Maybe you're better off not remembering."

"But don't you see?" the girl insisted. "I've got to find out what happened to Jack. Was there any way . . . that is, could it have been some sort of an accident?".

"It could. There is also the theory that Frant is only fooling and will pop up at breakfast and yell 'Surprise!' "

"What I mean is, was all that curse business just a coincidence, or did Jack have heart disease?"

"Not unless it's catching and being choked half to death is one of the symptoms."

"What are you talking about?"

"Simply that Frant's heart trouble got into my room last night and nearly broke my neck."

"You mean somebody tried to kill you, too?"

Rogan nodded. The movement brought a swift stab of pain. He grimaced. Nancy was sympathetic but insistent.

"I'm sorry if it hurts you to talk, but I've got to find out things. Who did it?"

"It was dark," Mr. Kincaid admitted, "but you can take your pick of our local phantoms. At the moment Undine seems to be favored."

Nancy's brow wrinkled. "Jack said something about Undine last night. Wasn't she sort of a fairy?"

"It seems there are undines and undines. You'll no doubt get a clearer idea if I tell you this one may be described as a cross between a jellyfish and a toad."

Nancy looked at him sharply.

"I haven't the least notion what you're getting at."

"Neither have I, if that's any comfort to you. But perhaps you are acquainted with the Hangman's Handyman?"

The girl shivered. "No, and I don't want to be. Who is he?"

"I wish I knew. My point is that whatever tried to kill me last night showed a decided preference for the neck. That rather indicates the assistant hangman."

Nancy pointed an accusing finger at him. "You're making it up."

"If so, I got black and blue doing it. Miss Makepeace mentioned the Handyman last night. Don't you remember?"

"He sounds horrible. What's he like?"

"She was chary of details, but he sounds like a cheerful fellow—the sort that whistles at his work and can tie a noose or pull a customer's heels with equal alacrity."

Nancy put a soft hand over his mouth.

"It must hurt you to talk, so don't waste it on nonsense. Besides, I've got to get out of here before somebody comes in and finds me."

"Why?"

"On account of because I have no clothes on. You just shut your eyes and listen."

Not unreasonably, Mr. Kincaid kept his eyes where they were.

"You say Jack was murdered," she went on. "Just where does that leave us?"

"Rallying around a mattress wishing I felt better."

She made a face at him.

"You'll get over that. But, don't you see, if somebody killed Jack, we're likely to be playing 'clap in and clap out' with the cops before long?"

"Well?"

"Well, nothing! The other people in this house are big bugs and their relations. Three guesses who's going to be locked in the pigpen as material witnesses?"

"You, for one."

"And you too, big nose, unless you do some tall thinking."

"I wasn't here."

"I never met a cop yet that could tell an alibi from a confession. What do you say we team up?"

"Wouldn't you be wiser to pick someone with a little more local pull?"

"I'm going after that, too, as soon as I have time to turn around."

"Turn slowly," Rogan counseled, "so they can get a good look from all sides."

"I'll take care of the sex appeal, but I want some brains to back me up. How about it . . . are we partners or not?"

"Partners, it is," he agreed. "I warn you, though, my brains aren't up to much this morning."

"I'll risk that. Where do we start?"

"Tell me as much as you can about Frant."

"I didn't know him awfully well, really. I met him at a party last fall, and he seemed a pretty good guy. I can't think what got into him last night. He always treated me swell."

"See him often?"

"Only when he was in New York. He'd hit town for a few days, or a week, and then be gone for a month or two."

Nancy sat down on the edge of the bed.

"You know," she said frowning, "there's something queer about this."

Rogan chuckled.

"Would you consider me bromidic if I hinted that you don't know the half of it?"

"No. I'm talking about Jack and that curse story. None of the rest of you knew him like I did, except maybe Dr. Braxton, so you might not have noticed it. Jack was the greatest fellow in the world for making up stories. He'd spend hours telling the biggest whoppers you ever heard."

"Unfortunately, most of his came true."

"Not all of them, I'll bet. I don't mean I ever caught him out. But the kind of lies he told, he didn't expect you to believe. Well now, that curse story was just like one of Jack's regulars."

"Are you trying to suggest that Frant was an accessory to his own murder?"

"No, but it could have been some fancy way of committing suicide. I'll tell you something else too—something I'm sure of. Jack framed that superstition business."

"What do you mean?"

"Well, remember I told you how his lordship broke my mirror?"

He nodded and Nancy went on.

"It was a put-up job. Jack told me he wanted to play a joke on his brother. He had me stand where Evan would bump me if he turned around. His highness didn't do much turning, and it was a long time before the trick worked. But it was Jack's idea. I can swear to it. I think that's why he invited you down here, too."

"To break mirrors?"

"No, to make thirteen at table. That's how many there'd have been if you and the Wests had gotten here. Even as things turned out, he dragged it into the conversation by the heels."

"Perhaps, but we couldn't prove any of it." Mr. Kincaid was skeptical. "Besides, if Frant killed himself, who choked me? You can't expect the cops to look at my throat and believe that nothing happened to me but a bad dream. Speaking of cops, you'd better take a look out of the window while I try to think up another angle."

"I'll bet you can't see a cross-town block in this fog."

Nancy rose and moved to the window. The mist had thinned a little, and she managed to make out a small boat about a quarter of a mile away.

"Ship ahoy." She turned to Rogan. "And I'm laying heavy money it's the boys in blue. Got that idea yet?"

"Yes, but it's not a very good one. Just a thought to keep the cops busy and give you time to turn around." He pointed to the robe the doctor had loaned him. "There is a key in the pocket of that. It fits the door of a storeroom that opens off the kitchen. Get dressed as quickly as you can. Go down and unlock that door. I caught a man prowling around last night and locked him in there. Don't let him see you, but open the door wide so he knows he can get away."

"But if you found . . ." Nancy's thoughts tumbled over one another faster than she could speak. "Maybe he killed Jack."

"Maybe he did, but the more time the police spend chasing him, the longer we'll have to think up some good reason for not being thrown in jail as material witnesses. Get going."

"O. K., but if anybody sees me coming out of your room, my good name will be str-r-ipped from me."

"If you take off anything else, you'll be stark naked."

10

Dr. Murchison Has His Doubts

MAKEPEACE, as the lawyer in the party, felt it his duty to greet the police on the dock. Dorsey, the sergeant in charge of homicides, was a heavily-built individual and on that account seemed short for a policeman. He looked like a typical Carolina farmer come to town in his store clothes, but the men who climbed out of the boat after him treated him with respect. Makepeace began to hope fate had sent them neither a fool nor a bureaucrat, but a hard-working cop who knew his job.

Dorsey stood on the little dock and introduced the others as they came ashore: chubby, shabby Doc Murchison, the coroner's physician; Paul Quinn, photographer; Jacob Feldmann, technician and fingerprint expert; and Nelson and Ordway, plain-clothes men. The remaining man turned out to be one of the Bailey's Point fishermen. It was his boat.

The lawyer's greeting was interrupted by a roar overhead. He looked up. Out of the zenith a seaplane appeared, diving straight at the dock. In Makepeace's mind sprang the sudden conviction that he had become insane—that Frant's horrid death, the dripping phantom that crawled through a bronze screen and choked Kincaid into unconsciousness, and now this mad aviator bent on suicide against the wharf on which the lawyer stood surrounded by policemen were all part of a waking nightmare. He even had time for the fear that he was damned to a future that would be one long succession of impossible terrors.

Then, perhaps fifty feet above their heads, the craft leveled off, settled lightly on the water, and swung around with the easy grace of a ski runner. At rest it showed as a tiny two-seater, and already a figure was scrambling out on one wing in an effort to reach the boat.

"You damn fool!" roared Dorsey. "I'll have your license!"

The man on the wing held on to a strut with his left hand and wagged the forefinger of his right at the sputtering policeman.

"Oh, no, you won't."

"What makes you think so?"

"Because I haven't got any."

The speaker made a wild leap for the gunwale of the boat, missed, and fell into the water with a splash.

The plane swung around and Dorsey saw that the man in the water had been passenger and not pilot. While he still floundered in the waves the aviator gunned his motor and, without even a backward glance, took off from the crest of a swell and departed northward. The aircraft was no more than a mote in the gray sky when the boatman succeeded in catching the passenger's collar with a boathook and holding him against the tug of the treacherous current.

Dorsey, whose wrath cooled quickly, jumped into the boat and helped drag the newcomer over the side.

There were a hundred policemen in New York and a thousand representatives of other professions who would have advised anyone who hooked Dan Collins out of the water to throw him back—first, because he was manifestly undersize and, second, because he was sure to cause more trouble than any long-suffering detective sergeant could conveniently absorb.

Collins was no beauty. His gleeful gargoyle's face looked out from under a tangle of red curls, and he weighed exactly a hundred and three pounds wringing wet. This latter fact is known because there were scales on the dock and he tried it. Whether the wetness improved his appearance was open to question.

"That's Pancake Pitts," he said, pointing after the disappearing plane, "the guy that put the joy in joy stick."

"He's a goddamn fool," said Dorsey.

"Wish I was. Pitts seems to get a lot of fun out of it."

He scrambled to his feet and held out his hand.

"I'm Dan Collins of the New York *Record.* Hope you haven't been waiting too long for me."

Makepeace turned to the sergeant.

"I asked Mr. Yeager particularly to keep the press out of this until you had finished your preliminary investigation."

"I didn't tell the papers," retorted Dorsey, "if that's what you're driving at. The news must have leaked from this end. Now he's here, I don't reckon there's much you can do about it."

The sergeant, after learning that there was a speedboat belonging to Frant at the island, dismissed the fisherman who had brought him. He turned to Makepeace.

"Where's the dead man?"

"At the house."

"Everybody else up there, too?"

"Everyone but my sister. We thought it best not to inform the servants of Mr. Frant's death until daylight, otherwise we'd have had a panic on our hands. She's with them now in their quarters over the boat-house."

Dorsey nodded. "She'll have her job cut out for her anyway, I reckon. Well, we'd better be gettin' up to the house."

The long-untended rose bushes had grown over the path, so that the little party was forced to proceed in single file. This gave the sergeant an opportunity to work out his plan of campaign. His worst fears had been confirmed by Makepeace's attitude. This was obviously going to be one of those cases where you couldn't take a step for fear of treading on tender toes, and where all concerned would say as little as possible for fear of involving themselves or their friends in any publicity.

Well, Dorsey had a trick to beat that. It had worked before. You got the dumbest witness alone and started on him. That usually gave you leads right away, and if any story had been fixed up you could spot it in a minute. Besides, the others wouldn't be sure what the first witness had told, so they wouldn't know how much they could hold back.

Dr. Braxton met them on the front steps. He greeted Murchison warmly and acknowledged the latter's introductions.

"Thank you for being so prompt, Sergeant," he said as he shook hands. "Will you look at Mr. Frant first or would you rather question us?"

"Where'd the death take place?"

"In the living room. However, the body's been carried upstairs."

Dorsey frowned. "You oughtn't to have let that happen, doctor."

"I wouldn't ordinarily, but the circumstances are most unusual."

"No help for it now, anyway. Will you show Murchison where it is? Don't go in the room. I want him to do his own work." He turned to his technician. "You go too, Jake, and take Paul with you for pictures."

As they passed into the living room Dorsey frowned at the evidences of wealth that confirmed his worst fears, but the sight of Bobby cheered him. The blond youth seemed to have been designed by nature for the role of first witness in the type of investigation the sergeant had planned. First, though, it would be necessary to get rid of Makepeace. Dorsey turned to the lawyer.

"How many people are on the island—not counting the servants?"

"Eight. Mr. Frant's half brother, Lord Tethryn; Dr. Braxton and his granddaughter; my sister, myself, and Mr. Chatterton—who is our nephew. There are also two others, a Miss Garwood and a Mr. Kincaid. I know nothing about them except that they were personal friends of Mr. Frant."

"They aren't local people, then?"

"No. The Garwood girl lives in New York, I believe. I have no idea where Kincaid comes from."

"We'll find out. Would you mind showin' Nelson here where the phone is an' stayin' with him while he calls up about the reports? He'll probably need information, so it'll save time if you're there to give it to him."

The lawyer's annoyance was evident, but he went. Dorsey watched him pass through the library door and then motioned Bobby to a chair.

"Now, Mr. Chatterton, while we're waitin' for the rest of the folks suppose you tell me what went on last night."

"I don't know exactly . . . that is . . . you see . . ."

"You were here, weren't you?"

"Yes, but . . . well . . . I didn't understand . . ."

"Suppose you leave that to me. Just tell me what you saw."

Bobby complied. In two minutes the unfortunate sergeant was regretting his decision to avoid hearing Makepeace's version first. The lawyer might have been misleading, but he would at least have been lucid. One thing, however, seemed clear from the Chatterton boy's story—Frant had quarreled with his half brother just before he died.

"Did they fight?"

"Oh, no, how could they? Mr. Frant was a lot smaller than Evan."

Dorsey controlled his temper. "Go on."

"Well, there wasn't much more really . . . you see . . . Evan cursed Mr. Frant."

"Was that what made Frant mad?"

"He wasn't mad. He asked Evan to curse him."

"Wait a minute. Are you telling me that Frant actually asked his brother to swear at him?"

"Oh, Evan didn't swear, he cursed."

The sergeant closed his eyes and counted ten. Then he said, "What happened next?"

"Mr. Frant died."

Dorsey choked. "Died—just like that?"

"It wasn't like anything I ever saw before."

"What killed him?"

"That's what I can't figure out."

The sound of feet on the gallery above saved the sergeant from apoplexy. He looked up and saw Dr. Braxton descending the stairs with Evan. In reaction from the feeling of helplessness brought on by Bobby, he strode across the room and planted himself in front of the doctor.

"I want to know what killed Frant," he demanded.

"I'm afraid that's something I can't tell you."

"Can't or won't?"

Evan stepped between them.

"Is it necessary to badger these people, Officer?"

"I'm not here to badger anybody," Dorsey growled. "But a man's dead and it's my job to find out how he died."

"Then ask your questions of me."

"Why you?"

"Because Jackson Frant was my brother. I killed him."

The sergeant's jaw dropped.

"Say, what is this?" he demanded. "First I get a lot of double-talk from the kid, then the doctor says he can't tell what killed Frant, an' now you claim you did it. What am I supposed to do? Laugh the whole thing off?"

Suddenly Evan's self-control snapped.

"You fool!" he shouted. "You purple fool! I killed my brother. I cursed him and he died. Isn't that enough for you?"

Dr. Braxton took Evan's arm.

"I think you'd better let me handle this, Sergeant."

Dorsey opened his mouth to reply when the return of Murchison stopped him. Before the plump coroner's physician reached the bottom step Dorsey had him by the arm.

"Come on, Doc. You're just the man I'm looking for." He pushed open the nearest door. They passed through kitchen and pantry into the dining room beyond.

Dorsey flung himself into a chair.

"Sit down, Doc, an' let's have the dope."

"I'd rather stand by an open window and air myself if you don't mind. It's going to be a long time before I smell like Four Roses again."

"Suit yourself, but listen. I'm used to havin' fast ones pulled on me, but the people here are tryin' to run me round in circles. The worst of it is they're prominent folks, and I'm in a spot. If I let 'em get away with it the D.A.'ll raise hell, but I can't bear down on 'em without havin' the real dope. So give me all you can. What did you find out about Frant?"

"He's dead."

"What killed him?"

"How should I know?"

"That's your job, ain't it?"

Murchison left the window. "Listen, Tom. That corpse upstairs is *plenty* dead. It would take an anthropologist to tell it ain't a nigger."

"You're drunk!"

"The practised eye might discover that I was drunk yesterday, but I'm unpleasantly sober now. Here's a guy been dead a month or so, an' you ask me to take a quick look and say what killed him."

"You've got the D.T.'s. That guy died last night."

"If that's so," said Murchison imperturbably, "he certainly hasn't wasted any time since."

A voice from the doorway asked, "May I come in?" The fat man turned and saw Julia Makepeace advancing toward him. He pulled out a chair with one hand and gestured with the other.

"Glad to see you, ma'am, and sit down. My name's Murchison. Tom Dorsey here is confused on a small point, and I'd like you to set him straight."

The sergeant grinned, and Miss Makepeace decided that she approved of him.

"Doc's been tellin' me Frant died a month ago," Dorsey said. "Any truth in that?"

"If that's his opinion, he's certainly wrong."

"How about takin' her up and lettin' her identify the body, Doc?"

Miss Makepeace turned to the coroner's physician.

"Could I?" she asked slowly.

Murchison chuckled.

"You got this case all wrong, Tom. Nobody's goin' to identify that body by lookin' at it. It ain't that kind."

"What's the matter with it?"

"Pretty nearly everything."

"I'm afraid, Sergeant," said Miss Makepeace, "that the way you heard our story started you off on the wrong foot. I am told that you got your information from my nephew and Lord Tethryn. No doubt you thought they were lying because what they said sounded impossible. My version will sound equally impossible, but I think I can at least make you understand it as well as I do."

Dorsey leaned forward. "That's good enough for me, ma'am."

When she came to the point where Frant's body had been carried upstairs, the sergeant asked:

"You seen it since?"

"No."

"Then who told you what had happened to it?"

"No one. That's why I asked Dr. Murchison. But the men knew. You could tell by the way they acted this morning—my brother especially. Besides, there was something else. The worst thing of all, I think. It took place just before Mr. Frant died, but to help you understand it I must begin with a rather trivial incident that occurred yesterday afternoon.

"One of the servants here brought his dog with him. I went for a walk before dinner and came on the animal rolling on its back in the remains of a dead sea gull. I made the dog stop, but it followed me back to the house. Even outdoors a strong smell of dead bird still clung to it."

Dorsey nodded. "Dogs are like that."

"Mr. Frant's death was very sudden, but it wasn't quite instantaneous. We were all trying to help him when I suddenly remembered the dog. It was hardly the time to think of such things so I put it out of my mind till after Mr. Frant was dead and Lord Tethryn had carried him upstairs. There was still a faint, unpleasant odor in the room. I looked about for the dog, intending to put it outside, but I couldn't find it. That was strange, because all the doors were shut and we would surely have seen the animal if it had followed Lord Tethryn."

"Did anybody else notice anything queer?"

"They were all too occupied, I think."

Dorsey scratched his head. "You mean the first time you noticed this—er—odor was after Frant fell down an' *before* he died?"

Miss Makepeace nodded.

"Wait a minute, ma'am," Murchison protested. "Do I understand you're askin' the sergeant and me to believe it wasn't the death that caused the decay, but the decay that caused the death? That might be all right with gangrene, or somethin' that took a week or two, but you say Frant was alive last night!"

"It's what the curse called for, wasn't it?" she reminded him.

"Surely, ma'am, you don't take that curse business seriously?"

"I've stopped trying to be logical, and so will you after you've been here awhile."

"Did his lordship stay with the body?"

"No. He must have gone to his own room and changed his clothes. He was dressed differently when I saw him again."

The chubby coroner's physician hunched himself forward in his chair to get a little slack in the seat of his pants.

"You don't happen to remember what Mr. Frant had on last night, do you, ma'am?"

"Yes—a white dinner jacket and a white tie, which I thought was in very bad taste. Everything he wore was white except for some broad black clocks on his hose."

Dorsey rose.

"On your feet, Doc. We got to go up an' look for an explanation."

"There ain't any," said Murchison. "Oh, I know I look like a bum, and I'd be on relief if my brother didn't control the third ward, but I've been cutting up dead men for thirty years, and I know a lot about 'em, when I'm sober. The post-mortem evidence is right out of line with anything in recorded medicine. When I was on the wagon, about ten years ago, I started writing a book on methods of determining the time of death. I never finished it, but I did a pile of research on the speed of putrefaction. I read every reported case I could lay my hands on, and I learned a lot. Some things speed it up—heat and sunlight and moisture; but you can take it from me, nothing on earth would account for what's wrong with that body upstairs."

"Good God, man, the thing's happened," Dorsey protested. "There's no use stickin' your head in the sand like some kind of scientific ostrich."

"You explain it, then. I'm a doctor, but I ain't a witch doctor."

"You could be a horse doctor for all the help you are. We got to take a look, anyway. Get movin'."

They met Collins coming out of the room that held Frant's corpse. Dorsey glared at him.

"What the hell are you doin' here, mister?"

The little Irishman cocked an untidy eyebrow.

"Temper, temper!"

"Beat it."

"Not until I've had a chance to sit at the feet of Gamaliel. You wouldn't recognize that. It's from the Bible. Put in the vulgar tongue, I seek to learn who will be arrested and when."

"I don't know yet. You'll learn when I find out and when I get ready to tell you—not before."

"What a quaint idea. Read tomorrow's *Record* for a complete analysis of the case—names, motives, and pictures."

"You're bluffing."

"Maybe." Collins moved away from the door. "But I can tell you one thing right now. Take a deep breath before you go in."

11

The Body on the Bed

IN SPITE of all he had heard, Dorsey was utterly unprepared for the thing on the bed. Standing beside it, he felt his hold on all that was sane and sensible slipping from him. Even without the pudgy physician's knowledge of medicine, he realized that the sight before him was starkly impossible.

He glanced up from the body to where Paul Quinn, the police photographer, and Jacob Feldmann, the technical expert, were putting away the last of their apparatus. The technician was a German Jew, driven to this country by the Hitler regime. There was a stolidity about him wholly Teutonic. He was amazingly good at his job, and his thoroughness was a standing joke among his colleagues. Dorsey realized his worth, although he was frequently annoyed by Feldmann's tendency to view his own findings, and even his mistakes, as divinely inspired. Now, standing there beside Frant's body, the sergeant found his assistant's imperturbability singularly comforting.

"Folks downstairs say this man died at nine-thirty last night, Jake. What do you think?"

"It is not possible." The technician went on to quote from memory a list of the periods after death at which the various symptoms of dissolution appeared.

Dorsey scratched his nose. "Learn anything else?"

"Not yet. But I have found a matter which it is my work to check. Could I please call one of the bureaus of the government at Washington over long distance?"

The sergeant waved him away. "Sure. But come back. I want to talk to you."

When the door closed behind the retreating technician, Dorsey turned to the photographer.

"What's Jake got up his sleeve, Paul?"

"Damned if I know. Maybe he thinks he can prove the corpse had measles in 1903. You know Jake, Chief."

"You got everything you want?"

"Yeah. And a lot of stuff Jake wanted, too. I'm going down now and get some shots of the living room. O.K.?"

When the photographer had left, Murchison walked over to the windows and lit a cigar.

"Got that explanation, Tom?"

"Yeah. This ain't Frant's body."

"You don't believe that, do you?"

"Hell! What else can I believe? Damn it all, the thing happened. There's got to be some way of explainin' it."

"Maybe. But that don't mean there's any use in an explanation that don't work. Look at the clothes on that stiff. They're Frant's all right, 'cause there's a tailor's label with his name on it in the pocket. The shape that cadaver's in, you can bet nobody put those clothes on it last night without leaving plenty of traces . . . 'specially the socks. Look at 'em."

The sergeant scowled at Frant's ankles.

"Besides," Murchison continued, "you remember what Miss What's-her-name said."

"Yeah, but that don't prove anything. You wouldn't have any guesses yourself, would you, Doc?"

"Your English friend's all ready with a confession."

"Yeah. And Shirley Temple shot McKinley. Can't you picture me and the D.A.? 'Well, Sergeant, what killed the man?' 'Please, sir, a couple of swear words!' Come on, Doc, you got to have some ideas."

"No, I don't. My job's to report my findings, and all I can find in this case is that the body is in an advanced state of decomposition."

"An' half-a-dozen people ready to swear he was alive last night! Damn it, if this is Frant, he must have been poisoned, and it's up to you to find out what with."

Murchison shook his head.

"There's no poison in the books to account for that kind of galloping gangrene."

"Maybe it's a poison that ain't in the books."

"Maybe. But that don't help you any. Think of the fun the defense lawyers would have: 'Do you write scenarios in your spare time, Sergeant?' You'd better fall back on the curse idea. It may be nutty, but it's the only theory that explains your case—explains every bit of it with nothing left over."

"Hell," said Dorsey. He was still of the same mind ten minutes later when Feldmann returned.

"A report came from Hartford." The technician held out a folded paper. While Dorsey read it, the coroner's physician spoke to Feldmann.

"You say this stiff couldn't have been alive yesterday, Jake, but everybody in the house swears he was. How do you account for that?"

"They are lying."

"They couldn't all be in it together."

The technician raised his shoulders. "There is no other explanation possible."

"What about poison?"

"It is not possible."

Dorsey looked up from his report.

"Damn it, stop talking like God. How can you be so sure?"

"I have studied under our Professor Zimmer in Berlin."

Murchison laughed.

"I haven't had your advantages, Jake, but I don't think it was poison myself."

"Well, then," snapped Dorsey, "what about the clothes? Maybe Frant was wearing them last night, and the murderer took them off him and put them on another body."

"That is not possible, either. I will show you." Feldmann became unpleasantly technical.

"God damn it, Jake," Dorsey interrupted him. "It's got to be either poison or substitution. Those people downstairs can't all be in on a lie. I'd almost as soon take Doc's idea that it's witchcraft."

Without moving a muscle Feldmann managed to convey his opinion of the coroner's physician. Murchison watched him for a moment and then asked, "Do you believe in dowsers, Jake?"

"What are dowsers?"

"Water finders."

Dorsey was interested. "You mean old fellows that run around with a forked stick lookin' for a place to dig a well?"

The fat man nodded.

"But that ain't witchcraft, Doc. It's instinc'. Like the birds findin' their way north."

Feldmann tittered.

"Pardon me, Herr Sergeant. It is not witchcraft, nor is it instinct. It is not anything. Water finders are like unicorns—they exist only in the imaginations of uneducated fools."

Dorsey bristled. "Who're you callin' an uneducated fool?"

Murchison jerked ashes in the direction of the technician.

"Everybody else," he said.

The sergeant snorted.

"I don't lay claim to much education, but it just happens I know somethin' about water finders. When I was a kid up in Sligo Falls my granddad tried to dig a well. He sunk more holes than a woodchuck, an' every one of 'em was dry as a sermon. Then he got hold of an old loony that claimed he could find water. I watched him work. He ran around the place with a hazel stick in his hands, an' in less'n an hour he picked a spot not thirty feet from one of granddad's holes. When we dug there we had the best well in the county."

The fat man grinned at Feldmann.

"Another one of your uneducated fools wrote the *Encyclopaedia Britannica* article on divining rods, Jake. He knows they work, too."

Feldmann's fleshy nose wrinkled, but the sergeant broke in before he could retort.

"All right, Doc. You've made a monkey out of Jake. That's easy, but what of it? I believe in divinin' rods because I've seen one work, but that don't make me believe in witchcraft. I've seen pigeons find their way home, too."

"Jake's like you," said Murchison. "He thinks with a sort of sieve that sifts out all the facts he doesn't want to face. He won't believe in dowsers for the same reason he won't believe in unicorns. He doesn't want to. Even if a unicorn came up and butted him in the pants he still wouldn't believe in it. Before he forms a theory he makes up his mind what facts to select. It's the oldest trick in the world to argue a thing don't exist by denying the facts that prove it."

"You . . . you . . ." sputtered Feldmann, "you talk of science! I am not a man of science because I do not believe in witchcraft?"

"Not because you don't believe it, but because you won't examine it."

"It is not necessary. If a fool tells me he discovers how to square the circle, do I have to waste time to prove that he is wrong? Scientists do not examine the lies of witches for good reason. We have, through the experiments in our laboratories, proved that the world is a colossal mechanism wherein each effect is produced by a set of interrelated causes, and thus, by definitely establishing the mechanical nature of the universe, we are able to state definitely that any phenomenon where effect is not founded on cause does not exist."

"Your science is out of date, Jake. Eddington and Jeans and the other atomic-physics boys say every fact is a long way from a gear in a universal machine. They laugh at the law of cause and effect. Did you ever hear of the principle of indeterminacy?"

"Kreuzdonnerwetter! Warum bestehst du darauf immer wieder diese englischen Mystiker anzuführen, die sich nur Wissenschaftler schimpfen. Deutsche Politiker sind vielleicht der Abschaum der Erde, aber Deutsche Wissenschaftler sind—"

"Shut up, Jake," ordered Dorsey. He turned to Murchison. "What are you drivin' at, Doc?"

"Just this. You've got a tough case on your hands. You can't solve it by looking for facts to fit a theory. The theory has to fit the facts."

"Maybe, but my job ain't makin' theories. The D.A.'s due back in town this afternoon, an' I've got to find him somethin' to work with. As far as the D.A.'s concerned, the curse business is worth about as much as a campaign promise."

Feldmann interrupted him.

"Pardon me, Herr Sergeant, the doctor is wrong. There is only one theory. All these people are lying. There is a way to prove it. Six of them are old friends. They are of two families, and Lord Tethryn who is Miss Braxton's suitor. They will all tell the same story. These are the ones to whom you have already spoken. But there are two more. I have made inquiries. There is a man named Kincaid. He is extraordinarily smart and you will not find out too much from him without much difficulties. There is also a girl by the name of Garwood. She was Frant's woman. She may not tell you the truth, but her lies will not be the same as those of the others. Hans Gross says—"

Dorsey slapped his thigh. "That's an idea! Where is she, Jake? Do you know?"

"In the kitchen getting breakfast for herself."

"Let's get goin'."

Left alone, the coroner's physician pulled up a chair and sat puffing on his cigar and staring at the body.

Murchison was a lazy man. He avoided effort whenever he could, but, as with many lazy people, once a problem took hold of him it would not let him rest. The cadaver fascinated him. It was all very well to accept the curse as the cause of death, but that left the *modus operandi* of the curse itself unsolved. Still, you could diagnose a case as cancer without knowing what caused the cancer. He imagined an article in the *A.M.A. Journal:* "The Faulkland Curse—Its Pathology; by H.L. Murchison, M.D.," and smiled. Nevertheless, the body was an all-too-obvious fact, and logically one could not deny the curse precedence over Dorsey's theories. He began testing the idea in his mind. After all, the curse hypothesis was only tenable as long as nothing pointed away from it. One little fact would be enough to put it out of court.

The coroner's physician rose and was about to bend over the bed when a slight sound caught his attention. He looked up to see a tall figure standing in the doorway. Murchison grunted.

"Friend of the deceased?"

"Guest. I'm Rogan Kincaid. I have a little snooping to do if you don't mind." He closed the outer door behind him and strolled into the bathroom. Murchison followed.

"What's the idea?"

"One of the theories is that somebody poisoned Frant's pills. It's not likely, but I thought I'd check up." Rogan opened the wall cabinet. "Yes, here they are. You might settle the point by analyzing them."

"I've already got my lifework laid out. Dorsey wants me to analyze *that.*" Murchison indicated the figure on the bed. "Got any idea what these are?" He took the pill box from Rogan and opened it, disclosing a half-dozen white capsules.

"Several drugs were mentioned last night: bichloride of mercury, calomel, dinitrophenol, oxalic acid, potassium cyanide. However, it will probably save time if you start testing for alum and run right down the white powders until you come to zinc sulphate."

"You start handing ideas to Dorsey, and my job'll be hereditary." The coroner's physician snapped the top back on the box and dropped it into his pocket. "If I've got to look over this cadaver I might as well get started. You wouldn't care to help me undress it? No? Anyway, it didn't do any harm to ask."

He waddled over to the bed and bent down without interrupting his monologue.

"For the time being, I'll have to confine my examination to the face and hands. I won't find anything there, of course, but it will help pass the time."

"If you care to pass the time in a little private conversation with me . . ."

"I don't like you. You found stuff for me to analyze, and what good will it do? Suppose somebody did switch pills on our friend here. The chances are they switched 'em back again later, just so I'd have to spend hours testing a box of aspirin . . ."

The last word ended on an odd note of surprise. Murchison took a wooden tongue-depressor from his pocket and flicked one of the blackened hands away from the breast of the corpse so that it lay palm up on the edge of the bed.

Side by side they bent over the dead hand. *The skin had been removed from each finger tip.*

Murchison straightened with a grunt. "Damn neat job, too. I'll say that for him!"

12

Man Hunt

DORSEY FOUND Nancy finishing her coffee and took her to the dining room for questioning. She added almost nothing to his knowledge of the dead patent-medicine manufacturer. "Lots of men," she explained, "don't like too many questions, and a girl learns to be careful." Yes, she had been out on parties with Frant when he entertained buyers, but they rarely talked business. When they did, she paid no attention.

On the other hand, she confirmed Miss Makepeace's account of the little man's death in a manner that left no room for doubt. Her story was annoyingly vague and she seemed to have noticed all the wrong details, but its very faults showed that it was an eyewitness account and not a memorized lie.

The sergeant sank back in his chair, damning Feldmann for suggesting the interview with Nancy and himself for putting hope in it. It was the technician's habitual misfortune to appear when he was most unwelcome. He did so now, pushing through the pantry door with an expression of self-satisfaction on his ugly face that made Dorsey clench his fists under the table.

"I have a report," Feldmann began, "which proves conclusively what I have already told you about the identity of the body." He placed a closely-written sheet in front of his superior.

The sergeant read it, scowling. "You're sure of this?"

"I have checked every point."

As the technician left, Dorsey turned back to Nancy.

"Got any more to tell me?"

"I've got plenty to ask you. What do I do now? I'm stranded with this turkey, and it's an eight-hundred-mile walk back. Any suggestions?"

"I'm married."

"I didn't mean it that way."

"I did." He rubbed his chin. "That's all, I guess. You can go now."

In the kitchen Nancy found Bobby and—to her surprise—Dan Collins, whom she knew by sight.

He greeted her cheerily. "Hello, Buttercup. I always said I'd like to be cast away with you on a South Sea island, and here we are! My friend here has just been showing me a parlor trick, but we can skip that. Tell me all."

Nancy was glad to see the little reporter. Somehow he broke the spell of brooding horror that hung over the old house. There was a wholesome magic about his rumpled clothes and pepper-colored curls that turned nightmare to nonsense and blood to red ink. The girl perched on the edge of the kitchen cabinet and swung her legs. She smiled at Dan.

"You seem to be working hard."

"I am," he replied, eying the legs with honest admiration. "The phone's in the pantry and I can hear half that goes over it. As a matter of fact, I've got so much stuff on this case now my paper won't have room for the ads."

"You'll have Winchell gnashing his teeth."

"Down to the gums. But come on, baby, give. Is it true that this earl guy is so superstitious he thinks it's bad luck to walk under a black cat? And what about Kincaid—did somebody really beat him up last night?"

She nodded, and the reporter whistled.

"Whew. Then it must have been King Kong. That fellow Kincaid is sudden death. I saw him clean out a poolroom once with eight guys in it. Some of 'em had guns, too. He could throw pool balls faster than they could shoot, and the way he handled a cue would make your mouth water."

The phone in the pantry rang. Collins put up his hand.

"Shhh! Let the sergeant answer it. It won't do to let these hick cops find out that little pitchers have ears like Clark Gable."

He turned and saw Dorsey standing in the pantry door, laughing at him.

"On your way, Collins. I hate to have my talks on the telephone misquoted." As Dan rose to go, the sergeant added, "An' if you see Miss Makepeace, ask her to come to the dining room, will you?"

Collins and Bobby went in search of Miss Makepeace, leaving Nancy alone in the huge living room. The crouching shadows of the night before were gone, but day had brought no honest sunshine—only the murky twilight that lives in wrecked ships and sunken cities. The girl shivered.

A furtive sound from the library caught her ear. Suddenly tense, she crept to the door and peered in. A woman's figure, clad in black, stood in one corner. Its head was turned from her and seemed bent with a curious intentness over some hidden object.

For a moment Nancy was frightened. Then she recognized Miss Makepeace and in her relief blurted out, "The sergeant's looking for you." There was a sharp click, and the older woman turned slowly like an automaton. She kept her hands behind her, and her face held an expression that the girl could not fathom. "He wants you to come to the dining room," she added uneasily.

"Why?"

"I'm not sure. That fellow Feldmann found out something about the body, I think."

"Was it poison?"

"He didn't say."

"Perhaps the sergeant will tell me." Miss Makepeace moved toward the dining room, then turned at the doorway. She smiled dryly. "Thank you for letting me know."

Nancy glanced at the corner and saw that the object Miss Makepeace had been hiding was a telephone. She recalled the attitude of rapt attention in which the older woman had stood and realized that she must have been eavesdropping on Dorsey's conversation.

As Nancy started for the living room, a line from a rôle she had once played rose in her mind—'Poison is a woman's weapon.' She looked quickly over her shoulder, but Miss Makepeace was gone.

When the sergeant re-entered the dining room he found Julia Makepeace seated with her hands folded primly on the table in front of her.

"Thanks for comin', ma'am."

"I was glad to. Miss Garwood tells me you have made some new discovery about the body."

"Yeah, an' I'm worse off than ever. When I first saw what was upstairs I figured it wasn't Frant's body. Figured somebody had it in for this English fellow, an' made a switch so's it would look like the curse really came true. Now Feldmann—he's the one that does my technical work for me—claims it's really Frant."

"What evidence has he?"

"Pretty good, I reckon. The body must have been dressed the way it is now before decay set in. Well, Feldmann found a tailor's label in the coat and phoned about it. The tailor says he made that white tuxedo for Frant and claims it's the only white one he ever made."

"How can he be sure it's the same suit?"

"I don't understand that myself exactly, but it's on account of the way the sewing is done. Feldmann says there's no question about it, an' he don't often make mistakes on technical things like that. Besides, there's the ring. Both Frant's brother and the doctor identified that. It's old and worn. Feldmann claims that sort of thing couldn't be faked."

Miss Makepeace nodded. "If he's right, it leaves you with a miracle to explain."

"Yeah." The detective got up and walked to the window. It was nearly nine now. The clouds had thickened and the fog was drifting toward the house in long streamers like dead men's fingers. Already the trees on the mainland were wreathed in mist. They'd have trouble getting back to town. Silently he blessed the pre-depression extravagance that had thought nothing of laying a quarter mile of private cable. He turned back to Miss Makepeace.

"I wanted to talk to you again, ma'am, because you strike me as a pretty levelheaded lady, an' I have a hunch I've been goin' at this case half cocked. That's my own fault, I guess, but you've gotta admit the facts are out of the ordinary."

She nodded. "I'll help in any way I can. What do you want me to do?"

"Well, most cases, I take a look at the body an' then ask all the questions I can think of. I been doin' that this time, of course, only I started with the Garwood girl, thinkin' . . ."

"Thinking," she finished his sentence, "that the rest of us might have agreed on a lie, but you could frighten the truth out of her."

Dorsey came as near blushing as his leathery face would permit. Miss Makepeace continued.

"I don't blame you. Probably I'd have done the same in your place. But we couldn't lie about this case. Lies have to hide behind complications, and there weren't any complications."

She unclasped her hands and spread them palms down on the table.

"Think of it, Sergeant. You can put the whole story in two sentences. Two men quarrel and one curses the other. He dies and rots in two hours. It's as simple as that."

Dorsey scratched his chin.

"If we look at it that way, ma'am, we never will find the answer. But take it another way, an' it ain't simple at all. There's a whole lot o' little pieces that don't seem to go together. Yet they all have to fit in somehow. Sometimes a fellow in my job can take a look at two or three of the parts and make a pretty good guess at the whole picture. Other times he has to gather all the pieces together an' then keep tryin' 'em two by two till he finds out how they fit. That's a hard way an' a slow way, but it's bound to work in the end."

"I'm afraid it won't this time."

"What makes you say that, ma'am?"

"Because either there was a real supernatural—or at least supernormal—force at work, or the whole thing was a kind of magician's trick. I don't know much about murders, but I happen to know something about conjuring because my nephew is quite an expert. He tells me that most of his tricks could not be solved by the jigsaw-puzzle technique because he always hides one piece of the puzzle."

"Just how do you mean, ma'am?"

"Well"—it was Miss Makepeace's turn to blush—"my repertoire isn't extensive, but I believe I can do one of Bobby's tricks for you. Have you any kitchen matches?"

The sergeant took a half-dozen from his pocket and offered them. She chose one.

"The idea is to balance a match on the table, butt end down. Try it yourself first and you'll see how hard it is."

Obediently Dorsey made the attempt. After three failures he gave it up.

"It can't be done."

"Oh, yes it can. Look." She stood her own match on the shining mahogany and took her hand away. The match remained vertical. "And to prove it isn't stuck—" Miss Makepeace blew against the match, which promptly fell over. "You can examine it if you like," she added.

Dorsey looked at the end of the tiny stick of wood and then touched it with a horny finger. He found nothing. He tried standing the match upright. It fell over.

"What's the catch?"

"It's a very simple one. While you were fooling with your match I dampened the end of mine. There was so little moisture that it didn't show, and it dried out before you tried to balance the match yourself. The point is that a tiny drop of saliva made all the difference between a match that would stand up and one that wouldn't. It was the part of the puzzle you didn't know about."

"An' you think it's the same way with Frant's death?"

"Yes. You say that most murders are like puzzles. Find all the pieces, put them together, and you have the answer. But if Mr. Frant's death was murder you can't solve it that way, because, strictly speaking, it wasn't a puzzle at all but a conjuring trick. One of the pieces—the important one—has been hidden."

Dorsey frowned. "If you're right, ma'am, we can't ever solve it."

"Yes you can. Only you must use a different method. Instead of trying to find the missing piece, you have to guess what it looks like."

"How'm I goin' to know if I guess right?"

"Because the right guess will make all the rest of the puzzle fall together. A poor guess will only solve part of it."

The pantry door burst open, and Sue rushed in. Dorsey sprang to his feet.

"What's the matter?"

"The murderer!" she panted. "At least he may be the murderer! Mr. Kincaid caught him last night and he's gone now."

"Show me!"

The girl led the way to the storeroom. Nancy had opened the door, and except for the cushions there was no evidence of Hoyt's occupancy. Dorsey turned to Sue.

"How'd you find out this fellow was gone?"

"I started to get him some breakfast."

"Tell me about it."

The girl outlined the events of Hoyt's capture. "His things are here," she finished, pointing to the cracker box where Rogan had left them. Dorsey dumped the contents of the box on the kitchen table and began examining them.

"Mr. Kincaid took the cartridges out of the pistol, but everything else is here," Sue explained. "Only"—she began looking through the little pile on the table—"I can't find . . ." She turned a white face to Dorsey. "The poison's gone!"

"What poison?"

"The man we caught had a capsule of some white stuff he said was cyanide. He must have taken it with him! Do you suppose he's killed himself?"

"He may be saving it for someone else," Miss Makepeace suggested dryly. "You'll have to find him, Sergeant!"

"Yeah," Dorsey assented. "If he's still on the island." He stepped to the door and shouted for Ordway. The big detective came on the run.

"They caught a man prowlin' around here last night an' locked him up. He broke loose. Get Nelson and find him."

"What's he look like?" asked Ordway. Sue described the little photofinisher.

Dorsey stepped to the door and gazed sourly out at the rocks and bushes that covered The Kraken.

"I'll give you a hand. It's goin' to be a tough job." He disappeared with Ordway on his heels.

After they had gone, Sue stood looking at the storeroom door.

"You know," she said, "there's something awfully queer about this, too. How did the man we caught get out of here? Mr. Kincaid was supposed to have locked him in last night. He couldn't have forced his way out because there aren't any marks, and he couldn't have picked the lock because the keyhole doesn't go all the way through."

"If you're implying," Miss Makepeace began, "that this is parallel to Mr. Kincaid's—"

"It's more than parallel," Sue interrupted. "It's the same. What's the simplest explanation of this door being opened? That Mr. Kincaid never locked it! And what's the simplest explanation of Mr. Kincaid's door being locked? That he locked it himself."

"And strangled himself."

"And *pretended* to have strangled himself. It all fits." Sue started toward the back door. Miss Makepeace put a hand on her arm.

"Where are you going?"

"To find that detective. Last night Mr. Kincaid tried to make me believe Evan murdered his brother, and all the while he and this other fellow were up to some game together."

"Aren't you jumping to conclusions?"

"Maybe I am, but at least this gives me a chance to spike Mr. Kincaid's guns before he tries to poison the detective's mind against Evan."

The older woman took a deep breath. "There's plenty of time for that. Come back and sit down. There's something I want to tell you."

"But . . ."

"Please, Sue, this is serious. Did your father ever talk to you about your uncle Michael?"

"Of course, but what's that got to do with Mr. Kincaid?" Suddenly the girl's eyes widened and she added scornfully, "That's nonsense!"

"What is?"

"Why . . . why . . ." Sue faltered. "I suppose I was conclusion-jumping again, but I thought you were trying to say that Mr. Kincaid was Uncle Michael come back after all these years, and"—she smiled—"that would have been nonsense, wouldn't it?"

"I only wish you were right."

"But . . . but . . . he couldn't be. What makes you think he is?"

"He told me so."

Sue snorted. "He was probably lying."

"Not about that. The family resemblance is too clear, once you've noticed it. You must have seen it yourself unconsciously, or you'd never have guessed what I was talking about."

Sue sat down suddenly. "Does Grandfather know?"

"Not yet. I'm not sure I want him to." Miss Makepeace put a hand on the girl's shoulder. "It isn't altogether easy, dear. Your uncle Michael is a pretty black sheep. He . . . he makes his living gambling, and . . . I suppose I may as well tell you everything . . . he's been in prison."

"Whew!" Sue thought for a minute, then asked, "How do you know?"

"I had a talk with him last night."

"What's he trying to do—*get* money out of Grandfather?"

"I'm afraid it's something worse than that. It's quite possible he killed Mr. Frant."

"But," the girl objected, "he wasn't even here."

"We don't really know that, and Sergeant Dorsey has had a report on him from New York that worries me. Besides, there's no one else here that could have done it."

"How did you find out? About the report, I mean."

"I listened on the telephone," Miss Makepeace confessed.

"What was it?"

"That Garwood woman came in before I could hear it all. But it was something about a man who was poisoned in Saigon."

"You mean Uncle Michael poisoned him?"

"I don't know. But if he did, or if he killed Mr. Frant, we've got to find out all we can, to protect your grandfather."

Sue started to speak, but the older woman's quick ear caught the sound of steps. She clapped her hand over the girl's mouth and then took it away as the living-room door opened and her brother entered with Collins and Bobby in his wake.

"Do you know what's going on outside?" the lawyer asked. "I heard a shout and now the police are running all over the island."

Miss Makepeace had barely finished her explanation when Dorsey stamped back into the house, banging the door behind him.

"He's still on the island," he announced, "unless there's a boat we don't know about."

"There are two in the boathouse," Sue told him.

"We found 'em—a fine speedboat an' an old tub. We got the boat he came in, too. The tide left it high on the rocks where he couldn't move it."

"You've got him then, Sarge," said the reporter, "and an escape's as good as a confession."

"To you, maybe," the harried detective growled. "I've seen your kind before. You don't give a continental curse about findin' facts or solvin' cases. All you want is plenty goin' on, so you can have somethin' to print under the pictures the mugs that buy your rag look at."

Dorsey turned to Sue. "Who locked this guy Hoyt in the storeroom?"

"Mr. Kincaid."

"Where's he hidin' himself?"

"He isn't hiding. He was hurt last night, and—"

"Dr. Braxton's with him now, Sergeant," Arnold Makepeace put in, "looking after his injuries."

"Kincaid's well enough to talk, isn't he?"

"Why yes. As a matter of fact—"

"Good! I can see him an' ask the doctor a few questions at the same time. Which room are they in?"

13

Cambodian Interlude

To DORSEY'S surprise, Rogan and the old doctor were not alone. Paul Quinn stood beside the door with his camera in his hand.

"What you doin' up here, Paul?"

"Takin' pictures—for Jake. That guy's tastes run into money, Tom."

Dr. Braxton looked up from his examination of Rogan's throat.

"I'll be with you in a minute, Sergeant. I've been wondering when you'd get around to me. Or is it Mr. Kincaid you want? By the way, I don't think you've met him yet."

Dorsey acknowledged the introduction, then ambled over to a chair and sat down.

"No harm talkin' to both o' you at once." He pawed in his pocket for a cigar.

"I in your way?" Quinn asked.

"Go right ahead." Dorsey bit the end off his cigar and licked the wrapper back into place.

"Kincaid," he began, "Miss Braxton tells me you caught a man prowlin' around downstairs last night."

"Yes. What do you make of him?"

"Nothin'. He got away."

Dr. Braxton broke in. "What's that, Sergeant? I hadn't been informed of any capture."

"Tell us about it, Kincaid."

"There wasn't much to it. His name is Hoyt. Miss Braxton, young Chatterton, and I caught him in the kitchen. He had a gun and told us he was going to shoot Frant for selling his wife a fat cure."

"What!" Dr. Braxton's voice was sharp with incredulity. "Why should he accuse Frant of such a thing?"

"Why not? That's how Frant made his money." Rogan sounded surprised. "Didn't you know?"

"That can't be true. Frant was a reputable chemist, not a vendor of nostrums. Besides, why should this Hoyt want to kill him?"

"Because Mrs. Hoyt took too much of the stuff. She died of it."

The doctor sat heavily on the edge of the bed. Dorsey looked at him curiously.

"What do you make of that, doctor?"

"I don't know what to make of it. There is some mistake, obviously. Frant was in the drug business. His firm may have issued a new product without adequate investigation and so caused this woman's death. However, that does not mean he would stoop to the cheap quackery of an obesity remedy."

"Ever buy any chemicals from him yourself?"

"No. I believe I suggested it once, but Frant did not carry the particular line in which I was interested. I did not try again."

"Hunh!" Dorsey snorted. "Frant's *only* line was the reducin' truck. Read that." He handed the doctor a folded paper. "It's my report on him from Hartford."

Dr. Braxton took the paper to the window, read it slowly, and returned it.

"I suppose there is no possibility of a mistake in this report, Sergeant?" Dorsey shook his head, and the doctor went on. "In that case, Frant must have been a very plausible scoundrel."

"He was a scoundrel," Rogan put in, "but I wouldn't call him plausible."

Dorsey turned to the gambler.

"Maybe you'd better not talk too big," he said. "I got a report on you, too—from New York. The boys up there seem to think I won't make a mistake if I pull you in. They sort of hint that folks you don't like have short lives."

Rogan smiled. "You can't connect me with Frant's death, Sergeant. I wasn't even here when it happened."

"Can you prove that?"

"You can't prove I was. Besides, I hardly knew Frant and had no reason to kill him."

"You can't prove that either, can you?"

"No, but with that sort of reasoning you can suspect the whole world. Anyway, how am I supposed to have committed this murder? I didn't do it with my little hatchet, I assure you."

For answer, Dorsey took another paper from his pocket and handed it to the gambler. "Ever see that before? New York just phoned it down."

Kincaid unfolded the sheet and read in the sergeant's large but surprisingly well-formed hand:

De Spain once used his knowledge of native Cambodian poisons to collect a gambling debt. A Portuguese named Queiroz had lost over two thousand piasters to him at baccarat, and refused to pay on the ground that he had been cheated. Many gamblers would have simply shot the Portuguese down—the age-old penalty for 'welching'—but not de Spain. He offered Queiroz a drink, and then informed him that the liquor had contained *nuoc-mam*, a native poison which the Khmers had used to punish their slaves. *Nuoc-mam*, it seems, acted on the nerves to produce agonizing pain which started in the extremities and worked toward the heart. The special feature of the poison, however, was the existence of an antidote as quick and sure as insulin. When the Khmers thought a slave had been punished enough, they gave him the antidote and he could be put back to work in half a day. De Spain promised to give Queiroz some of this medicine when he paid up.

The Portuguese had never heard of *nuoc-mam* and laughed at the idea that any such poison existed. Even when the first pain began ten minutes later he was not convinced, but consulted a world-famous physician who happened to be visiting Saigon at the time. The doctor could find nothing wrong with him, although the symptoms had by that time reached knees and elbows, and the agony was fearful. Under the circumstances Queiroz had no option but to pay de Spain. The gambler then administered the antidote. It proved so effective that he was able to persuade his victim to sit down an hour later and be cheated out of another five hundred piasters.

Rogan handed it back.

"Somebody's feeding you flapdoodle, Sergeant. *Nuoc-mam* isn't poisonous, though you might think so from the taste." He smiled. "Actually it's a kind of fish sauce. In fact that whole pain-poison business is a fairy tale, and the rest of the yarn is garbled out of recognition."

"Then why did you write it?"

Mr. Kincaid's head snapped around to the detriment of his damaged throat.

"Say that again!"

"Why did you write it?"

The gambler leaned back on the pillows. "This is a new kind of game to me, Sergeant. I won't play unless you explain the rules. What makes you think I wrote any such Sunday-supplement outburst?"

"Anyway, you admit it's a supplement article?"

"I don't admit anything, but it's obviously the sort of thing the Great American Public would rather read than go to church."

Dorsey stood.

"Look here, Kincaid, I'm not playin' games. Centre Street dictated that to me over the telephone. It's from the Record for December 5th, part of a story called *Look Out for Greeks,* and your name was signed to it. What's the good o' denyin' it?"

Rogan burst out laughing.

"Sorry, Sergeant. I forgot Ames' penchant for what he calls 'fearless journalism,' which means he isn't afraid to put his lies into anyone's mouth. I furnished the groundwork for his *Look Out for Greeks* series . . . sat up all one night telling yarns so a stenographer could take them down for some hack on Ames' staff. Probably I told the real story about de Spain. It's rather good, as a matter of fact. But the point of it is that the pain-poison existed only in de Spain's imagination. What he really gave the Portuguese was chopped bamboo in his food. That's agony all right, only there's no cure for it. Queiroz didn't find that out until after he'd paid de Spain off."

Dorsey glowered down at him.

"You seem to know some pleasant people."

"Lots, but I don't know any magic poisons . . . there aren't any."

"An" you expect me to believe this is the first time you've seen that article?"

"Of course. Ames paid me for telling the stories, not for reading them. I suppose his hack thought he could give the *Record's* readers a cheap thrill by pretending the 'strange Cambodian poison' was real, even though it meant killing the point of the story. As a matter of fact, if the *Record's* version came out in December, I couldn't have read it because I wasn't in America. I met Frant on the trip going out."

"I suppose Collins could prove all this?"

"I doubt it. He runs a column on crime for the daily. You might ask him, though. He certainly knows how Ames handles that supplement of his."

Dorsey turned to his photographer.

"Mind callin' the redheaded runt, Paul?"

When the door closed behind Quinn, Rogan asked: "Why all the fuss about the supplement article? Whatever killed Frant, it wasn't this mythical pain-poison."

"Frant was poisoned with somethin'. You can't get away from it. Believe me, I've tried. An' it was a mighty queer somethin', too. I guess New York figured anybody that knew about one thing like that might have more up his sleeve. At any rate, they thought enough of the *Record* story to give it to me over long distance."

"You know better than that, Sergeant. Somebody in Centre Street had heard of me and remembered the article. He stuck it in to pad out his report."

"The report on you didn't need paddin'," Dorsey retorted dryly. He returned to the doctor. "Just how well acquainted were you with Frant, Dr. Braxton?"

"Not at all, apparently, though I thought I knew one side of him rather well. I met him some years ago when he was a patient in Johns Hopkins. He was suffering from a rare glandular disfunction in which I was interested at the time, and I was called in as a consultant. Frant was my only patient in Baltimore, and as he was a very interesting conversationalist I saw a good deal of him. However, Frant was an excellent chemist, so our talks were usually confined to that subject. It did not occur to me to pry into his personal affairs."

"You must have found out more about him later."

"Very little, I'm afraid. I never saw him again until yesterday. What acquaintance we had was carried on by correspondence, and the letters were largely technical. Frant's laboratories made periodic efforts to find a harmless substitute for some dangerous drug or other. Such work is out of my line, but I like to encourage it when I can."

"Hmm." Dorsey came back to Rogan. "You say you hardly knew Frant. If that's true, why'd he invite you down here?"

"You'd have to ask him that. But get it out of your head that I'm a suspect in this case. I'm not. I'm a victim."

Dorsey's chin was thrust forward. "You're what?"

"If I killed Frant how'd I get this?" Rogan bared his throat.

"Miss Braxton said you got in a fight with Hoyt."

Kincaid laughed. "It wasn't a fight, and Hoyt couldn't hurt anybody. Wait till you see him. No"—he gestured toward his throat—"this came later."

"Tell me about it."

"You wouldn't believe me if I did, but when they found me this morning I was out cold, and the door was locked and bolted on the inside. Apparently Frant's friend Od paid me a little visit."

Dorsey rose and waddled over to the door like an angry bear. The bent bolt and the splintered jamb told their own story. To the unfortunate sergeant this was the last straw. If he did not show to advantage in what followed, it was not so much that he was out of his depth as that he was out of his world. Accustomed to deal with a routine of witnesses and clues, he was unequal to a case in which there were, in the usual sense, neither. No fingerprints, no bullets, no bloodstains. And the witnesses could only testify to the bare facts of two happenings—both of which were, on the face of them, impossible. To add to his troubles, Mr. Collins chose that moment to arrive. The little Irishman was at his breezy worst.

"Case all solved, Sergeant? No? Then you've sent for the right man. The boys in New York do the same when they're stuck. 'Case-cracker Collins,' they call me, the 'savior of Centre Street' . . ."

"Shut up, sit down, an' read that!" Dorsey thrust the *Record* article at him.

"Dear me, was I wrong? A confession already?" He read a few lines. "No, evidently not."

"Ever see it before?"

"In a word, no."

"Your paper printed it."

"Where?"

"Sunday supplement."

"I never read the magazine section," said the reporter with some pride. "But I'm not surprised. This is down to their usual standard."

"He thinks I wrote it, Dan," Rogan put in, "because Ames signed my name to it. Tell him that's not beyond Ames."

"Nothing," said Collins with conviction, "is beyond Ames."

Dorsey roared at him. "Do you mean to say your paper would make up this poison business and stick Kincaid's name on it?"

"Sergeant, all that Ames' rewrite men need is a vivid imagination and a knowledge of the law of libel. I'm expecting any day to learn they invented Kincaid. He's just their style." Dan leaned against the foot of Rogan's bed. "You know," he continued, "you boys on homicide would have plenty of grief with this case if it weren't for me."

"What makes you think so?"

"Because you can't get a conviction without a *corpus delicti.*"

"I got one—a honey."

"You just think you have. Let me tell you a story. Awhile back, you may remember, I was in the kitchen. Newspapermen, like snakes and armies, travel on their stomachs. In the kitchen I met young Chatterton. Sez I to he, 'What's to eat?' Sez he to me, 'Have a cookie,' so we sat and ate cookies. When they were all gone I noticed that Master Robert had placed a dime on the cookie plate. I said, 'Taking up a collection?' He said, 'Would you believe I could knock that dime through the plate with a box of safety matches?' I said, 'No.' Very laconic, us Collinses. Well, the kid spun the coin and slapped the box down on it. He picked up the box and the coin certainly wasn't in the plate. When he lifted the plate there was ten cents in hard money lying on the table, and old man Collins staring at it with covetous eyes."

"Has this got anything to do with Frant?"

"I'm coming to that. I asked the kid how he did the trick. He said that if you spun a dime and slapped an empty safety-match box on it face down, the dime would go right through the wood of the box. He opened the box and there was a dime. The dime under the plate was a plant. Do you follow me?"

"I'm way ahead of you. He used two dimes, so you guessed there might be two bodies. Do you reckon I didn't think o' that? I didn't need any half-wit to help me, either."

"The kid's brighter than you think, Sarge." Mr. Collins sounded grieved. "Anyway, what's wrong with the idea?"

"Plenty! The body we got is wearin' Frant's clothes an' Frant's ring. What's more, it was dressed in 'em before it began to rot. If it isn't Frant's body, then it's a million to one the rottin' was perfectly natural. That means the killin' must have been planned a long time. Whoever did it had to get hold of Frant's clothes an' ring at least three weeks ago. He had to palm off duplicates on Frant without his findin' out! Can you answer that?"

"I can answer anything. Go on."

Dorsey took a firmer grip on his cigar and glared at the reporter, but he continued.

"All right, answer these." He ticked off his points on stubby fingers. "One: Frant was a little shrimp, way under average. How'd his killer get hold of a body the right size? Two: how'd the killer know Frant an' his brother would be down here about now with a house party? Three: how could he tell Frant would bring up the family legend and that his brother would curse him?"

Mr. Collins put his hands on his knees and leaned forward with interest. "Elementary, my dear Watson. Is that all?"

"Not by a jugful. Maybe you can say why the killer should pick such a crazy scheme when there were a dozen things that could've gone wrong with it. Maybe you know why Frant died the very minute his brother cursed him. An', if the body in the next room belongs to some other fellow, maybe you can tell me where Frant's own body is now?"

Collins waited until Dorsey paused for breath and then said, "Yes."

The stocky detective's face became apoplectic.

"By God, Collins, if this is some more of your sauce—"

"Not sauce, Sarge—ratiocination, a thirteen-letter word meaning brains. Take your last question first, for example. 'Where is Frant's body now?' Easy. He's running around in it."

14

Mr. Collins States a Theory

DORSEY CHOKED.

"You mean Frant's still alive?"

"Sure, think it over. You asked the wrong questions. Frant could have gotten hold of his own clothes and ring easy enough. It was simple for him to come here and invite his brother and his guests. It was even simpler to bring up the curse story. Falling down when his brother cursed him was simplest of all."

The sergeant was still stunned. "Sure I admit all that, but what good did it do him?"

"Look." Dan's voice took on the tone of one explaining things patiently to a small child, so that Rogan longed to kick him. "Frant was in a tough spot. He had a couple of dozen damage suits on his neck already with criminal charges and Federal boards from *A* to ampersand in the offing. On top of that, this crazy goop Hoyt was following him around the country, looking for blood. With all that against him it won't do Jackson B. any good to run. He has to drop right out of the picture."

Disbelief and anger were fading out of the detective's craggy face. One could almost see his mind leaping forward. Dan raced on to keep ahead of him.

"Disappearing isn't easy these days—not with newspapers and radio. Frant had to die and his remains had to be found. He got hold of a body, and dressed it up in his clothes and waited. If the stiff was fresh, do you suppose anybody'd take it for Frant? That's why he came here where he had a whole island to himself. But he needed more than just a spare body. The cops have quit believing every unidentifiable corpse they stumble over belongs to the clothes it's got on. Frant had to find a way to *prove* the body was his. He found one. If you can think of a better way I'd like to hear it."

Dorsey slapped his thigh.

"By God, I believe you've got it!"

"Sure I have. I've answered all your questions and one you didn't think of."

"What's that?"

"Everybody here says Frant was a great lad for spinning wild yarns. Three people told me that what happened last night sounded exactly like one of his own stories. He made it up from start to finish."

Dr. Braxton broke into the conversation.

"That is a very ingenious explanation, Mr. Collins, but I'm afraid it's impossible." He paused for a moment, and when he went on there was a slight change in the timbre of his voice. "Frant told the story of the curse to Mr. Kincaid some time last winter. You can hardly claim a disappearance plan went back so far."

That was not what the doctor had started to say, and Rogan knew it. It puzzled him.

"Furthermore," Dr. Braxton continued, "Frant read the curse legend to us last night from a copy of some family records. The story is nearly three hundred years old. Frant could not have invented it."

The reporter was unconvinced. "If what he showed you only pretended to be a copy, he could have faked that easy enough. But suppose the story really is old. That makes it still simpler. Frant got his idea from the legend. What's wrong with that? The more kosher the curse seemed, the better his idea was. Maybe he invited Kincaid down here just to prove that someone had heard the yarn quite a while back."

"But why pick such an improbable story?"

"That's easy. A guy acts the way he is. From all I hear, Frant was the type who would make up a tale about being captured by bandits to explain why he was late for dinner."

"I question that. However, I'd like to hear your reconstruction of last night's events."

"All right," said Collins, "I'll tell. But remember I work for a morning paper, so don't let this leak to the other rags before I've printed it. If anyone does, I'll give him a write-up that'll leave his face red for so long he'll have to sit with the Indians on the day of Judgment."

He fished in his pocket for one of Bobby's cigarettes.

"I'll have to go back further than last night, though. It's like you said—this thing began about three weeks ago. Frant had a duplicate set of clothes made for himself and another ring. Just how he got hold of a dead body I don't know, but it could have been worked." Dan grinned. "Maybe another one of his customers died and he wanted to get rid of the evidence. Anyway, he stuck the stiff in the trunk of his car and brought it down here. Then he dressed it and built some sort of coffin arrangement to put it in."

"What makes you say that?"

"There must have been something of the sort. The clothes wouldn't have been so neat if the body had been tossed around like a football dummy. The coffin didn't need to be elaborate, just a box of white pine and celotex, with tissue paper packed in it to keep the stiff from shifting around. The whole thing had to be weatherproof, of course. He couldn't keep the body in the house."

"An' I suppose you know where he did keep it?" The sergeant was sarcastic.

"I've got a good idea, anyway. There's a ledge outside one of the windows in Frant's room. It's on floor level, so you can't see it unless you stick your head out. You can't see it from the ground, either, because of the way the land on that side drops away from the house. Besides, there's another thing. That window is the only one on the whole floor where the screen isn't screwed shut. I checked it."

That last item sounded as if the reporter knew what he was talking about. Dorsey leaned forward. "If this box thing lay out on that ledge for three weeks," he said, "Feldmann ought to be able to find marks."

"On the window sill, too," Dan agreed. "Fresh ones. But I'm coming to that. When Frant got back here yesterday he was all set. He started in right away, talking about superstitions and quarreling with his brother, until he had everybody worked up and ready to expect anything. Then he sprang the curse legend on 'em, with a copy of an imaginary manuscript to back it up. He'd already planted in Nancy Garwood's mind the idea that he took medicine after his meals. That gave him a perfect excuse to go upstairs and set his stage. It wouldn't take long. All he had to do was bring the coffin in through the window, lay his stand-in on the bed, and burn the coffin."

He noticed a change in Dorsey's expression and broke off. "What's the matter?"

"Nothin'. You're doin' fine. Miss Makepeace gave me some reason for thinkin' Frant began to spoil before he died. If he'd just been handlin' that corpse, I can guess where he picked up the perfume."

Rogan checked off a point in his mind. That explained why the Poe volume was open at the Valdemar yarn. Miss Makepeace had probably thought of the tale's likeness to what she believed had happened to Frant, and looked it up in the hope that it contained a useful idea. Probably she had dropped the book when the over-vividness of its last horrible sentence struck home to her.

"I told you this idea cleared up everything." Collins grinned at Dorsey. "Even things I hadn't heard about. I've got more evidence, too. There are fresh ashes in the fireplace in Frant's bedroom."

"It sounds like you've got it all worked out," the detective conceded, "but I'm not so certain Frant could have handled a body his own size and a coffin to boot."

"Why not? The coffin could have been very light, and the stiff doesn't weigh a lot. Not nearly what it did when it was alive. I doubt if the whole thing, coffin and all, came to over a hundred pounds."

"I guess he could have managed that much."

"Sure, and the rest was easy. Frant went back downstairs, worked up the big scene with his brother, and pretended to kick off when the earl cursed him. His lordship carried him upstairs. Then all Frant had to do was to wait around until the house was quiet and then slip out. He probably had a boat stashed in the bushes somewhere and rowed the quarter mile to the mainland as soon as the storm died. What's wrong with that?"

Dr. Braxton answered him.

"A great deal. For one thing, dead bodies do not grow on bushes, as you seem to assume. It would have been practically impossible for Frant to procure one."

"Still," Dorsey objected, "I've had insurance-fraud cases where guys managed to get hold of a stiff."

"Perhaps. However, there are at least two other points on which Mr. Collins' ingenious theory falls to the ground, and both are beyond controversy."

"What are they?"

"The first concerns Lord Tethryn. He carried Frant to his room at a time when, according to Mr. Collins' theory, the substitute body was already on the bed. If that were the case, Lord Tethryn could hardly have overlooked it!"

"Who says he overlooked it?" Dan was enjoying-himself how, springing his big surprise. *"His highness was in on the game!"*

"What!" Dr. Braxton had risen and stood towering over the reporter, a picture of righteous indignation. Collins, who had been sitting on the edge of the bed, rolled over on his back like a threatened puppy and lay there grinning.

"Gosh, doc, don't get sore. I know the earl's a friend of yours, but that doesn't mean he wasn't mixed up in this caper. You say yourself it couldn't have been worked without him."

"Nonsense. Why should Lord Tethryn lend himself to any such gruesome swindle?"

"Because he got plenty," Collins retorted. "You can bet your last pants button Frant had a pile stacked away where the bankruptcy court wouldn't find it. Anyway, what could his lordship lose? He could always crawl out of it by proving the whole stunt was a fake. There's no law against disappearing, unless you're a fugitive from justice. Frant's not that yet, so the earl isn't even an accomplice."

A knock on the door cut short the doctor's reply, and Sue's voice came through the thick panels. Dan pulled the door open, and the girl entered. Her eyes sought the bed where her uncle lay and then turned to her grandfather's troubled countenance.

"Has . . . has anything happened?"

"What's the matter, Miss Braxton?" Dorsey's voice showed his surprise at her question.

"Oh!" The girl caught herself. She tore her eyes away from the old doctor and turned to Collins. "Your editor's on the phone. He wants you."

"He always does."

As Dan slid off the bed, Dr. Braxton spoke.

"Do you intend to give this harebrained theory of yours to your paper, Mr. Collins?"

"Not this trip, doc, so keep your socks on. If I tell all I know now the rewrite boys will have a field day with it. I'll feed Ames the local color and save my big news until just before deadline. Then he'll have to print it right off the wire."

When the door banged behind the reporter, Dr. Braxton looked at Dorsey.

"I hope you approved of my leading him on, Sergeant. I had no idea he was pointing to such a ridiculous climax, and there was always the possibility that he might have stumbled on some useful suggestions."

"I guess he did at that. That business about the ledge outside Frant's window, an' about the screen not bein' screwed in, sounds like the McCoy."

"I hardly see how these facts can have any significance except on Mr. Collins' theory that Frant is alive, which of course is absurd."

"I don't see why."

"Good heavens, man! Don't tell me you take any stock in this wild idea?"

"Sure I do. It's the only solution that fits the facts. I can't turn it down just because Lord Tethryn's a friend of yours. Besides, I've got the D.A. to think of. He's runnin' for governor an' if I don't take him some sort of reasonable answer he'll have a hemorrhage. Nobody in politics wants a case like this stuck at 'em unless they've got an explanation all lined up."

Dr. Braxton stiffened. "I'm afraid Mr. Collins' 'explanation' will not help the District Attorney's ambitions. You seem to forget that the one thing we do know about this case is that Frant is dead."

"You can't be sure of that."

"Of course I'm sure. I examined him myself last night right after he fell. Do you suppose I can't tell a dead man when I see one!"

15

Murder Made to Order

DORSEY'S JAW DROPPED. He scratched it. "Don't get the idea that I'd pull a fast one to help the D.A. win an election, doctor. But it's only natural for me to want to clear this business up, an' Collins' idea sounded good to me. Still, I guess Frant's dead if you say so. If he is, it sure puts a crimp in any idea he was mixed up in this business himself. That brings us back to the fact that he must have been poisoned."

"Tut, Sergeant." Mr. Kincaid was scornful. "Why swap one difficulty for another? There's no poison on earth that could turn Frant from a routine undertaker's job to the most famous thing in the state of Denmark in less than two hours."

"I'm not so sure. Every day you read about something new and queer in the drug line. An' even ordinary things do funny tricks sometimes. When you were a kid, did you ever put salt on a slug and watch him melt away like lard on a hot griddle? You wouldn't believe common salt would do a thing like that if you hadn't seen it."

"Perhaps. But when you get into the 'possible impossibles' you give yourself a wide field. You might as well drag Od back into the picture. And, speaking for myself"—Rogan caressed his throat—"I've met that gentleman once too often already. Why not give Collins' theory another whirl? It has its merits."

Dorsey grunted. "It don't make sense now. We know Frant's dead."

"You can't be sure of that. With all possible respect for the doctor's authority, the conditions under which he made his examination last night were far from ideal. He took very little time and the light was bad. Under the circumstances, a mistake was a distinct possibility. Once we admit that, Collins' idea explains everything else."

"Hardly," Dr. Braxton objected. "It doesn't even explain Mr. Collins himself. His claim that he flew here in this weather merely because of Frant's bankruptcy is ridiculous. Then why did he come? I'll tell you. Someone in this house phoned his paper last night!"

"Oh!" Sue looked at Rogan. "Bobby was right. That's what you were doing downstairs!"

As soon as the words were out of her mouth she was sorry she had spoken. Calling attention to her uncle in that way could only do harm.

Rogan read her expression and realized that she knew his identity. Inwardly he damned Julia Makepeace for a busybody.

Dr. Braxton scowled at his son. "What made you do such a thing?" he demanded.

Actually the gambler had wanted an inside position from which he might control, or at least color, the inevitable publicity. He had made the call before learning the full extent of the evidence connecting the doctor with Frant and had acted as much in his father's interest as in his own. However, he could hardly point that out now. He said:

"News is a commodity. I had some to sell. I thought Ames of the *Record* would buy. He did."

"I suppose he pays well?" The doctor's voice was scornful.

"He does. It's his one virtue. Counting the tip last night and the inside dope I can pass on, my cut will run over a thousand dollars, which I shall find useful."

"Yeah," Dorsey contributed. "I guess you will. The New York pawnshop detail reported you had to do business with Uncle to get here. For a fella that's used to big money, like you are, you must've run into some bad luck lately."

"It's only temporary, I assure you." Rogan turned to his father. "You see, doctor, I am poor but blameless. I take it there's no law in this state against consorting with the press."

The older man's eyes flashed.

"There is a law in this state—the law of hospitality. You accepted Mr. Frant's invitation. You were here as his guest. Yet within three hours of his death you used his own telephone to spread the news over the pages of some yellow journal."

Mr. Kincaid had grown up in a world in which publicity was as conscienceless as the weather. The idea that a dead man had any rights in the matter never entered his head. He concluded that the doctor feared a disclosure of his own relationship with Frant and was angry because Rogan's phone call had upset Makepeace's plan to delay the press. While the gambler was debating his own tactics in reply, the door burst open and Collins galloped into the room. The redhead was in high good humor.

"Ames is going all out on this yarn," he began. Then noticing the serious faces around him he waved a hand. "Hope I haven't kept you waiting. What's new?"

Rogan settled back. "The doctor says a peroxide rinse is no good for your filthy rag, Dan. It needs a platinum bleach."

"Tut, tut, doctor," Collins chided. "You know the *Record's* motto: 'The truth, the whole truth, and anything else we can think of!' But why worry? It isn't as if his lordship had broken the law exactly."

"The doctor," said Rogan, "claims we've broken the law of hospitality."

The doctor ignored their bantering tone.

"See that you respect the law of libel," Dr. Braxton warned.

Mr. Collins assumed the pose of one prepared to be reasonable at any cost.

"I know how you feel, doc, but this story is made to order for Ames. Anyway, why pick on me? Dorsey can't keep it quiet, even if he wants to. It's the only reasonable explanation of what happened."

"I don't know about that," the sergeant interposed. "The doctor's knocked a big hole in it. Besides, your idea don't account for what happened to Kincaid." He pointed to the battered door.

"That's easy. Frant didn't get away as soon as he'd planned. Maybe he hid in this room, thinking it still belonged to the Garwood girl, and Kincaid walked in on him in the dark."

The detective jeered. "I'll bet! An' then that little hundred-an'-twenty-pound shrimp chokes Kincaid unconscious an' slips through a locked door."

"I don't know how he managed to choke Kincaid," Dan admitted, "but the door was a cinch."

"Oh, sure!" Dorsey was scornful.

"Sure. Give me ten feet of string and a nail, and I'll turn the key and shoot the bolt, too."

"But you couldn't," Sue broke in. "It fits too well. Bobby proved it."

Dan shrugged. "There are plenty of other ways. Maybe Frant hid somewhere and slipped out while you were all fussing around Kincaid."

"That's impossible too," the girl said. "I stood in the doorway until after the room was searched."

"Well,"—Mr. Collins was undaunted—"I've heard of cases where the man in the room was unconscious and was killed *after* the room was broken open." Realizing that such a method did not fit the present instance, he went on hurriedly. "And people have been knifed through a small hole that you'd never notice, and . . ."

Rogan laughed. "Easy, Dan. One more bad guess and they'll think you did it yourself."

"Hardly that," Dr. Braxton amended. "Nevertheless, Mr. Collins' failure is significant. He is accustomed to thinking up some sort of explanation for anything, but he cannot find one for this. It was starkly impossible for anyone to enter this room, choke Kincaid into unconsciousness, and exit leaving the door locked and bolted behind him."

"There's got to be some sort of explanation," Dorsey protested.

"Not necessarily."

"Say, now . . ."

"I didn't intend to mystify you, Sergeant. What I mean is this: we don't have to explain it *because it never happened.*"

"Why, you told me—"

"That we found the door locked and Kincaid on the floor. So we did, but there was no sign of anyone else. Why? Simply because," the doctor answered his own question, "there never was anyone else. Kincaid did the whole thing himself!"

Rogan laughed. "You sound like 'stout Cortez' discovering the Pacific, doctor, but judging by the look on Miss Braxton's face you're a little late."

Dr. Braxton turned to Sue in surprise.

"Did you know that, my dear?"

The girl started to speak, but Rogan cut in ahead of her. " 'Know' is the wrong word, doctor. She *thought* of the idea just as you did. Only she didn't say anything because she realized that choking yourself unconscious presents difficulties."

Sue grasped at the excuse her uncle offered.

"That . . . that's right. Besides, I couldn't think of any reason for it."

Rogan made a mock bow. "Does that quell your suspicions, doctor?"

"Not at all. From the sergeant's attitude I gather that his report on you contained more material than the *Record* article—material which made you likely to be suspected. To counterbalance such a situation, you would naturally desire to provide evidence which seemed to point away from yourself. A simulated attack is a frequent device in such cases, I believe."

"And the locked door?"

"No doubt you felt that would increase the supernatural atmosphere and would therefore add to the confusion."

Rogan laughed again. "Really, doctor, your imagination puts Dan's to shame. Now if you can only explain how I managed to get these . . ." He displayed the marks on his throat.

"A resolute man could produce bruises like those on himself, I think. Certainly your unconsciousness could have been simulated."

"You didn't think I was faking this morning."

"I had no reason to suspect you then."

"Exactly. And you had no reason to suspect Frant last night."

"That was a different matter. There is no doubt whatever that he was dead when I first examined him."

Dan looked up at that, but Rogan spoke first. "Are you infallible, doctor?"

"Of course not. There are instances in which a medical man may be wrong about death, but Frant's case was not one of them. All the signs were too clear. I will stake my professional reputation that Frant was dead before his body was carried upstairs."

"That's what the doctors said about Washington Irving Bishop."

Collins snapped his fingers. "That's right, doc. He's got you there."

"Who was this guy Bishop?" Dorsey demanded.

"A mind reader," the reporter told him. "Made quite a sensation in New York about 1890. He was a fake, of course, like all the rest of 'em. But a lot of medical big shots thought there was something funny about his brain and longed to hunt around in it with their little knives. Unfortunately for Washington Irving B., he had cataleptic fits. One night, at the old Lambs' Club on West Twenty-sixth Street, he went off into a coma. There were three surgeons there and they saw their chance. They hustled Wash to the undertaker's and pronounced him dead in spite of the fact that he carried a card saying he was given to that soft of fits. The doctors said, Phooey. What does this guy know about it? He must be dead because we want to take his brain apart. We may not be around the next time he dies.' By the time they got through whittling on Wash, he was dead all right."

"That's true." Rogan decided it might be well to insert a warning that would keep his father from venturing too far. He added, "The doctors involved were all men of high standing. It wasn't as if they were technical advisers to a patent-medicine firm."

Dr. Braxton ignored the hint.

"Every profession has its renegades. There was no catalepsy in Frant's case, and simulation was out of the question. The convulsions that preceded his death were very violent. No living man could have controlled his breathing after an attack of that sort, to say nothing of his pulse. Frant was dead. I could not have been mistaken."

"I guess there's no gettin' around that argument," Dorsey announced. He turned to Rogan. "Well, mister, it looks like we might get a chance to chuck you back in the jug for a spell."

Dr. Braxton caught him up.

"What's that, Sergeant? Do you mean this man has been in prison?"

The detective nodded. "For a confidence game, New York says. Pretty smart one, too. Cost him two years, but I doubt if it taught him anything. Crooks never learn. That's why they're crooks."

"I also play cards for money." Rogan turned to his father. "I'm a very wicked man, doctor, but I don't see how that helps your argument. In fact, I'm a little vague about what you're trying to prove. As I understand it, you claim that I locked the door and choked myself to discount a possible accusation. Now I admit we ex-convicts are likely to be charged with anything that's going, but in this case I can't for the life of me imagine what I could be accused of. We've all taken turns in pointing out that this is a pretty fancy case. Before you can blame any of it on me, you'll have to figure out some crime I could conceivably have committed. More than that, you'll have to figure out a motive for it—a motive that takes into account all the queer doings that went on last night."

"I believe I can do that." Dr. Braxton's face was stern. "I might have spoken before, except that I was afraid of harming a possibly innocent man. Last night's crime was marked by two outstanding characteristics: it was ingenious and it was cold-blooded. I was puzzled because I knew of no one on the island who could be supposed to meet those requirements. Naturally you occurred to me as a possibility, but it seemed unfair to suspect you merely because I felt I could eliminate everyone else. What the sergeant has told us of your record clears up my doubts on that score, not because it shows you to have been a criminal, but because it raises a reasonable presumption that you are both cold-blooded and ingenious. That leaves me with only one question to ask. *Why did you come here?*"

"You're barking up the wrong tree on that one, doctor. I came because Frant let me think I could get a little poker here." Rogan snorted. "From the looks of this crowd, bridge at a quarter a corner would be more like it. Frant didn't tell me that. Maybe he didn't know it himself."

Dr. Braxton turned to the reporter.

"Mr. Collins, would you say I was justified in hazarding that Kincaid was reasonably prominent in his profession?"

Dan wished passionately to keep on Rogan's side, but as he could not see where the question was tending, he had no choice but to nod. The doctor spoke to Dorsey.

"All right, Sergeant. We are asked to believe that a big-time gambler (is that the phrase?), short of funds and anxious to recoup, would pawn his belongings to travel eight hundred miles, on an invitation given by a man he hardly knew. Furthermore, that he would do this on the off-chance of an opportunity to win enough money at poker to get back in a game with his usual type of victims."

"Frant played for fair stakes," Rogan objected. "I took about fifty dollars from him on the *Gigantic.*"

"Fifty dollars!" Dorsey was scornful. "From what New York tells me you couldn't buy chips in your regular game for less than a thousand."

"Thank you, Sergeant." The doctor went on. "Kincaid, if you'd only wanted to play poker you would never have left New York. You had a brand-new idea. You came here because you'd thought of something—something you could sell for the thousand dollars you needed."

"What have I got," asked Rogan, "that would bring a thousand dollars?"

"Murder!"

"If you think somebody paid me a thousand dollars to kill Frant, you're crazy."

"Somebody's going to pay you more than that."

"Who?"

"The New York *Record.*"

16

The Last Straw

FOR A DOZEN heartbeats no one moved. Dan Collins drew a deep rasping breath like a man being strangled. Rogan's glance flickered to Dorsey's face, and he saw that the sergeant was testing Dr. Braxton's theory with growing approval. That had to be stopped, and quickly. The stocky detective was judge and jury now, since he had the power to detain Kincaid as a material witness. In that case, and with the doctor's charges against him, Rogan knew he would find himself at the mercy of a district attorney with one eye on the governor's chair and with the firm conviction that ex-convicts were his natural prey.

The simplest move was to discredit the doctor by revealing his partnership with Frant. But for once in his life the gambler found himself hesitating over a course of action. He had, he told himself, no sympathy with the hypocritical code which believed that honor could be preserved by hiding a breach of it. Dr. Braxton had shared with Frant in the profits from the sordid traffic of capitalizing on the credulity of foolish women willing to dose themselves with unknown drugs. There was no reason now why he should be protected from the results of his treachery to his own high calling. Yet against all reason, Rogan decided to make one more attempt at defending himself without involving his father.

"Your suggestion is very clever, doctor," he began, "but even the long arm of coincidence has its limits."

"The cleverness was yours, Kincaid, not mine. Mr. Collins said this case was made to order for his paper. He was literally right."

"You credit me with superhuman powers." Rogan turned to Dorsey. "Try this little credulity strainer on your piano, Sergeant. I need money and hit on a scheme to sell Ames a murder story. Not having a corpse I decide to make one. Unfortunately, Ames can get ordinary murders in gross lots for a dollar. This has to be special. I set my stage in a house two centuries old. I assemble my cast. I invent a strange and subtle poison and a family curse. In an excess of realism I plan to get myself choked behind locked doors. By Monk Lewis out of Sweeny Todd, with Paracelsus and Madam Blavatsky for godparents. In three days all is ready. I am washing around in the waves, but no matter. Frant dies on schedule. I call Ames—a little past his deadline, but still in time for him to pull his front page. A thousand dollars, doctor? If you know anyone looking for a good phantasmagoria, complete with figures and a radio in every room, I am never knowingly undersold."

It will be noted that Mr. Kincaid's self-control had slipped.

The doctor's charge against Rogan marched with Dorsey's own convictions. Centre Street's report on the gambler had weighed heavily with him from the start. Nevertheless, his deep-rooted honesty forced him to admit the justice of Kincaid's contentions even though they contained references that escaped him. He shook his head.

"When he puts it like that, doctor, your idea does sound unlikely."

"Perhaps, but the strength of Kincaid's argument lies entirely in the way it is put, not in the facts themselves. He is trying to persuade us to reverse cause and effect through a trick of logic. If a man says it is cold in winter on account of the snow, you laugh, because you realize the snow is the result of the cold, not the cause. However, if an equally invalid statement is made in a complicated manner, such as the harangue Kincaid has just given us, the fallacy is much more difficult to spot."

Dorsey scratched his square chin. "I see what you're drivin' at, but I don't quite get how it fits in."

"Very simply. Kincaid pretends the charge against him is based on the theory that he *first* decided to murder Frant, and *then* worked up the curse scheme and invented a poison to match. Had that been the case, he would be justified in branding the accusation as absurd. Actually, however, the reverse was true. Presumably Kincaid already knew how to prepare the poison he used. Frant had told him of the curse legend, and he must have been struck by the similarity between the wording of the curse and the effects of the drug. When Frant met him in New York and invited him down here, Kincaid was in desperate need of money. No doubt the idea of selling more material to the *Record* had already occurred to him, but unfortunately another set of casual reminiscences would not bring the thousand dollars he required. The *Record* is a blatant tabloid, and the tastes of its readers run chiefly to spectacular murders. That fact must have given Kincaid the idea of raising the sum he wanted by staging a murder and selling the news of it to the paper."

Rogan sighed inwardly. If his father kept on at that rate there would be no alternative except to expose him in self-defense. He had already been given a warning hint that the gambler possessed knowledge of his connection with Frant, but it was just possible he had missed it. If so, something more definite might bring the dangers of his position home to him.

"Even your mastery of dialectic, doctor, can't disguise the fact that your case against me is founded entirely on unproved assumptions. You assume that I locked the door and choked myself. There is no evidence whatever for that; but you accept it, simply because you can't think of any better explanation. Your assumption that Frant died of some mysterious poison is even worse, since it is founded on the theory that Frant is dead."

Kincaid paused for a moment to make sure his next sentence struck home.

"Don't you think that if you examined the fingers of the corpse you might reconsider your findings?"

"What possible connection is there between Frant's fingers and his death?"

Dr. Braxton asked that without batting an eye. Evidently he felt that to retreat from a position once taken was to admit weakness. Rogan decided to afford opportunity for escape along a different line.

"There's another point, too, doctor. The motive you suggest for me has the charm of novelty, but it's not very practical. A couple of quiet stickups in New York would have been a lot safer way to raise money."

"Not at all. I think the main attraction of your plan was its apparent safety." Dr. Braxton swung back to the detective. "In ordinary police practice, Sergeant, I believe your chief method is to find the motive. Lacking that, you try to trace the loot. Am I correct?"

Dorsey nodded. "That's right."

"Do you see how skillfully both were hidden in this case? The motive for the murder—the *Record* story—apparently did not arise until after Frant's death—another instance of Kincaid's trick of reversing cause and effect. And the proceeds of the crime were to be, not stolen bills from one of the 'stickups' of which he speaks so glibly, but a check given in good faith by a New York newspaper."

Dorsey's expression showed that whatever doubts he had were falling rapidly before the doctor's ability to reply to any argument. Collins found that disturbing. He had no means of guessing at the basis of Rogan's strategy, but its failure was evident. That the gambler would get himself out of the hole, the reporter never doubted. But the *Record* was in this time—for a nasty scandal, if nothing worse. If Kincaid were pressed he might not attempt to pull the *Record* with him to safety. Dan decided to take a hand himself.

"Look here, doctor," he began. "You're aiming at Kincaid, but you're attacking my paper, too. That brings me in. If you think I'm going to hold my fire until I can see the whites of your eyes, you're one hundred per cent wrong. I have a theory of my own about this case, you know, and the only objection to it is your idea that Frant is dead. Maybe you're wrong about that, too."

"The signs of death were too plain for me to make a mistake."

"You made a worse mistake than that when you picked Kincaid for a fall guy. I don't know what he has up his sleeve, but I'm going downstairs and phone in my dope about the earl right now. Once that hits the street you'll have a hard time getting people to listen to theories based on a Dick Tracy motive like you've dreamed up."

He started for the door, but Dr. Braxton blocked the way.

"Sergeant," he said with a coolness that Rogan found himself admiring, "the case against Kincaid is not yet complete. But if we wait to complete it we shall give the *Record* an opportunity to do Lord Tethryn a wanton and irreparable injury. Is there no action you can take in the matter?"

Dorsey nodded, pleased with the opportunity it gave him to take Collins down a peg.

"Sure. There's enough against Kincaid so I'd have to hold him anyway. New York says he's broke. That means I can slap a vagrancy charge on him an' make it stick long enough for the D.A. to get a chance to look into this business. It's gettin' too mixed up for me to handle by myself, anyway."

Silently Kincaid cursed the reporter for precipitating the situation. However, it made no real difference. The gambler was convinced now that his father was a sanctimonious egotist secure in the belief that his professional standing rendered him invulnerable. If so, a more direct attack might shake his complacency. The excitement caused by Collins' outburst offered an opportunity to do that in a way which might escape serious notice from anyone but the doctor. Rogan smiled at Dorsey.

"You're going off half cocked, Sergeant. Don't grab whatever suspect is offered you last. There's so little evidence in this business that I could make a case as good as the doctor's against anybody on the island."

Dr. Braxton broke in. "Kincaid should be given every opportunity to defend himself, Sergeant, but not at the expense of his fellow guests. He is proposing now to invent baseless slanders in the hope that Collins will publish them and cloud the real issue."

Rogan was annoyed. The doctor seemed bent on making things difficult. Perhaps he would be easier to handle if the threat against Tethryn were removed.

"Don't be worried for your friends, doctor. To prove my generosity, I'll show you that Collins' theory doesn't necessarily involve the earl. Frant's closet is seven feet deep. It runs the full width of the bathroom. If he stored the body in that closet while he was downstairs, there wouldn't have been anything to make Tethryn suspicious."

"Lord Tethryn needs no defense," Dr. Braxton replied in a voice that conveyed to his son's ears a deliberately affected pompousness, "except from the newspapers, and I think even that may be managed. Now, Sergeant—"

"Wait a minute," Rogan interrupted. "I told Dorsey I could make out a case against anyone on the island. I insist on demonstrating. Let's take the most unlikely person—you, doctor, to begin with. You were the only local guest who knew Frant. He was socially undesirable, yet you made him your friend. You tried to cover that by describing him as plausible, although everyone else spotted him as a liar on sight. To cap it all, you told us he was a fine chemist, but I happen to know he couldn't tell calomel from bi-chloride."

The thrust was so direct that the gambler fully expected his father to beat a retreat, but Dr. Braxton's aplomb was perfect. He faced Dorsey.

"If you have made up your mind to arrest Kincaid," he suggested, "let me urge you to do so at once. Then you can give the case against him to the news services so they can send out their stories for publication this afternoon. In that way you can gain half a day's march on the *Record,* which is a morning paper."

Collins was frantic.

"Try it," he shouted, "and I'll burn up the wires giving my dope on Tethryn to every rag in the country! If you think they'll print a story about Kincaid when they can get one on an honest-to-Roosevelt earl, you're crazy."

"Sit down, Dan," Rogan directed, "and stop acting like the power of the press. Your precious theory's wrong, anyway."

Mr. Collins was staggered.

"Just because the doctor says Frant's dead . . ."

"I know. It doesn't prove a thing. Oh, I admit you had the right idea in general. Where you went wrong was in picking Frant's accomplice. It wasn't Lord Tethryn!"

Rogan paused to give his father a last chance to withdraw, but there was no change in the doctor's face. Evidently he had decided he could discredit the gambler and bluff it out. Rogan gave up. He turned to Dorsey.

"Look, Sergeant. When Collins first told you that last night's shenanigans were a stunt to help Frant disappear, you believed it. Why? Because it was the only explanation that didn't drag in mysterious poisons or ghosts or some other nonsense. But after you had accepted Collins' theory you gave it up. Again why? *Because Dr. Braxton told you that Frant was dead.* There's only one answer to that. The doctor was lying! He lied because he was in the game himself!"

Collins caught fire.

"By God, you've got it! That explains where the body came from, too. Bodies may not grow on berry bushes, but the medical schools are full of 'em!"

Dr. Braxton's calm broke. "Be careful what you say, sir! Why should I have been in league with Frant?"

Before Collins could answer, the stamp of feet sounded in the hall and the door was burst open. Ordway and Nelson entered, carrying between them the limp figure of a man. One pair of handcuffs held his wrists and another encircled his ankles.

"Who's that?" asked Dorsey.

They dropped their burden to the floor and straightened up, grinning. Ordway answered, "Hoyt."

"What's the matter? Did he put up a fight?"

"Some." Nelson fingered a swollen eye.

"He won't now. Let him up."

Released, the photofinisher struggled to his feet. Dorsey barked at him.

"Why did you come here last night?"

"I knew Frant was here. I'm going to kill him. Him and his partner—the doctor that invented the stuff that killed my wife."

Sue gasped. "It's not true!"

Hoyt swung his manacled hands toward her.

"It is true!" he yammered. "You told me so yourself!"

Collins smelled victory. "Answer that one, doc!"

His glance identified Dr. Braxton, and Hoyt leaped at the doctor, screaming. While Nelson and Ordway struggled with Hoyt, Sue grasped the sergeant's burly arm.

"Don't you see the man's crazy?"

"Yeah? What's this poison he's talking about?"

"Dinitrophenol. It's—"

"Dinitrophenol!" the old doctor repeated. He walked over to Hoyt and looked down into the thin bruised face. "Did Mr. Frant sell your wife dinitrophenol?"

Hoyt's red-rimmed eyes glared back with concentrated hate.

"Him and you. Put it up in bottles and sold it at the drugstores . . . dollar a bottle . . . death for a dollar. You burned her to death! Hell's too cold for the two of you." His voice rose in shrill crescendo. "She loved me . . . I tell you . . . my wife, my beautiful wife . . . and you killed her!" He broke off suddenly, closed his eyes, and collapsed on the floor in an untidy heap.

Collins was triumphant.

"You asked why you helped Frant, doc." He pointed to Hoyt. "There's your answer!"

Dr. Braxton paid no attention to the reporter. It is doubtful if he heard him. As Hoyt fell, the doctor had swung around to fumble in his bag, which stood open on the chair by Rogan's bed. Dorsey was beside him in a flash, grabbing his wrist.

"What are you after?"

"Spirits of ammonia, Sergeant. The man needs medical attention."

"An" he'll get it. But not from you." He barked at his two assistants. "Take this guy in another room an' have Murchison fix him up. An' send Feldmann in here. I want him." He released Dr. Braxton's wrist and stepped back. "Sorry, doctor, but I'm not takin' any chances. Hoyt will be safe with

Murchison lookin' after him. Safer, maybe—if you were in this patent-medicine racket with Frant, like he said."

Dr. Braxton seemed dazed.

"I can't understand it," he murmured. "This accusation . . . I never saw the man before."

Involuntarily Sue's eyes sought Rogan's face. Finding no help there, she went over and put her arm around her grandfather.

"Don't worry about Mr. Hoyt," she urged. "He's crazy, I think. Last night he told us how his wife died, and I said he must be wrong because you'd suggested dinitrophenol to Mr. Frant, and . . . he must have thought . . ."

"That I was Frant's partner," the doctor finished. "I see."

Feldmann's turkey neck poked around the edge of the door.

"Did you send for me, Sergeant?"

"Yeah." Dorsey explained Collins' theory of the coffin on the window ledge and sent the technician to look for evidence. Then he returned to the doctor.

"Tell me somethin' about this dinitro—stuff."

"It is a drug that increases the rate of metabolism and thereby reduces surplus flesh. Some years ago it was recommended in medical journals, but it later developed that the proper dosage varied widely for different individuals, and an overdose might cause blindness or even death. Such dangers can often be eliminated by chemists, and I suggested to Frant that his laboratories might well undertake the problem. I had no further connection with the matter."

The old doctor's bearing might have had its effect on Dorsey had not Makepeace chosen that moment to enter the room.

The lawyer's practice lay largely in the intricacies of probate law, and he had not seen the inside of a police court for years. He came through the door with indignation wrapping him like a cloud. A worse mood in which to deal with the stubborn Dorsey could hardly have been found.

Makepeace wasted no time in preliminaries.

"Sergeant, your men tell me you have accused Dr. Braxton of some sort of complicity in this business. They were vague as to the exact nature of the charge, but that hardly matters. Any theory whatever that involves the doctor is ridiculous."

Dorsey's jaw tightened.

"You've no cause to take that attitude, Mr. Makepeace. I'm only a bull out of harness, but it's my job to clear up whatever happened here last night. I'm tryin' to do it in a way that's fair to everybody."

"Then see that you are fair to Dr. Braxton. And in case you have any doubts as to what that means, I've sent for Dr. Murchison."

"Why does Murchison figure in this?"

"Because he's a friend of yours and you are more likely to listen to him than to me. I want him to tell you something about Stirling Braxton's standing both in our own city and in the country at large. When Murchison has done that, I hope you will realize how insane it would be for you to indulge in any loose talk against a man in Dr. Braxton's position."

The door opened, and Murchison's shiny red face appeared. He was very drunk. Both Makepeace and Dorsey stiffened at sight of him.

"Is it all ri' f'r me t' come in?"

The sergeant swore under his breath and then said aloud:

"I guess so, Doc, but we're pretty busy."

"It's all ri', Tom." The coroner's physician slid into the room, smiling like a red-eyed cherub. "It's business I come on." He had lost his spectacles, and his round bloodshot eyes wandered over the faces before him without recognition. Dorsey put an arm around him.

"Sure, Doc, sure. But we've got everything under control. You run along."

"Can't go yet." Murchison shook his head like a stubborn child. "Got t' give evidence. 'Bout Dr. Brax'on. Dr. Stirlin' Brax'on."

"Yeah, Doc. I know. Mr. Makepeace told me."

"No, he didn't. Not Makepeace. I'm the only one 'at knows, but I'll tell you. 'S 'bout body in next room. Dr. Brax'on, th' great Dr. Stirlin' Brax'on, cut off all th' fin'erprints."

Dorsey grabbed the chubby coroner's physician by both shoulders and shook him.

"What do you mean by that?"

Murchison sought to bring his own finger tips together in a gesture of explanation.

"Fin'er tips. He cut 'em all off."

"Off Frant?"

" 'Tain't Frant, else why should he cut off fin'er-tip fin'erprints?"

"What makes you think Dr. Braxton did it?"

"Prof—profesh—" Murchison groped for an easier word. " 'S good job. Couldn't've done so good m'self. Orn'ry layman—'mpossible." He waved his hands to demonstrate just how impossible the ordinary layman would have found it.

Dorsey swung the coroner's physician around and tipped him into a chair. Then he turned to Dr. Braxton.

"What have you got to say to that?"

"I don't even know what he's talking about."

"No? Well, he says the body isn't Frant's, because somebody cut the finger tips off to keep it from bein' recognized. And he says it was a professional job, so you must have done it."

"He's hardly in a condition to give an opinion."

It was Dorsey's turn to be indignant.

"An' do you know why he got that way? It was because it took a lot o' liquor to get him to a point where he could accuse a man he'd always looked up to. He wasn't drunk when he noticed the finger tips. You can bet on that."

He pulled the door open and yelled for Feldmann.

"What are you going to do, Sergeant?" Makepeace asked.

"I've got me one fact, now. The first one since I came here. If Jake's report on that window sill matches up, then it's goin' to look a whole lot like the doctor's been helping Frant swindle his creditors."

Dr. Braxton stood up. The first shock had passed, and the old doctor faced Dorsey proudly. Rogan found himself admiring his father. Quack and hypocrite he might be, but he was meeting a difficult situation with a calm dignity that the gambler had never before encountered.

"I understand your position, Sergeant." Dr. Braxton's voice was as level as if he were discussing a problem in chemistry. "I hope you will understand mine. The evidence on which you base your accusation does not point to me, however much it may seem to. I hope I shall be able to prove that. But you speak of a swindle as if that were the principal charge laid at my door. Believe me, the allegation that I was a partner with Frant in his infamous traffic is far more serious, though it may carry no legal penalty. All my life I have fought the battle of humanity against disease. All my life I have fought for the integrity of my profession. I have developed nearly a hundred diagnostic techniques and turned them over to science. Is it conceivable that I would now stoop to making a few dollars selling poison by the bottle to unfortunate women?"

Jake Feldmann's ugly face was thrust into the room like a cautious periscope.

"Did you wish me?"

"Yeah. Got that dope yet?"

"Not from the fireplace, but I have covered the ledge and the window sill. However, even about them I did not have time to be thorough."

"Never mind. Tell me what you found."

"Well, there was something rectangular on the ledge beyond the window—perhaps a window box. I cannot say how large it was, because there was a mark left only at one corner."

"What about the window sill?"

"There were also marks there, but they were not definite. Perhaps a box was dragged in. Perhaps something was shoved out."

"Were the screens screwed shut?"

"All but that one."

"You'd better check the others on this floor. It may be important. You can get after the ashes later."

The technician moved over to the nearest window and began examining the screws through his thick glasses. Dorsey turned to Dr. Braxton.

"Well, doctor, what you got to say now?"

To Sue the talk in the room had been infinitely harder to bear than the Grand Guignol horrors of the night before. She had been so overcome by hearing her uncle and grandfather accuse each other of chicanery and murder that she had scarcely attempted to follow the details of charge and defense. Perhaps for this very reason she came to realize, slowly but more clearly than any of the men, that the crux of all their arguments lay in the identity of the body in the next room. Dorsey and her uncle seemed to feel certain that the clothes and the removal of the finger tips settled the matter—that the corpse was that of a stranger. But that pointed toward some fraud on her grandfather's part, which was impossible. Surely there must be another solution. She closed her eyes and racked her brain for an answer. When it came, the enlightenment was so violent that she spoke her thought aloud.

"That's it! He didn't do it!"

Dorsey turned to her in surprise.

"Who didn't do what?"

"Grandfather. He didn't cut off the finger tips."

Murchison roused himself.

"Yes, he did. Must've."

"You didn't see him do it, did you?"

"Nup, but it was a neat job. Couldn't've done s' good m'self."

"When was it done?"

"Las' night . . . 's morning maybe."

"Don't you see?" Sue swung back to Dorsey. "If Grandfather and Mr. Frant had been trying to disguise the body, finger tips would have been the first thing they'd have thought of. Anything they did to the hands would have been done long ago."

The sergeant shook his head. "I'd take more stock in that, Miss, if there was anyone else on the island could have done it."

"But there is. There is!"

"Who?"

"That man over there!" Excitedly Sue pointed to Feldmann who, oblivious to all around him, was methodically examining the screwheads in the screens.

"By God, I forgot all about Jake. That would be just like him."

He shouted, and the technician turned.

"You want me, Sergeant?"

"Yeah. Murchison says somebody cut the finger tips off the corpse. Did you do it?"

"Naturally."

Dorsey gulped.

"Naturally, hell! What was the idea?"

"The papillary ridges on the outer surface of the skin were destroyed. The patterns go all the way through the skin, which is why it was necessary to examine the inner side. In cases of this sort fingerprints are the preferred means of identification."

"They are if you've got something to compare 'em with."

"Oh, but I have. That was why I told you I must phone Washington."

"Wow!" Collins chortled. "Ames will love this. G's identify secondhand stiff!"

"No, no. Not the Federal Bureau of Investigation, Mr. Collins, but the Veterans' Bureau. I will explain."

"Never mind," said Dorsey. "We get it. You phoned in the formula. All right. How long will it take you to get an answer?"

"I already have one. The identification is now positive."

"Good God! An' you didn't tell me!"

Feldmann's eyes widened.

"Why should I trouble you with details when you already knew the facts? Didn't I inform you this morning? The body is that of Mr. Frant!"

17

Thicker Than Water

A MOMENT EARLIER the room had been clamorous, but Feldmann's announcement stunned it to silence. Rogan studied the faces of the others. He had plenty of time. The shock rolled over them in waves. First came surprise. The evidence that the body was not Frant's had been built up to a practical certainty, and to have it collapse at a word left the group breathless. Then the sheer impossibility of the thing began to make itself felt. Until a few minutes before, most of them had been prepared to accept the identification of the corpse with their host as a tenable theory. Now that it had become a matter of cold fact, each in his own way seemed suddenly to realize that it could not be. Except for Feldmann himself, no one doubted that Frant had been alive the previous night. There were too many witnesses. Besides, Kincaid himself had seen the little man in New York three days before. No, there was no way out. The transformation in Frant's corpse was horrible, it was impossible, but it had occurred.

As usual, Makepeace was the first to speak.

"I'm afraid I don't understand all this, Sergeant. Where does the Veterans' Bureau enter the picture?"

"The Bureau has all the ex-soldiers' prints. Frant was forty-five or so, and Feldmann probably guessed."

"I do not guess, Sergeant." The technician was indignant. "I know. There was a button in the lapel of one of Mr. Frant's suits—"

"You'd better know." Dorsey cut him short. "If there's any mistake about this, I'll . . ." Suddenly he became suspicious. "How'd you ever get two-hour service out of anybody in Washington?"

Feldmann smirked. "I have a friend. He—"

"So that's it!" Dorsey exploded. "You have a friend. Hell! I know those Washington boys. You gave him the formula an' he stuck it in his pocket an' went to lunch. Then he figured you were probably right anyway, an' why bother? So he called you back an' said, sure the prints were Frant's. If you ever catch him out on it he can always claim he'd made a mistake because the army did a rotten job takin' the prints in the first place."

Dorsey's diatribe served only to increase the technician's smugness.

"I also know government clerks, Sergeant, so I do not put any trust in them. Besides, it is not necessary. I do not give my friend the formula of the cadaver's prints. Instead I ask him the formula of Mr. Frant. When he telephoned it to me it was:

19	I 13	U	IOM	21
	I 18	R	OOI	

That way I do the comparison myself. It checks."

Dorsey shook his head. "I guess that settles it." He sat down on the bed. Makepeace expanded.

"In that case, Sergeant, I take it that an apology to Dr. Braxton is in order."

Dorsey groaned. "Listen, mister. If you want to do the doctor, an' me, an' everyone else a favor, go somewhere an' read a book."

"But surely if Dr. Braxton is cleared . . ."

" 'Surely' hasn't a thing to do with this case. An' the doctor isn't cleared. Only I've stopped believin' he's guilty. That doesn't mean I believe he's innocent . . . just that I've stopped believin'. I don't even know what killed Frant. It might have been poison or it might have been his lordship's cussin', or maybe the niggers in the boathouse killed him with cunjur spells. I'm goin' back downstairs an' start takin' statements from every mortal soul on the island an' turn 'em over to the D.A. when he gets back to town this afternoon. After that, it's his headache."

Sue stayed in her uncle's room after the others had left. When the door closed behind Dorsey she burst out.

"I don't understand."

Rogan smiled at her.

"I don't either, if it's any comfort to you."

"Oh, I don't mean about Mr. Frant. I mean . . . about you."

"Miss Makepeace told you, didn't she?"

Sue nodded. "But that's it. How could you accuse your own father?"

"He accused me."

"But he didn't know you were his son."

"What difference does that make? *You* think of your family just as you think of your arm—as a sort of extension of yourself. And you're right. It is. But the family isn't a part of me. I broke loose too long ago. The only thing we have left in common is the power to disgrace each other. That's why I never tried to come back. In most ways I'm proud of my life. By my standards it's been a good one. But by yours I'm a blot in the family 'scutcheon".

"You're my father's brother."

"Which means your pride would have made you act as if your family were above the things you count right and wrong. But inside, you would all have been ashamed of me."

"You've been ashamed, too, or you'd have come back before."

"No. I am ashamed of my mistakes, but they aren't the same things you'd call wrong. They aren't things that would count with you at all. You feel it's dishonorable for me to make my living at cards. I'm proud of it because it's something I do unusually well. On the other hand, I feel humiliated by being broke right now. Not that the money means much—I can get more—but because I was swindled by a trick I should have guarded against. If someone cheated you, you might feel anger but not shame." He settled down a little on his pillows. "You're never going to understand me. We don't belong to the same world."

"You're my uncle," Sue insisted.

"No, I'm not. Not really. It's not birth that makes families. It's background—having a community of outlook. I'm not denying heredity. Coming of good stock gave me a sound brain and a sound body. Maybe it gave me the will to come out ahead that people call 'blood' in a horse. But it's ideas that make the man. Mine don't come from the family. They come from the carnival lot, and the card table, and the crooked little Swiss that brought me up and taught me that if you want to be cleverer than the other fellow you have to work at it."

"You're right about my not understanding," Sue admitted. "But even if you don't feel you need to stick up for Grandfather, that's no excuse for trying to get him arrested."

"I had my own skin to look out for. Whether you realize it or not, my father's theory made me the sergeant's number-one suspect. I probably still am, for that matter. As soon as Dorsey can gather himself together, I expect the cops to come back and walk all over me in their hobnailed boots."

"Anyway, you didn't have to tell people Grandfather was Mr. Frant's partner in the patent-medicine business."

Rogan shrugged. "That couldn't have been kept quiet, anyway. Nancy Garwood knows. Frant told her before they came down here."

"But it's not true. You said yourself that Mr. Frant was a liar."

"He was. However, I'm afraid the only lying about the partnership was done by my honorable father. I don't think he murdered Frant, but there's not much doubt he was Frant's partner."

"But why should he have been? Grandfather was always fighting the patent-medicine people. Why should he turn quack at his age?"

"There was money in it. Frant may have died broke, but I gather he made a pile in the last few years."

"But money doesn't mean a thing to Grandfather. He's always had more than he could use. Besides, half the Dundas estate came to him when Grandmother died. Mr. Frant could no more have tempted Grandfather with money than he could have tempted a sailor with a bucket of sea water.

Grandfather's always complaining because his investments take too much time from his medical work."

"You're certain about that?"

"Of course I am. You know it yourself. You said something last night about my being 'the rich Miss Braxton.' "

"I supposed you had plenty, but I assumed it came through your mother, or that your father had made it."

"Father and Mother are well off, but nothing like Grandfather." Sue dropped on the side of the bed and put her hand on Rogan's. "Please believe in Grandfather. He's the finest man in the world. I've been very close to him all my life and I've never known him do a single thing he couldn't be proud of."

"If the doctor has money, that kills his motive for going into the quack-medicine business," Rogan agreed. "But why did he lie about Frant? And why does he act so much like a confidence man talking himself out of a jam?"

"Haven't you got it backward? It's the confidence men who try to act like Grandfather."

"Perhaps you're right," Rogan admitted. "I haven't had much experience in solving problems where my emotions were involved. Besides, my mind doesn't seem to function today. If I give it a rest it may start working again."

The girl sighed.

"You'll be too late to help Grandfather, I'm afraid. That redheaded reporter is sure to publish what he knows."

"What harm will that do? The only possible case against the doctor broke down when Feldmann proved the body was really Frant's. Dorsey may still count him as a suspect, but he isn't going to do any thing about it himself, and by the time the District Attorney—"

"But it isn't the case that matters," Sue insisted. "It's the quack-medicine business and the fact that Grandfather told Mr. Frant about dinitrophenol. That's just the sort of thing a man like Collins will print, and then everybody will be sure there's more to it than that. It will kill Grandfather . . . really it will."

"I'll make Ames publish a denial."

"Nobody reads denials."

"Then the only thing to do is to stop Collins. Send him up to me and I'll fix him."

Sue jumped to her feet.

"Promise?"

"Promise."

18

The Locked Door

MR. COLLINS stuck his head in Rogan's door. "Want to see me?"

"Figuratively. Ames didn't by any chance give you a check for me, did he? I could use it."

Dan shook his head. "They don't trust me with anything but carfare. But what's all this about your being broke? Is it a gag?"

"I wish it were. I got swindled in Rio."

The reporter whistled. "I didn't know anybody could pull a stunt like that on you and live."

"They can't. But I didn't get my money back." It was said so quietly that for a moment Collins missed its implication. Then he remembered stories he had heard—stories of men who had tried conclusions with Kincaid and of the sudden misfortunes that had come to them. He changed the subject.

"Poor old Dorsey's falling back on routine. He's questioning everybody, one at a time. He won't get to first base that way and he knows it. This case is too much for the sergeant."

"I suppose it's a setup for you?"

"Sure it is." Collins sat down on the small of his back and stared at the ceiling. "I don't want a solution—yet. The longer the case lasts the more I'll be able to print. As a matter of fact, things are coming too fast for me now. I like 'em spaced."

"Whom do you expect to feature, now that the doctor's out of it?"

"He isn't out of it so far as I'm concerned. He's a name, and names make stories."

"They don't unless you've got something on them."

"Who says I haven't got plenty on the doc? He told Frant about that di-nitrophenol stuff, didn't he? As a matter of fact, Ames won't like that part, but he'll print it just the same."

"Ames," Rogan stated with conviction, "would print his father's divorce evidence and love it."

"He would," Collins agreed, "if the old boy had ever married. It isn't smells that Ames objects to. But Frant ran his ads in the *Record*. The business staff will howl their heads off because all the other patent-medicine accounts will kick. Suppose you read a liver-pill ad in a paper that carried stories about how some woman had died from taking Frant's junk. You wouldn't buy liver pills—you'd see a doctor. The liver-pill man would lose and so would the *Record*. Doctors don't matter. They don't advertise."

"Then why should Ames print the story?"

"He'll have to. The case is too big to let anything go. Ames' only problem is spreading it out. Think of it: the curse, the bankruptcy, Frant's half brother being an earl—a dozen stories shot in one day's paper. Ames will need all the follow-up he can get. He can't let the yarn peter out. That's why he'll want names."

"Dr. Braxton isn't a name. Nobody but doctors ever heard of him."

"True, but he's the stuff that names are made of. When I get through with him he'll be a household word."

"He'll love that."

"Can I help it?" Collins protested. "I've got nothing against the doc personally, but, after all, news is news. Besides, that finger-tip business didn't let old Braxton out. He's still in this, right up to his eyebrows, only now it's murder."

"Sure, he's practically in the death house. All you lack is motive and method."

"There's plenty of motive." The reporter was affronted. "You said yourself he was Jackson B.'s partner. All right. If Frant pretends to die and runs away he'll live to blackmail another day. But a little poison would fix that up fine, especially as the stage was all set for this curse business to act as a blind."

"So Dr. Braxton invented the poison on the spur of the moment."

"Not at all. The old boy's been dabbling with chemicals all his life. He might have stumbled on the stuff years ago and let it slide because he couldn't find any practical use for it."

"The poison idea still strikes me as fantastic."

"Phooey! Any other explanation is out. Frant didn't go funny all over just because his brother swore at him. You know, maybe this whole curse business was the doc's idea. Maybe he talked Frant into it and promised to provide a corpse, only he kept the idea that he had Jackson B. cast for the rôle as a sort of surprise."

Collins sat up.

"By God, this idea gets better and better the more I think about it. There's another thing. Everybody agrees that the murderer had to be ingenious. Well, the doc's that, plus. His business is inventing medical whatnots, and he's smart about other things, too. That motive he thought up for you was as cute as they make 'em."

He sank back in his chair. "Yep, the doc's guilty, all right. I only hope he doesn't commit suicide when we prove it on him."

"The wish does you credit."

"It's not that, but when a suspect dies, the bottom falls out of the story. Look at Hauptmann. Look at Sacco and Vanzetti. Until they were executed they filled up the front page. Afterward—bang! back on page eight, and a week later you couldn't find a line. A murder case never outlives the guy that did it. That's why you don't see any editorial writers yelling for quick trials and snappy hangings like the English pull off. If Hauptmann had killed a British kid, there'd have been ten million less words to the story. That counts."

There was a gentle rap on the door. Collins shouted, "Come in," and Bobby entered.

"Mr. Chatterton himself!" Dan greeted him. "Thanks for that trick with the dimes, kid. Your idea didn't work out, but it started me thinking."

"I just came up to tell you—" Bobby spoke to Rogan. "The telephone won't work."

"What!" Collins jerked himself upright. "What's the matter with it?"

"That technician fellow thinks the cable broke."

"How the hell could that happen?"

"Sergeant Dorsey says the Hangman's Handyman might have done it."

Dan opened his mouth, then closed it again and turned to Rogan.

"You ask the next one. All I do is feed cues for 'The House That Jack Built.'"

"Did Dorsey tell you who the Hangman's Handyman was?" Rogan inquired of the boy.

"Oh yes, and I knew you were interested, so I came up. It isn't a who—it's a what—that is, it's a current."

Mr. Collins threw up his hands. "If this has a lot of electricity mixed up in it you needn't explain. Just take it as read."

"Oh, no," said Bobby. "Not watts and current—I said—"

"All right." Rogan chuckled. "I get it. There's an ocean current that runs north along the shore here," he explained to the reporter, "sort of Gulf Stream in miniature. Makepeace says it sometimes carries drowned bodies to a place called 'Gallows Cove.' No doubt that accounts for the name."

"That's right," Bobby agreed, "and Sergeant Dorsey says that putting a body in the sea around here is just like delivering it to the morgue."

"The Hangman's Handyman is unfair to hearses," Dan contributed.

Bobby kept on going. "Sergeant Dorsey says that after a storm like we had last night the current's as strong as a millrace."

"Davy Jones' Locker—with free delivery service," said Collins. "Sailors' wives must find it a convenience."

"At least that settles one thing," Rogan put in. "It wasn't the Handyman that strangled me last night."

"Did you think it was?" Dan asked.

"I toyed with the idea. As long as I had only the name to go on, the connection seemed logical."

The reporter leaned forward. "Just what *did* happen to you, anyway?"

"I wish I knew. When I got back to my room last night after locking up Hoyt, I heard a noise—a wet slither—the kind of sound you might expect a sea snake to make dragging itself across the window sill."

"Don't you know what it was?"

"No, but you'll have a tough job making me believe it was Dr. Braxton. At the time, I was about two-thirds convinced it was my old friend Od. What happened afterward didn't encourage skepticism. The thing and I played blindman's buff in the dark for quite a while and once I touched it. It was cold, and wet, and that was all. There was no substance to it. Then it dropped on me, as if it had been hanging from the ceiling. It smothered me. I could feel it on my head and around my legs, but it didn't keep me from moving my arms. It was as if I were swimming in something like thick water, and yet I could still breathe a little. I fought, but there was nothing to strike at. Finally some tentacle of the thing wrapped itself around my throat. That was real enough." He pulled open the neck of his pajamas.

Collins whistled. Then he caught himself and grinned.

"Did you ever hear the one about the man who ran into a door in the dark?"

"I don't expect you to believe me. Feldmann didn't either. But he couldn't figure out what sort of thing made the marks on my throat."

Bobby edged toward the door.

"Well," he said, "you know about the Hangman's Handyman now."

"Thanks for telling me. Don't run off."

"Maybe I'd better. You want to talk to Mr. Collins, and I'm sort of a wet blanket."

"Not at all," said Dan. "We like you. Besides, I've got some questions to ask."

"I guess I'd better go." The boy pulled at the door and added, "It fits so tight it sticks."

"Never mind," Rogan told him. "Don't leave yet. Maybe you can help us."

There was a new note in his voice. The reporter looked up.

"What have you got now?" he asked.

"Hold of one end of the mystery, I think. I've just remembered something. *I didn't lock my door last night.*"

"What's that got to do with . . . ? Wait a minute. I get it. A spook might have been able to seep out of a closed room, but it certainly wouldn't have needed to lock and bolt the door behind it!"

"Exactly."

"But," Dan's excitement died, "how does that help? We knew all along it was some sort of trick."

"If you'd felt what I did last night, you might not have been so sure." Rogan turned to Bobby. "Tell us exactly what happened when you broke in this morning."

"Aunt Julia heard you fall," the boy said. "She yelled and that woke the rest of us up."

Collins nodded. "I can see how it would."

Bobby kept on. "Uncle Arnold looked in the keyhole and saw the key was on the inside."

"Did you see it, too?" Rogan asked.

"Oh, yes. It was there all right." Bobby went on to describe his attempt to obtain the key; how Evan, impatient at that, had thrown himself against the door; and how Dr. Braxton had suggested breaking in with an ax.

"Didn't anyone think of getting a key from one of the other rooms?" Rogan asked.

"Aunt Julia did, but I guess Evan was in too much of a hurry to wait."

"Did you try the knob yourself?"

Bobby nodded. "The door was fastened all right."

"Well," said Rogan, "I didn't do it."

"Let that be a lesson to you," Collins admonished. "Always lock your door in a strange house."

Kincaid frowned. "Now that you mention it, there was no key in my door last night. I could have bolted it but not locked it."

The reporter went over and examined the shattered jamb.

"It was bolted *and* locked this morning," he said, pointing out how the hasp of the hand bolt had been torn loose from its screws and how the bolt of the lock had pulled loose its metal 'strike' and split the woodwork when Evan broke in.

While the others talked, Bobby wandered around. He found a tumbler in the bathroom and was hunting for something else when Rogan noticed him and asked what he wanted. Bobby answered, "Piece of paper," and set the tumbler on the table.

"Maybe there's some on the shelf in the closet," Dan suggested. "What do you want it for?"

"I just thought of a trick."

Mr. Collins was pleased.

"Shoot," he said.

The boy found the shelf paper and tore off a piece. This he proceeded to wrap tightly around the tumbler so that the shape of the glass was evident. Then he drew a chair to the table and sat down, placing the parcel in front of him. He looked up at Collins.

"You wouldn't believe I could knock that tumbler through the table with the palm of my hand, would you?"

"Oh, yes, I would."

Bobby smiled sheepishly and brought his hand down on the paper smashing it flat. The glass dropped to the floor and broke.

"Gosh!" said Bobby.

"I know," said Collins. "You used two glasses."

"Shut up," Rogan snapped. He turned to the boy. "How did you do it?"

Bobby fingered his mustache. "It's easy, really. You see, I held the tumbler upside down. And I didn't put the paper over the mouth at all. Well—no matter how tight I wrapped the paper the glass could still slip out, because the mouth is bigger than the bottom. I let the glass fall in my lap when I sat down. You didn't know that because the paper kept the same shape, and it looked as if the glass were still inside. Just as I set the paper down I knocked the glass against the table with my knees, so you would hear a little bump and think the tumbler was still in the package. When I hit the paper I dropped the glass from between my knees at the same time. I'm sorry it broke," he added apologetically.

"Solid through solid," said Collins. "Question: if young Robert here can knock a glass through a table, can X pass through a locked and bolted door? Somehow I doubt it."

"Keep quiet, Dan," Rogan commanded. "Go on, Chatterton. What's the point of that trick?"

"Well," Bobby stammered, "you see, you took the form for the substance. That is, you believed the shape of the wrapper proved the glass was inside and—"

"Hold it, son! Hold it!" said Collins. He swung back to the door. "Uncle Dan has a thought."

He bent and examined the door jamb carefully, musing to himself.

"If the lock was . . . but the bolt . . . but before that . . . it could have been done . . . jimmy."

"How well you put things," said Mr. Kincaid.

"No, listen, I think I get it."

"Who cares? What's the sense in conducting a guessing contest when all you have to do is to ask Chatterton what he means by his little parlor parable."

"No need. Suppose the door had been locked, but not bolted, and the key hadn't been on the inside of the lock? There'd have been no mystery, would there?"

"Go on. It gets harder."

"Not for me. Will you admit I could put a thread through the keyhole and still work the lock with a key from the outside?"

"Yes, but I don't believe you could fasten another key to the inside end of your thread and pull it into the lock."

Collins' face fell.

"There's got to be some way around that."

"There are probably dozens, but where would they land you? The door was bolted."

"Never mind the bolt yet. Help me over the inside-key difficulty if you can."

"That's easy. The simplest way would have been not to put the inside key in the lock at all, but merely to hang it in the keyhole by the wards. That wouldn't have kept the outside key from turning."

"Yes, but would it have fooled Makepeace and the kid here into believing the key was really in the lock?"

"I don't see why not. They weren't solving puzzles. They were trying to get in."

"Anyway, the key wasn't in very tight," Bobby contributed. "It fell out when Evan hit the door."

"Good," said Collins. "That's it, then. Now listen: we've proved that the lock alone was easy. Haven't we?"

"Yes, but the bolt by itself was plenty."

"Then why turn the lock at all?"

"The whole thing was a dodge to make people think I'd been killed by our old friend Od. Two bolts made it more impressive."

"Maybe, but how do you know the hasp for the hand bolt wasn't broken off *before the door was shut?* Nobody even though of the bolt until they got inside and found it bent and the hasp torn loose."

"You mean the bolt didn't function at all?"

"Nope." Collins was exultant. "It was just a blind to keep us from thinking too much about the key and the lock."

"The trouble is there wasn't time to bend the bolt. Chatterton says Miss Makepeace started screaming when I hit the floor."

"The bolt could have been fixed beforehand, couldn't it—before you came upstairs at all?"

Rogan nodded. "I believe you've got it, Dan. You'd better keep Chatterton around to think for you."

"What about you?" Collins retorted. "At least I could take a hint. The door trick was the kid's stunt worked double. We took the shape of the paper for the glass. Same here. The lock made us think the bolt was kosher, and the bolt kept us from guessing that the lock was really the whole works."

"Not to cast any doubts on your theory, but just to make sure, hadn't you better see if you can find tool marks on the bolt? It must have been bent with something like a monkey wrench."

The reporter stooped to examine the bolt.

"Can't tell anything here," he admitted. He had better luck with the hasp. There were marks showing where it had been prized up with a heavy screw driver.

"That clinches it then," Rogan agreed.

"You bet it does." Collins was jubilant. "I wonder how Fritzy Feldmann missed it."

"Maybe he didn't. Overlooking things isn't his kind of mistake. But let's talk about something really important. Does anybody in this house smoke a pipe?"

"What difference does that make?"

"Lots. I want some tobacco."

"Oh." Bobby held out a blue tin. "I'm sorry. I meant to offer you some before. That's one of the reasons I came up."

"How did you know I needed tobacco?"

"I was here when they found you this morning. I saw your pipe . . . and well . . . I mean . . . you couldn't have had any dry tobacco . . . that is . . . not after you fell overboard." He brought the pipe from the table where Rogan had placed it. "That's Mr. Ordway's," he added, indicating the blue tin. "I hope it's all right."

"It's fine, thanks."

"Match?" asked Collins, holding out a packet he had borrowed from Quinn.

"You are both too kind. Now if I had a drink everything would be perfect."

"Quite," added the reporter.

"I'll get you something if you like," Bobby offered. "There's plenty downstairs."

"Make it Scotch and soda."

"And *two* glasses." This from Collins.

"And," continued Rogan, "see if you can find some big kitchen matches. I don't like these paper doodads. Thanks a lot."

"Glad to help." Bobby started for the door. When his hand touched the knob Rogan stopped him.

"There's one thing more. I noticed a *Britannica* in the library. Would you mind bringing me up the volume containing the article on"—he paused for a moment and then finished—"poker."

When the boy had gone, Mr. Collins put his head on one side and made a clucking noise with his tongue.

"What do you want the *Encyclopaedia* for? I thought you knew more about poker than the man who wrote the book."

"There are plenty of other articles in the same volume. One about poisons, for instance."

Mr. Collins started to ask what Rogan meant by that and thought better of it. Instead he inquired, "What do you think of the Chatterton kid?"

"I like him."

"So do I, but I can't make him out. To look at our Robert you wouldn't think he had sense enough to be a state senator, and he talks like he was tongue-tied, but he's got some kind of brains somewhere. What I can't figure out is where he got the idea of doing little tricks and making you guess, instead of saying things right out."

"I think I can understand that," said Rogan. "The boy looks like one of Wodehouse's saps, and he probably seemed even dumber when he was a kid. But it's inhibitions he suffers from, not inability."

"You mean he has an inferiority complex?"

"Not in the ordinary sense of the term. I believe he's got a fixed idea that he isn't very clever, and he's probably morbidly sensitive about having people tell him how stupid he is."

"Yeah, but I don't see why it makes him act the way it does."

"Well, suppose you were in a world managed by people slower-witted than you are and who didn't understand you at all."

"I am," said Collins. Rogan ignored him.

"Suppose you suddenly woke up to find yourself arguing about radio with a tenth-century college of cardinals. Every time you tried to explain something, they'd laugh at you, particularly if you were as bad at putting things into words as Bobby is. You'd probably get to a point where you'd be afraid to make a suggestion for fear of being thought crazy, but that wouldn't keep you from having ideas just the same and you probably couldn't help trying to pass them on. I think Chatterton feels just that way, though I doubt if he understands himself because he sincerely believes that the world is entirely made up of people with more brains than he has."

Dan scratched his tousled thatch.

"You mean if he comes right out with an idea, he's afraid of being kidded, so he does parlor tricks instead. Then if people think they're just tricks, at least they don't laugh, and when every once in a while somebody gets the point that's all to the good."

"Exactly."

"Maybe," Collins admitted, "but he's a queer specimen."

Rogan winked. "You know, you're passing up a good suspect there. Locked rooms are young Chatterton's meat."

"No motive."

"Oh, yes. I think he's in love with Miss Braxton. Suppose he killed Frant and tried to throw the blame on Tethryn?"

"Too thin," Collins pronounced.

"Well, what about the Makepeaces?"

"Where do they come in?"

"They used to own this island. Perhaps they figured that with Frant out of the way, they could get it back. Besides, brother Arnold's an expert on the spook business."

Dan shook his head.

"Nope. I'm going to pin my money on the doctor."

"I wouldn't if I were you." Rogan sucked at his pipe. "He couldn't have pulled the locked-door trick."

"How do you know he didn't?"

"Because I know who did."

"Who?"

Rogan blew a smoke ring and watched it dissolve in air before he answered.

"Tethryn."

Dan stared at the gambler.

"What is this—a gag?"

"Not at all."

"But damn it! The only thing everybody agrees on in this case is that whoever did it had to be ingenious. I spent half an hour this morning talking to the earl, and if he's ingenious I'm handsome."

"I doubt if the ingenuity was supplied by his lordship. Nevertheless, I repeat: he pulled the locked-door trick."

"What proof have you got?"

"Think a minute. Remember what Bobby said? 'Aunt Julia'— that's Miss Makepeace—'wanted to get a key from one of the other rooms, but the earl went right on breaking down the door.' "

The reporter's eyes widened.

"That's right. The door had to be broken in or there wouldn't have been any mystery. The smashed hasp and the bent bolt would have given the rinkus away if he'd let the old girl use a key."

"Exactly. It's just possible that Tethryn stepped in and saved somebody else the trouble, but I'm tired of having coincidences suggested in this case."

"Anyway," Dan conceded, "he'll make a lot better suspect than the doctor."

"I thought you'd see it that way."

"Do you believe he murdered his brother?"

"That," said Mr. Kincaid, "is one of the points I haven't decided yet. But I feel sure he knows a great deal more than he's told so far, and I'm going to get it out of him."

"You think he's bluffing with all this talk about believing in the curse? After all, he claims he killed his brother that way. That's a pretty risky stunt if it's a bluff."

"Why? No one will pay any attention to him as long as he claims he did it by magic. On that basis he could confess to every murder from Abel on down. However, for all I know, he may believe in the curse story. That's one of the things I want to find out. How about sending him up here? Give me thirty minutes and then bring up Dorsey. Whatever I get out of Tethryn I want to pass on to the sergeant while it's hot."

"O.K." Collins' eye fell on the black bag. "Looks like the doc forgot his medical kit. I'd better take it down to him."

"Let that alone. Maybe I can find a use for it."

"What's on your mind?"

"Beat it and get Tethryn."

"He's practically here." The reporter turned in the doorway. "Your plan for handling this guy had better be good. Suppose he goes high hat on you? 'My-dear-man-I-am-the-Earl-of-Tethryn-your-   insinuations-are-beastly' sort of thing?"

"Ever hear of the third degree?"

"You wouldn't dare try it—not on his lordship. Besides, it'll take more time than you've got, just to soften him up."

"Want me to work out on you for practice?"

" 'S not necessary." Dan started for the hall, but before he could leave, Bobby arrived with book, matches, and a tray holding a decanter, seltzer, and two glasses. Rogan thanked him. Collins picked up the whisky.

"Just what I need to keep off the ague."

Rogan said, "Put that down. Liquor that wasn't mixed in a bathtub will kill a reporter quicker than soap will a Russian. Besides, you're in a hurry."

For a moment Dan was angry, but one look at Kincaid's face told him the other was serious. He lowered the decanter with a sigh.

"Oh, all right." He took Bobby's hand. "Come on, son. Let's go look for dandelions."

19

Caffeine and Psychology

AFTER THE DOOR closed behind them, Rogan lay still for a moment, checking over his plans. When he made sure that no point had been omitted, he crawled painfully from his bed. Standing up, he was seized by an attack of vertigo and had to wait for that to pass before he could move. His first step was to rummage through Dr. Braxton's bag. In it he found a box of quinine capsules, two of which he dropped into the pocket of his pajamas. Next he opened the box of matches and put a pile of them on the chair by the head of his bed. The tumblers he left on the table beside the decanter and siphon.

At the cost of another spell of dizziness, he knelt and picked up two splinters of glass from the wreck of Bobby's tumbler. Returning to the doctor's bag he took out a bottle of iodine and carried it and the crumbs of glass into the bathroom. He placed the glass fragments on the shelf of the basin and poured the iodine over them. When they were well soaked, he picked them up gingerly and cleared away the results of his labors. Back in the bedroom he put the bits of glass on the chair by the bed. As he was returning the iodine bottle to its place in the bag, his eye fell on a vial marked 'gr. 1/2 caffeine.' Grinning to himself he counted out a dozen tablets and dropped them into the decanter of whisky. His preparations were barely complete when he heard a knock on the door. He slipped into bed and called, "Come in."

"Hello," said Evan. "Feeling any better?"

"Much, thanks. Do you mind fixing me a drink before you sit down? Mostly seltzer, and have one yourself."

Tethryn charged Rogan's glass, splashed a liberal amount of whisky into his own, and then sat down on the side of the bed.

"I hear you've had a bit of excitement up here."

"Yes. The sergeant got hold of an article about a mysterious Cambodian poison. He thought I'd written it, and that gave Dr. Braxton the idea I'd murdered your brother to make a front-page story for the *Record.*"

Evan nodded. "The doctor told me about it. Still, if you don't mind my saying so, that was hardly an excuse for you to accuse the old boy yourself. Blood's thicker than water, you know."

"Too well." Kincaid eyed the other. "Has Sue been going around telling people Dr. Braxton is my father?"

"Of course not. Only me. Strict pledge of secrecy. You can count on Sue to do the right thing."

"At the moment she seems to be counting on *me* to do the right thing. We had a talk after the rest left, and she convinced me that I was a heel to clear myself by putting my father in a jam. I promised I'd get him out of it."

"He can do with a spot of help."

"Sue thinks so, anyway. Do you care enough for her to lend a hand?"

"I'd be glad to, but what can I do? The police won't believe me when I tell them I killed Jackson."

"You still believe it yourself, then?"

"My dear man, what else is there to think? Jackson was alive last night, and you saw what happened to him. No one can suggest another explanation that will hold water. Makepeace admits that now. He's had experience in that sort of thing, even if he is an old ass. But the sergeant won't listen."

"I have a plan to make him listen. Suppose you tell Dorsey that you were the one who strangled me last night?"

Evan coughed over his drink.

"Good heavens, man, why should I do that? Besides, he'd never believe me. He'd be sure to ask how I got through a double-locked door. What a fool I should look when I wasn't able to tell him!"

"Ah, but you *can* tell him. That's where my idea comes in. Simply say that before you choked me, you pried off the hasp and bent the hand bolt so that when the door was locked and then broken open—"

"I dare say your suggestion is very ingenious," Evan interrupted, "but, see here, I'm in a rather peculiar position. I've been talking with old Makepeace and, well, he says the only thing that keeps me from being a pretty serious suspect myself is the supernatural element in the business. So naturally . . ." He stopped in confusion.

"I see. You feel the supernatural element is your chief protection, and you hesitate to diminish it by giving a rational explanation of the locked-door matter."

"You've got it in one."

"Well, I can't blame you for that. Perhaps I shouldn't have asked your help. But last night I understood you were anxious to give yourself up to the police."

"I was. But I've thought it over since and decided Jackson wasn't worth going to jail for."

"That's no reason to let the doctor suffer."

Tethryn rose and refilled his glass.

"Look here," he blurted. "I wouldn't tell this to everyone, but I know I can trust you. The fact is, I'm not so certain the doctor is innocent. You see, I happen to know he held it against Jackson for dragging him into the patent-medicine business."

"They really were partners, then?"

"Not exactly. But your father supplied the technical brains."

Kincaid shrugged. "I fail to see how the doctor's guilt or innocence enters into the matter. After all, he's Sue's grandfather."

"Oh, come now, is that fair? It isn't as if I were engaged to her, you know. Besides, you're hardly in a position to talk. You got him into this mess."

"I did," Rogan concurred. "And I'm going to get him out of it. Furthermore, you're going to help me. Even if I have to use force."

Tethryn smiled. "You're flat on your back."

"Moral force. Or perhaps you'd call it immoral force. I've been thinking about you ever since I learned you were half American and had been in this country from the time you were twelve. Yet you still kept that Piccadilly accent. That doesn't make you a phony earl, but it does prove you're a phony person. And phonies are my meat."

"I'm afraid you'll find me a bit indigestible."

"Perhaps. But that won't alter the fact that you are going to tell Dorsey you choked me."

"Why should I?"

"Because you *did* choke me. You practically confessed a few minutes ago when you didn't wait for me to finish explaining how the locked-door trick was done. If you hadn't pulled it yourself, you'd have wanted an explanation."

That was more than a shrewd guess. It was knowledge, and Tethryn recognized it. He got up and put his glass back on the table.

"It looks," he said, "as if I'd better tell you the whole story. I don't know what you've heard about the quarrel I had with Jackson last night. Anyway, it couldn't have been the real truth because no one here knew the background. Jackson hated me all my life because my father was a cut above his socially and had more money. When the governor got his earldom, that put the lid on it. Of course, I thought that was all over when the old boy died bankrupt and Jackson wrote that he'd look after me if I came to the States."

Evan took his cigarette case from his pocket and opened it before he went on.

"He looked after me, all right. But he took precious care to get his own back by ragging me every chance he could find."

Rogan nodded. "I figured that out last night."

"Smart, aren't you?" He started to offer his case, saw Rogan's pipe, and took a cigarette himself, closing the case with a snap. "Well, it's the truth. I'm not really superstitious, but it's always made me furious to have anyone accuse me of being. And Jackson knew that. It was his favorite game. When he started ragging me yesterday, I realized he was in one of his worst moods. I didn't know what was wrong, though, until he told us he was stony. You can guess how I felt then."

"Easily. He'd lost the money that gave him the whip hand. Yet he was still laying it on."

"Even when he started in on the family curse," Tethryn continued, "there wasn't a thing I could do. The curse is just a silly legend, of course. Still, I know from experience that saying so would only make Jackson worse. I kept getting madder and madder, until by the time he dared me to curse him, I hardly knew what I was doing. But I meant that curse—meant it as I never meant anything in my life—meant it so much that it hardly surprised me when Jackson died. His death fitted my mood so perfectly that it made the whole thing seem real."

"When did you realize it wasn't?"

"Not till I'd carried him upstairs. I had a chance to think then, and I understood three things: that I hadn't killed him; that someone else had; and that poison must have been used. Naturally I thought of the doctor."

"Why?"

"That's not hard, is it? Only three of us had ever seen Jackson before. Since I knew I wasn't responsible, that left only the Garwood wench and Dr. Braxton. And the girl was out of it from the start."

"Yes. She'd hardly have committed a murder in a place where she didn't know the ropes."

"I couldn't picture her using an out-of-the-way poison, either. On the other hand, I knew the doctor had good reason to hate Jackson. And I knew he was an expert on all sorts of unusual drugs—things no one else ever heard of."

Evan sat down on the edge of the bed again.

"Well," he went on, "I'm no hero, but I knew how Sue would feel if her grandfather were accused of murder. That's when I made up my mind to take the blame myself. It wasn't as quixotic as it sounds. You see, I felt sure I was safe as long as I pretended Jackson had been killed by the curse. Naturally I tried to do everything I could to add to the supernatural atmosphere. When you showed up I got the idea of choking you and leaving the door double-locked behind me. It wasn't fair to you, I admit, but you looked tough enough to stand it. Anyway, you were a stranger and I was trying to help Sue's grandfather. As it turned out, you struggled so hard I had to choke you more than I intended."

"Was the story about the dead kitten part of your supernatural propaganda, too?"

"Yes. It carried the curse story back for years and made it seem real. Now you can see why I can't afford to have it known I strangled you. That would make all the magic business look silly. I'd be in the soup and so would your governor."

"I understand. But there's one thing you haven't taken into account."

Rogan knocked the ashes from his pipe and began to refill it slowly.

"That pain-poison article in the *Record*—I lied when I told Dorsey I didn't write it. I did. And the poison itself exists. I had some once. A native priest gave it to me for helping him out of a scrape in Cholon. The stuff causes the most exquisite agony, but the antidote acts like magic."

Evan was wary. "You're trying some trick!"

"Oh, no. It's real enough. I knew you wouldn't take my word for it. That's why I had young Chatterton bring up the *Britannica* article on 'Poisons.' There's a paragraph about it in there. Fortunately, Dorsey never read it."

As Rogan had hoped, the other crossed his left leg over his right to make a rest for the large volume. While he turned the pages, Rogan put his pipe in his mouth and struck a match, but instead of lighting the pipe, he held the flame under Evan's left foot. It was the old 'hot foot' trick of the boxing camps. In a short while the heat penetrated the leather. Tethryn leaped up with a cry, grasping his aching foot. The pain was so intense that tears stood in his eyes. Rogan blew gently on the match as if he were putting it out after lighting his pipe.

"What's the matter?" he asked innocently. "I just had a terrible pain in my foot."

"Maybe an ant bit you."

Evan took off his shoe and looked inside. Nothing. While he examined the sock, Rogan picked up the shoe and, under pretense of feeling for a nail, planted his bits of glass in the leather of the insole.

"Nothing there," he said, and returned the shoe to Evan, who put it on. "Still hurt?"

"Yes."

Rogan nodded. "It always starts that way. Has it begun in the other foot yet?"

Tethryn looked up at him sharply.

"No. Why should it? What are you talking about?"

The gambler smiled. "You didn't believe in the pain-poison. There's no proof like a practical demonstration."

Evan stared.

"Wha—what?" he faltered. "You mean you gave me some?"

"I'm surprised you didn't taste it in the whisky."

There had been an odd taste to those drinks. For a moment Tethryn struggled between uncertainty and belief. Then he realized the absurdity of the idea and managed a feeble grin.

"You're pulling my leg. You drank some of that whisky yourself."

"Only a sip. You had two highballs. But don't worry. I told you there was a perfect antidote." Rogan held up the two quinine capsules. "You may have one of these if you're reasonable."

Evan was convinced enough to feel frightened.

"You crazy fool! Why should you want to poison me? I never did you any harm."

"No? Why do you suppose I'm on the flat of my back? You forget injuries quickly, my lord—other people's injuries."

Tethryn gasped. "Are you getting back at me for last night?"

"Oh, no. But you strangled me to help the doctor. I thought I'd help him by poisoning you. Tit for tat."

"How can that help him?"

"By speeding you up. I got my father in a jam. If I'm to get him out, I need information. I'm in a hurry. I can't waste time having you lie to me."

"I haven't lied!"

"Oh, yes you have. Sue's probably told you I'm a professional gambler. I'd starve to death at that if I weren't a pretty good mind reader. There's nothing mystic about mind reading. It's largely a matter of watching for unnatural reactions and interpreting them. Awhile back I started to give you an explanation of the locked-door trick. You weren't interested. That was abnormal. It meant you already knew the solution. Then I told you I'd lied to Dorsey about the *Record* article and that the poison itself was real. The normal response to that was to jump to the conclusion that I had a hand in your brother's death. You gave the secondary reaction first. You doubted the reality of the poison. That proves you know I didn't kill Frant. Therefore you must know who did kill him—and how it was done."

"I told you I suspected your father!"

"That would have been enough to make you wonder—later. But not to change your first response."

Tethryn stared at Rogan for a minute, trying to read the gambler's eyes. That was a game at which shrewder men had failed, and Evan realized it. Suddenly he reached a decision.

"All right, damn you. You asked for it. You'll wish you hadn't, but that's your lookout. Here it is. You're right about my knowing who killed Jackson. It was your father. I saw him do it. Jackson fell down when I cursed him. He must have been under a long strain over the bankruptcy business, and perhaps the excitement of ragging me was too much for him. Or maybe the fall was just part of the rag. Anyway, it happened. While we were all trying to help him I saw the doctor stick a hypodermic needle into Jackson and right after that he died. God! I was nearly crazy. I knew it would kill Sue if it came out that her grandfather was a murderer. That's why I carried the body upstairs—to keep anyone else from finding the mark of the needle."

"I suppose it never occurred to you that Dr. Braxton might have been giving your brother an injection to help him? Or did the doctor's expression give him away?"

Tethryn drew a deep breath.

"If you could have seen his face! There wasn't any doubt about it." He held out his hand. "Suppose you give me one of those capsules. Not that I believe in your bloody poison, but just to be on the safe side."

"If you really feel you've earned it . . ." Rogan grinned suddenly. Evan regarded him for a minute and then said sheepishly, "It was just a leg pull, wasn't it? About the Cambodian stuff, I mean."

"Of course. That's what makes your nerves so tense."

Tethryn puzzled over that as he stood up. His weight drove the iodine-covered splinters of glass into his already damaged foot, and he winced at the pain. At that exact moment Rogan said:

"When I pull a man's leg it hurts 'way down in his toes."

Tethryn whirled to face the gambler. Kincaid's eyes were narrow slits and his mouth a straight line. He spoke without moving his lips:

"So you don't believe in my 'Cambodian stuff'?"

"Then you did poison me? You rotten swine!" Evan took a step toward the bed, and again the sharp glass pierced his foot. Caution overcame anger, and he dashed blindly for the bathroom, where Rogan heard him retch violently in an effort to rid his stomach of the imaginary poison.

Kincaid swung out of bed and made his way painfully to the bathroom door. His head throbbed in slow agony, but he knew he must force the pace to keep the advantage he had gained. When Evan looked up he saw his tormentor leaning against the jamb of the bathroom door, blowing smoke rings.

"It's too late to get rid of the stuff now," Rogan told him. "Even a stomach pump wouldn't help. Only these." Again he held up the two capsules.

"You crazy fool!" Evan shouted. "What are you after, anyway?"

"The truth."

"I've told you the truth!"

"Oh, no. Think a minute. You said you invented the kitten story to add to the supernatural atmosphere and lay a false trail away from the doctor. *But you told Sue that story before Frant died!* That makes a lie out of everything else you've said. It won't be so easy to lie now. Not when you know the strength of the virus that's working in you." His smile was bleak. "Ordeal by torture. It's very effective. Wait till the pain works up to your knees."

Mr. Kincaid's left foot jerked suddenly and he managed a very convincing wince.

"It hurts, doesn't it? That was my first twinge. However—" He put one of the quinine capsules into his mouth and after a moment managed to swallow it. Then he winced again. "I wonder how long it takes the cure to work."

Evan plucked up courage and started forward.

"Get out of my way, damn you," he shouted. "I've got to see the doctor."

Rogan knew he would never be able to stay on his feet if Tethryn rushed him. The trick was to keep the other on the defensive. He held the remaining quinine capsule in front of his mouth.

"Believe me, this is the last grain of the antidote in America. After a few hours of that poison even hell will seem narcotic. There's no opiate on earth that will do you the least good. Remember, I've seen white men die of the stuff, and I know what I'm talking about. Has it reached your knees yet?"

Evan was convinced. There was no doubt about the pain in his foot. That was violent and real. The caffeine he had taken in the whisky was beginning to have its effect as well. The dose was too small to be felt definitely, but there was an odd jumpiness about his nerves that could only be the effect of some drug. However, the crowning touch was Rogan's voice. Tethryn had once heard a vivisectionist describe what he was going to do to a rabbit. There was the same complete absence of doubt as to the ability of the speaker to carry out what he planned. Above all, there was the same indifference as to the feelings of the victim. Evan held out his hand.

"Give me something to stop this damn pain, and I'll do anything you ask."

Rogan dropped the capsule into his pocket.

"Talk first. But remember, I want the truth. One more lie, and I'll smash the capsule and scatter the medicine on the floor. If I do, you'll spend the next six weeks in agony begging for the hangman."

Evan flinched at that. "I'll tell you what I know. Only let me go to the bedroom and sit down."

There was no relaxing of Rogan's grim jaw.

"Not till you talk. Suppose you begin by telling me how you killed your brother."

There was a long silence at that, a silence broken only by the sound of the fog-blanketed sea sucking at the rocks below. Tethryn let the air slowly out of his lungs with a whistling hiss that to the gambler's keen ears seemed a curious mixture of fear and relief. Still Rogan held his place in the doorway. Evan drew a deep breath before he spoke.

"I didn't kill my brother. I did choke you. I've admitted that. But I didn't kill Jackson. That's the truth."

And it *was* the truth. Kincaid knew that, with a conviction that admitted no possibility of doubt. Wryly he recalled the doctor's statement about the occasions when a mistake was impossible. Rogan realized he had been told lies about Frant's death—lies which he had failed to detect. But Tethryn was not lying now. That was certainty. And it left Rogan with only two people to suspect, Nancy Garwood—and his father.

If Evan had moved then—if he had coughed even, the case might have ended differently. But he remained motionless and so gave the gambler another moment for thought. In that moment the whole problem fell together in Rogan's mind, with the ease and simplicity of a shattered vase made whole again by a piece of camera magic in a motion picture.

Before Kincaid had time to consider details, he was interrupted by a knock on the door of his room. He moved to one side.

"You can go in and sit down now. But don't forget, you still need that antidote, and I'm not through with you."

Evan limped from the bathroom and dropped on the edge of the bed. Rogan called, "Come in!"

Julia Makepeace entered. She looked from one man to another, but the gambler forestalled her question.

"You're the very person I wanted," he told her.

"I suspect that's flattery, but never mind. I'm glad to see you on your feet. I knew nothing would keep you in bed long. I came up to find how you were."

"As a matter of fact, I was just going back to bed. Move over, Tethryn." Kincaid sat down against the pillows and swung his long legs under the covers. The movement brought back the agony in his head. He had to wait for it to subside before he spoke again. "Lord Tethryn has been kind enough to relieve my convalescence with a rousing game of 'I Doubt It,' and we are about to try a round of 'Truth and Consequences.' Will you join us?"

There was a hint of wariness in her answer.

"As long as I'm not 'it.' "

"Oh, but you are. The last comer is always 'it.' Suppose you begin by telling us what you know about Frant."

"Next to nothing. I never saw the man in my life until last night."

"What about your brother?"

"He'd never seen him either. Lord Tethryn conducted the negotiations for this house. None of the rest of us knew Mr. Frant or knew anything about him, except that he manufactured chemicals. Even Stirling only met him once."

"Thanks. That cleans things up nicely and brings me down to my final point. Dr. Braxton spoke highly of Frant, both as a person and as a chemist, until it became abundantly obvious that there was nothing good to be said about the man along either line. Then the doctor tried to explain his mistake by saying Frant was 'plausible,' although people far less astute sized the man up as a liar on sight."

Rogan paused for a moment and then spoke slowly to bring out the full meaning of each word.

"The natural inference from the doctor's actions is that he was lying. If he were, if he departed from the probity of a lifetime, then there is no way to escape the conviction that he was either the murderer himself or knew who the murderer was and was trying to protect him. In the latter case, *the person who killed Frant must have been someone very near and dear to Dr. Braxton."*

"That's nonsense!" Miss Makepeace was furious.

"Exactly. It is nonsense in the literal sense of the word. I can imagine the doctor telling lies, but not stupid lies like those he seemed to have told. All right, let's turn the case around. Let's decide that Dr. Braxton was telling the exact truth as he saw it."

"That's what I tried to get you to do last night."

"I know, and if I'd taken your advice I'd have saved myself a sore neck. However, I am wiser now. As I see the case, it boils down to a single question: granted the doctor is both honest and intelligent, why did he fail to read Frant's character when it was so obvious to everyone else?"

Before Miss Makepeace could reply, feet sounded in the hall. Dorsey thrust open the door and entered, followed by Ordway and Collins. The sergeant's eyes flickered over the room and came to rest on Rogan.

"What's goin' on up here?"

"Gathering of the clan. Do you mind asking Miss Garwood to join us?"

"Why should I?"

"Because I want to ask her a question. If I get the answer I expect, I'll break your whole case for you in ten minutes."

"You're pretty full of yourself, aren't you?"

"Nice of you to put it that way. Do I see Miss Garwood or not? I promise that there will be no deception, no double-talk, and no innuendo . . . everything open and aboveboard. How about it?"

"I'll take a chance." Dorsey jerked a thumb at his subordinate. "Get her, Ordway."

Miss Makepeace sat with her hands folded in her lap, her eyes alight with interest. Collins tried to make himself inconspicuous in a corner. The rest regarded each other warily, like strange dogs. No one spoke until Ordway returned with Nancy.

The girl was plainly frightened. She had never been certain that the gambler had taken their partnership seriously, and his long silence had fed her doubts. She barely stepped inside the room and, after a quick glance at the faces around her, huddled against the towering Ordway for support.

Rogan guessed at the cause of her uncertainty and purposely phrased his questions to put her on the defensive, so that Dorsey should not suspect him of prompting her.

"How long had you known Frant?"

"About a year." She turned to the sergeant. "I told you that."

Rogan kept after her. "Where did you meet him?"

"I forget."

"Think hard. It's important."

"I don't know. It was at some kind of a party. I remember that because he took me home. The man I went with was too drunk to care," she finished bitterly.

"Who introduced you to Frant?"

"It wasn't that kind of a party."

"Then how did you know his name?"

Suddenly Nancy's resentment at being questioned flared up. "He told me, smarty. Besides, I've met lots of his friends and they all called him 'Jack' or 'Frant.' "

"Say," Dorsey broke in, "what is all this, Kincaid? If you're trying to prove the body wasn't Frant's, you're crazy. Feldmann's got fingerprints."

Rogan nodded. "The body was Jackson Frant's. *The man who played host last night was someone else.*"

20

The Hangman's Handyman

NANCY LASHED OUT. "If this is a frame, you can't get away with it. You identified him yourself in New York!"

"As 'Frant,' " Rogan admitted. "Not as 'Jackson B. Frant.' "

"But everybody called him 'Jack.' "

"Exactly, and what does 'Jack' usually stand for?"

"Well, 'John,' but—"

"No 'buts' are needed. Jackson Frant had a cousin named John. It was John that you and I knew."

"You mean he'd been masquerading ever since I met him?"

"Not at all. You simply knew a man called Jack Frant. So did I. When he told us a few days ago that his full name was Jackson B. Frant, we believed him. Why not? We didn't care who he was."

"But why should he call himself 'Jack' when it was so much like his cousin's name?"

"Probably for that very reason. John was the sort that liked to have strangers mistake him for his wealthy cousin. It got him a certain amount of respect from people who had heard of Jackson but didn't know him personally. By introducing himself as 'Jack Frant,' John encouraged the idea and still left himself a loophole in case anyone knew the facts."

"But," Miss Makepeace protested, "even if that fooled you, it wouldn't work with people who knew the real Jackson Frant."

"If you're talking about Hoyt, he never saw Jackson. The only Frant he ever saw was John—yesterday afternoon."

"I'm not talking about Hoyt, and you know it. I'm talking about Stirling. It was Jackson Frant that he knew."

"Dr. Braxton *met* him," Rogan corrected, "five years ago, when Jackson was sick in bed. Do you think the doctor, with his bad memory for faces, could remember a man that long? It didn't even need a resemblance. Any small man could have passed himself off on the doctor as Jackson Frant."

"If that's true," said Miss Makepeace, "it would explain why Stirling thought Mr. Frant was a fine chemist."

"Exactly. The man he knew, Jackson, *was* a chemist—enough to put up a good bluff, anyway. John had no knowledge of the subject."

"That makes sense," she admitted, "but what about Evan? He certainly knew his own brother."

"Of course. Therefore Lord Tethryn was lying. It follows that he was mixed up in Jackson Frant's death, and took part in last night's charade because he wanted to hide the real facts."

Miss Makepeace whirled to Evan in amazement, and Dorsey barked at him, "What have you got to say to that?"

"Simply that it's ridiculous on the face of it, like the other wild theories that have been flying around here today." He started to rise, felt a stab of pain in his injured foot, and sank back on the bed.

"Sergeant," Rogan broke in, "getting the truth out of his lordship is slow work. Suppose you let me tell you what happened. Then if Tethryn wants to deny it he can. Somehow"—the gambler glanced at Evan's foot—"I don't think he will."

"All right, but I'm through with theories."

"I'll give you proof," Kincaid promised, "but take the story first. Dan Collins was probably right about Jackson being on the run. Only, Jackson started a month ago, and—instead of leaving a corpse behind—he planned to have John lay a false trail."

"How do you know that?"

"Because of the scheme John used later. If I'm right about John's weakness for encouraging strangers to mistake him for his cousin, Jackson B. probably knew about it. Certainly it gave him an ideal way to cover his tracks, particularly if Tethryn went along to vouch for the impostor. You know, 'This-is-my-brother-Jackson-B.-Frant- the-chemical-manufacturer' sort of thing. Jackson picked this island as a starting point because people connected his name with it and yet no one here knew him."

Rogan paused to re-light his pipe, and then continued.

"So far it's all speculation, but I'm sure of the rest. Tethryn and John both worked for Jackson. He ordered them to meet him here. Perhaps John found out he was being used as a decoy, and rebelled. In any event, there was trouble and he killed Jackson. The fact that Tethryn was here gave John some sort of hold over him, enough to make him help out with last night's fun and games, anyway."

"But," Miss Makepeace protested, "I don't understand. It's all been such a shock. What really did happen last night?"

"Collins was right. The curse business and the death were a put-up job. Where he went wrong was in thinking they had to provide a body. The real problem was to dispose of one."

"But they didn't dispose of it."

"They disposed of the wound. That was the chief thing."

"What wound?" Dorsey growled.

"There must have been one," Kincaid insisted. "Ask yourself what sort of injury shouts 'murder' at first and then is disguised by the natural lesions of decomposition. My guess is a knife stab in the back." He turned to Evan. "It's your turn now, and remember that 'honest confession is good for the sole.' "

It is doubtful if the grim pun, with its reminder of his still-aching foot, was needed to break Tethryn's resistance. The caffeine had tightened his nerves, and his belief that this was due to a strange oriental poison had exaggerated the effect out of all proportion to the small amount of the drug actually in his system. The result cost him that extra measure of self-assurance he would have needed to face Rogan's charge. He gave in.

"I don't know how Kincaid guessed, but he's got it right, even about Jackson's plan to use John and me as decoys."

"Guessing wasn't hard." Rogan shrugged. "John's specialty was inventing wild yarns on the spur of the moment. No one can *really* do that. Actually they take scraps of other stories and patch them together. It's like a dime-museum faker assembling a freak fossil out of a miscellaneous collection of old bones. John's material was all second-hand. Take what he told me about the curse eight months ago. John wanted to show off, so he said he had a titled relative. That was truth—once removed. He embroidered it with a few vague hints about the curse. Probably the only thing John knew about earls was that they have old castles and family curses. His other ideas were all picked up the same way. This house looks eerie by candlelight, and that must have suggested the idea of creating a supernatural atmosphere by arranging a breakdown of the light plant. The library is full of books on elementals, and perhaps John made Od an undine because we're surrounded by water. No doubt those books supplied most of the yarn he wrote in the manuscript."

"They did," Evan admitted. "I spent all one night looking up outlandish words."

"It wasn't hard to find a source for every element in the whole story, except one—the impersonation stunt," Rogan went on. "Yet that was the most elaborate part and could hardly have been worked without some sort of collaboration from Jackson himself. That made it likely that Jackson had thought of the idea in the first place."

Dorsey eyed Rogan. "Where do you come in?"

"Identity witness chiefly. John wanted people who'd known him before any impersonation was possible and yet could be made to believe that 'Jack' stood for 'Jackson B.' Also I was supposed to add to the atmosphere by making up thirteen at table. We'd have been that many if the storm hadn't made me late and kept the Wests away. To top it off, I'd heard the first draft of the curse story, so John must have thought running into me was a stroke of luck. Inviting a near-stranger down here didn't trouble him. It was typical of the opportunism that marked the whole plan."

The sergeant turned to Evan. "Is Kincaid right about it?"

"Every word," Evan admitted. "Mrs. Hoyt's death was the end of things for Jackson. He ordered John and me to come here without telling us why. I was in a foul mood. The speed-boat was out of commission and we'd had to come across to the island in a leaky rowboat. Then, when we were getting our stuff ashore, somebody forgot to tie the boat up properly and it drifted away with half our provisions. We had nothing left but whisky and some tinned stuff. We didn't even have a proper gadget to open the tins. I had to use my *skean dhu.*"

"What's that?" Collins asked.

"A kind of Scotch dirk," Rogan told him. "The Highlanders wear them in their stockings and use them to bet."

"That's right," Evan agreed. "I won mine from an older chap when I was only ten. It was pretty battered and had somebody's initials cut in the hilt, but it was my proudest possession then. I got in the habit of carrying it around with me as a sort of lucky piece. That's how I happened to have it in my suitcase."

"Get on with the story," Dorsey commanded.

"Well, Jackson gave us our orders. We were to make a trip through the middle west, opening up new territory. John was to pretend to be Jackson, and I was to go along to vouch for him. We had a stack of post-dated letters, signed by Jackson. They were to be mailed from various points on our route to keep the police force from getting suspicious. Jackson didn't give any reason for the masquerade, but he was always up to shady tricks and never explained things to us, so we were used to that. After Jackson went to bed, John came to my room. He'd decided Jackson was up to something unusually rotten and that we were to be scapegoats. John suggested we turn the tables by taking the business away from Jackson while his back was turned."

"How could you have done that?" Collins inquired.

"I didn't believe we could, but John had it all worked out. I kept raising objections and finally John hinted that we might solve them all by putting Jackson out of the way. We had him here to ourselves. No one knew where he was, and it would be over a month before anyone would think of looking for him. I laughed at that, because I thought it was just one of John's stories, made up to see what I'd say. But it wasn't. After he left me, John went to Jackson's room and stabbed him in the back with my *skean.* The next morning we learned about the bankruptcy. John was a murderer for nothing."

"What I can't make out," said Dorsey, "is why John picked such a fancy scheme for getting rid of the body."

"Simplicity wasn't John's forte," Rogan reminded him. "Though I admit I can't see why he didn't dump the body in the ocean."

"That's easy. The Hangman's Handyman would have got it, an' then we'd have got John."

"The Handyman did get it." Evan was grim. "John took the fly-wheel off one of the motor boats in the boathouse and tied it to Jackson's body. Then he threw it off the end of the dock. That was about one o'clock in the morning, and I didn't find out till afterwards. The other boat was the better of the two, but even that was so dried out we were all day getting it to float. The moon was up by the time we launched it. We had no petrol, but we found a board and one of us paddled while the other bailed. It was slow work. After a while we saw the current was carrying us inshore, so we stopped paddling and drifted. The current wasn't straight toward the mainland, but more north in the direction of Bailey's Point. Even so, we were grateful for it—then."

Dorsey nodded. "Changed your mind later, I reckon."

"Not much later. The current was incredibly strong. It was like being sucked into a whirlpool. In about an hour I saw we were heading for a little cove, a mile this side of the point. The moonlight showed something black ahead of us. I sat on the gunwale to fend us off with my feet. When we got near enough I gave a great kick. The thing drifted away and I fell into the water. There was some sort of sand bar and the water was only a few inches deep. I waded over to see what it was I'd kicked. It was Jackson. His body was still tied to the flywheel. He had dragged that weight over a mile in less than twenty-four hours."

Evan took a deep breath before he went on. "My *skean* was sticking out of his back. There was a big cairngorm in its hilt and the stone gleamed in the moonlight like a huge diamond. I pulled the knife free and wrapped it in my handkerchief. I didn't dare throw it in the sea for fear that cursed current would wash it ashore."

"What did you do with the body?"

"Pulled it into the boat. We couldn't leave it. The current ended in a big eddy and we had to paddle to shore. John stayed with the body and I went on to the village to see if I could buy some petrol. I knocked up the storekeeper and told him I'd gone adrift down the coast, and that the tide had swept me up to the point. The fellow laughed at that. He said it wasn't the tide that had brought me but the Hangman's Handyman. I can even remember his exact words: 'Anything loose in the sea around here, the Hangman's Handyman drags it straight to Gallows Cove.'

"I'd never heard of the Handyman then, and I didn't know what he meant, but it finished me. I could feel the cold sweat running off my face, and like a fool I pulled out my handkerchief. The damned *skean* fell right on the counter. There was still blood on it. At least I thought there was. Anyway, I ran. I didn't stop for the knife or the petrol or anything."

Dorsey chuckled. "The Handyman earns its name all right— caught a murderer for me five years ago."

"The name of the thing's bad enough." Evan shivered. "Fortunately the petrol didn't matter so much because the rowboat we'd lost the day before had drifted into the cove and John found it. We dumped the body into it and sank the motorboat in a sort of marsh. Then we had to row back against the current. We were so tired we were barely able to carry Jackson up the hill to this house. The next morning we still had to get rid of the body—and the soil on the island is too shallow to bury anything. If you think the scheme we finally hit on was mad, try to work out a better one."

"But Evan," Miss Makepeace demanded, "why did *you* help with all this? Surely your duty was to bring your brother's murderer to justice, not aid his escape."

"Of course it was. I would have if I could, and John knew it. But he had the whip hand."

"How could he? All you had to do was to denounce him to the police?"

Evan shook his head. "It was the other way 'round. Jackson was stabbed with my knife. The storekeeper had the knife and he'd seen me. John was supposed to be in Florida. Besides, the knife was easy to identify. There aren't many like it in the States, and the initials on the hilt were I. D. A. My friends used to pretend that was a girl's name and rag me about it. There must be fifty people who would remember, and John knew it."

"He had you in a tough spot," Dorsey conceded, "but go on with your story. I want to know how you worked things last night."

"That was simple enough. John and I had rehearsed it like a play. When I cursed John he faked a fit and pretended to die. I carried him upstairs to keep anyone from finding out he was still alive, and to make it easier to substitute Jackson's body. John hid in my room until the house was quiet. Then we went down and launched a boat we'd hidden in the bushes. John rowed ashore in that."

"Did you go out the back door?" Rogan asked.

"Yes. Why?"

"Hoyt got in that way, and Chatterton said his uncle had locked it. I suppose it was when you were coming back that you frightened Sue?"

Evan nodded. "I was sorry about that, but I didn't dare give myself away. I had to hide in the shadows."

"You frightened me, too," Miss Makepeace added. "At least you left a wet trail on the floor, and that almost had me believing in undines."

"You weren't alone," Kincaid chuckled. "But we must have had our revenge if Lord Tethryn overheard me when I suggested that Jackson didn't die last night." He read confirmation in Evan's face and went on. "I thought he was still alive then, but you must have believed I knew how long he'd been dead."

Rogan grinned at Evan and then smothered a yawn.

"Well, it's all over now. Perhaps I can get some sleep. I'm only sorry I went wrong before and dragged Dr. Braxton into the picture. But he's out of it, so maybe he'll forgive me."

"I'm not so sure the doctor's out of it," Dorsey announced. "Ask him to come up here, will you, Ordway? We may as well finish this."

"Thanks, Sarge," said Collins, as the plain-clothes man departed. "I've been wondering about the doc myself. If he was Jackson B.'s partner, he must have seen him more than once."

Mr. Kincaid was annoyed. "Control yourself, Dan. The doctor wasn't Jackson's partner."

"John said so," Collins reminded him. "And he worked for the firm, so he probably knew."

"Not on your linotype. Jackson was the sort who didn't tell anyone anything. You heard Tethryn. John was lying to impress me. Or perhaps he knew the original dinitrophenol suggestion had come from Dr. Braxton, and since John wouldn't have given an idea like that away for nothing, he may have figured the doctor would have held out for a partnership at least."

"Still," Collins insisted, "the doc did tell Jackson about the stuff. You can't get away from that."

"Fiddlesticks!" snapped Miss Makepeace. "Dr. Braxton's always talking about chemicals. He mentioned some kind of poisonous acid last night. If I go in for a little quiet murder some day and use it, could you blame the doctor?"

Dorsey scowled at Kincaid. "This whole thing sounds screwy to me. If John left the island before you went to bed, who tried to strangle you?"

"Tethryn. He's already admitted it." The gambler turned to Evan. "Who thought up that locked-door trick—you or John?"

"It was one of the ideas John had while we were working out ways to get rid of the body."

"Oh, no, it wasn't." Rogan's eyes hardened. "That lock trick wouldn't have helped you to hide a body. It was part of a plan for murder!"

"I didn't kill Jackson," Evan stammered. "I didn't!"

"No?" Rogan's eyebrows rose. *"But you drew straws for it!"*

The shot told. Miss Makepeace read its truth in Evan's eyes and gasped in horror, but before anyone could speak Dr. Braxton arrived, followed by Makepeace and Ordway.

"You sent for me, Sergeant?"

"Yes. I want to check something. You examined Frant before Lord Tethryn carried him upstairs last night?"

"I did."

"Are you prepared to swear that he was dead at the time?"

"I am."

"Then, by God, you're in it, too!"

"In what, Sergeant? I don't understand."

"In John Frant's getaway."

"I know no John Frant."

Collins snorted. "The hell you don't!"

"See here, Sergeant," Makepeace snapped. "There have been too many unsupported accusations today. Suppose you explain what you are talking about."

Dorsey told them. They listened to the story of Jackson Frant's murder with growing horror and amazement until he came to the part Evan had played. Then the doctor interrupted.

"Sergeant, I don't know where you got this idea, but it is simply impossible. Lord Tethryn would never have shielded his brother's murderer."

"Wouldn't he, though?" Collins broke in. "I suppose you wouldn't either? Who examined John Frant last night and swore he was dead so he could beat a murder rap?"

Makepeace exploded. "The whole idea is preposterous. Why should Dr. Braxton do such a thing?"

"To get a title in the family."

Rogan decided it was time to interfere. "Wait a minute, Dan. You and the sergeant are going off half cocked. Neither Tethryn nor Dr. Braxton helped Jack Frant escape last night. In fact, he didn't escape at all."

"What do you mean?"

"Tethryn killed him instead."

There was shocked silence at that. Before the others could catch breath, Rogan went on smoothly.

"It was so easy. The stage was set. All he had to do was to poison John's medicine. Chatterton guessed that last night. Tethryn waited for the poison to take effect, and at the first sign he launched his curse. Probably John never knew what hit him. He may even have thought he was actually dying of the curse. Sardonic."

Evan snarled at that. "You're mad!"

"Oh, no. I'm not dead either, though you tried to kill me last night. You didn't strangle me for 'atmosphere.' You did it because you believed I'd put two and two together from Hoyt's story and had a fair idea of what really happened. You overestimated me. That isn't a common fault, but it's going to hang you."

"Evan!" Dr. Braxton exclaimed. "What's the truth of this?"

"There isn't any. I admit I helped John, but I didn't kill him. Why should I?"

Rogan answered that. "Blackmail!"

"For what?" Evan's frayed nerves were still driving him. "He'd made me help cover the murder, but what else could he get out of me? I haven't a dollar to my name."

"True, but you hoped to marry Miss Braxton for her money. I doubt if the idea of sharing with John appealed to you."

"You're crazy. Good God, I'd had enough trouble with Jackson's body! Why should I want another corpse on my hands?"

Instead of answering, Kincaid spoke to Collins.

"How about that dinitrophenol story, Dan? You've got enough without it."

"Damn it!" The reporter was almost frantic. "Don't you see, this yarn's too big to let go of *anything?* I'll need every scrap I can get."

He had been prepared to face Rogan's anger, but the gambler was ominously meek.

"I just wanted to give the doctor an antidote for the trouble I caused him this morning, but you're the boss." Kincaid glanced at Evan. "You'll need an antidote, too. Hand me my robe, will you?"

Tethryn nervously jerked the robe off the foot of the bed. Rogan's left hand went into the pocket and came out bearing the cartridges he had removed from Hoyt's gun, and the cyanide capsule. He dropped the cartridges into his right hand and offered them to Dorsey.

"You'll want these, Sergeant. They came out of the revolver you found downstairs."

As Dorsey took them, Makepeace burst out.

"See here, Sergeant, how long do you intend to permit Kincaid to make these unsupported accusations?"

"As long as he likes. I don't have to believe 'em until he gives me proof."

"They aren't unsupported," Rogan told the lawyer. "You heard Tethryn fake a long-distance call to John last night. He pretended John was leaving to take a job in South America. That phone call was dangerous. It brought John into the picture when otherwise we might not even have guessed he existed. There'd have been no point in making it *if John had been still alive.* But John was dead, and Tethryn needed to plant an excuse in case someone asked why John wasn't around any more."

"And so"—Makepeace grew sarcastic—"having just gotten rid of one body with the greatest difficulty, you think Lord Tethryn immediately saddled himself with another."

"Not exactly. This time he thought he had a hiding place that would keep his secret till doomsday."

"And I suppose you know where this mysterious hiding place is?"

"I know where it was. When Tethryn came back from 'seeing John off' last night he left a trail of sea-water on the floor. He didn't get that wet from launching a boat. And why do you suppose the telephone cable stood up all these years only to break just when it was needed for a murder case? *Because Tethryn tied John's body to it.* He thought John would stay there forever, but the cable was old and the Handyman is strong. It snapped the cable and pulled the body loose. They'll find John in Gallows Cove tomorrow!"

Blind with rage, Tethryn threw himself at Rogan's throat. The gambler made no effort to protect himself, but the thumb of his right hand found the nerve in Evan's knee. He saw the other wince and said, "Pain's worked higher now, hasn't it?"

The two detectives pulled Tethryn off. As they did so, Kincaid slipped the cyanide capsule into Evan's hand. "Take it," he said. Then as the other's fingers closed over the poison, he added, "Easy."

Dorsey jerked Evan to his feet.

"Thanks, Mr. Kincaid," he said. "I'm satisfied. We'll find the body, too."

"I'm sure of it." Rogan looked down at Evan's clenched hand. "I'm afraid they've got you, but"—he let his glance drop to the other's knee—"there are worse deaths than hanging."

Evan jerked his hand free, and put the capsule between his lips before the policeman could stop him.

"Poison," Collins shouted. "Get it out of his mouth."

Evan swallowed. "Don't worry. It's not poison. Just some medicine I had to take."

"You know, Sergeant," Kincaid remarked, "I'll bet that's the stuff I took from Hoyt last night and hid in the cracker box. Tethryn must have found it later."

The words told Evan he had been tricked. He hurled himself at the gambler again, but this time the police were faster. Whatever he tried to say was lost in the noise of the fight. Before they got him under control the poison took effect. It was a repetition of the death of his victim the night before. Dr. Braxton bent over the body.

"It's cyanide," he pronounced. "There's nothing to disguise the odor now."

"Poor chap," said Makepeace.

"To hell with him," said Collins. "He's knocked the stuffing out of my story."

"Maybe," Dorsey admitted, "but I can't blame him. It was sort of heroic in a way. By killing himself I figure he's saved Miss Braxton's grandfather a lot of unpleasantness."

"Sentimental nonsense," sniffed Miss Makepeace. "He may have cheated the hangman, but he couldn't cheat the hangman's handyman."

She looked fixedly at Rogan. He grinned back at her.

21

Exit Od

DAN COLLINS FOUND Rogan the next morning at the *Jeb Stuart Hotel*. It was ten o'clock, but the gambler was in bed, propped up on pillows as he had been the day before.

"Well, well," Dan greeted him. "Don't tell me you're still shattered? I thought you got here yesterday under your own power?"

"I did. But my dear old grandmother taught me always to stay down for the count of nine, so I'm taking it easy."

"I don't blame you. All the same you ought to be gladder to see me. I come bearing gifts."

"What gifts?"

"These." Mr. Collins pulled a wad of bills from his pocket. "It's your pay for the story tip. I had a hell of a time getting Ames to wire it down. He's sore at me because my camera got wet when I fell in the drink and I didn't send him any pictures. He's sore at you, too, for letting the earl sneak out of a trial. Ames damn near cried when I told him the yarn was washed up. To hear him talk, you'd think he believes you killed Tethryn yourself just to cheat the *Record* out of a story."

Rogan counted the bills and shoved them into the pocket of his pajamas.

"Speaking of killing stories, did you run anything about old Doc Braxton and the dinitrophenol?"

"Hell, no. There wasn't room. Not when I had to crowd the whole thing into one edition. Besides, I knew you wanted to protect the old boy. I had to mention his being at the house party, but I spelled his name wrong."

"I don't doubt it, but that was force of habit, not friendship for me."

Dan's retort was never uttered, for at that moment the door opened and Nancy Garwood walked in. She wore a suit of brown tweed that set off both her figure and her buttercup-yellow hair to perfection. A saucy hat with a feather in it was cocked over one eye. The reporter drew a deep breath.

"Remind me to ask you where you've been in that getup."

"You don't have to ask me. I've been down seeing the District Attorney. His name's McArdle and he's sweet. He's running for governor."

"I'll bet after one look he was running for you."

"Of course. He's going to give me Jack's car. Isn't that nice?"

Mr. Collins' mouth fell open. "Give you Frant's car?"

"Well, not give it to me, silly. But you see, when the cops brought it back from Bailey's Point yesterday, they found out it was a drive-yourself Packard that Jack had hired in New York. So I said, why not let me drive it north, on account of because I was going anyway, and so why send a policeman who'd only have to come home when he got there? So Mr. McArdle said all right, and I've got the keys. Only"—she turned to Rogan—"while I was there, Sergeant Dorsey was in the next room, talking to somebody named Yeager, and he said that they ought to subpoena you for the inquest, and that they'd better hold you as a material witness to make sure you showed up. I thought you'd want to leave before they get here, so I came back right away. You can drive to New York with me if you'd like."

"Splendid," said Dan. "I'll come, too."

"Shame on you," Rogan chided. "Don't you know that two's company?"

"Sure. You two could be company for me."

"Perhaps. But you wouldn't be company for us. You've got an expense account. Here's your chance to use it. Also"—Rogan took the money from his pocket and peeled off two bills—"get Nancy's bags and have them at the back door. I'll come down the fire stairs and pick them up. Pay my bill. Then go stand out front and watch for cops." He turned to the girl. "How long will it take you to get that car here?"

"Fifteen minutes. I'll meet you in the alley." She blew him a kiss and was gone.

Collins sighed. "Some guys have all the luck."

Exactly seven minutes later, Mr. Kincaid was carrying his bag down the stairway. A night's sleep had done wonders, but Tethryn's attacks had left the gambler shaky, so he was thankful he had only two flights to negotiate.

The stairs ended in a concrete-floored corridor that ran to the rear entrance of the hotel. A doorway led into the lobby, but the door was closed now. Rogan dropped his suitcase on the floor and sat down on the steps to rest and wait for Nancy. He had hardly taken his place when the lobby door opened and Sue Braxton came through it.

"Oh," she gasped. "You *are* here! Bobby said you might be. You see, the Makepeaces were subpoenaed for the inquest and Bobby thought you'd be, too. He didn't suppose you'd like it, so we came to warn you. We rang your room, but you didn't answer. Bobby guessed you'd heard already and left, but he went up to make sure."

"And in the meanwhile he figured that if I were trying to get out ahead of the police, I might prefer the stairs to an elevator. Smart boy."

Sue started to laugh at that and then changed her mind.

"Why yes, I guess he is. You know I never thought of him that way."

"You have plenty of company." Rogan smiled. "Thanks for coming to tip me off."

There was silence for a minute, and then the girl said, "I had to see you anyway—for another reason. I . . . I didn't know whether I wanted to thank you or hate you."

"Is it necessary to do either?"

"I suppose not. Only I couldn't make up my mind about you. The way you treated Grandfather, I mean. And Mr. Collins told me you wouldn't let him print anything about the dinitrophenol. Besides . . . well, I was almost engaged to Evan, you see . . . and I don't know what to think about him now."

"How old are you?"

"Twenty. Why?"

"Because the only certainty about being twenty is that the things that worry you today won't be the things that will worry you tomorrow."

The girl looked up at him, startled. "I suppose that's true, isn't it? Most people say, 'You'll get over it,' but that's not the same thing, is it?"

"Nothing is the same when you put it in different words."

Sue thought that over and then suddenly opened the bag she carried.

"You said you didn't have any money, so I brought you this." She took a roll of bills out of her bag and thrust it into his hand. "There's nearly a thousand dollars here. That's all I could get today. I'll send you some more later."

Mr. Kincaid caught his breath.

"Thanks," he said. And then, "That's one of the nicest things that ever happened to me. But I can't take the money."

"You're my uncle, aren't you?"

"Yes."

"Then why?"

"Because if I did, you'd think I needed more. Next you'd start worrying about how I was getting along, and there'd be no end to it. Besides, I have plenty." His hand went to his pocket and brought out the bills Collins had given him. "See? A week in New York and I'll have more than I can use."

He held up the money she had given him. "Do me a favor with this?"

"What?"

"Buy yourself something pretty—a ring, or a necklace—something that will keep. Then when you wear it, say to yourself: 'Wherever Uncle Mike is, he's well and happy.' Will you do that for me?"

"Of course." She took the money. "And I really believe you will be, Uncle Mike."

"Thanks. And another thing. Let's keep this uncle business secret. I had my passport made out to 'Kincaid,' and if the State Department finds out the name ought to be 'Braxton' they might be annoyed."

"I won't tell." She looked up at him and added, "Anybody."

"You're swell." He held out his hand. "And now I'd better be on my way before the police get here. Good-by."

Sue ignored the hand. "Down here," she told him, "nice uncles always kiss their nieces good-by."

He kissed her.

"Thanks for that, too."

There was the sound of feet behind Rogan, and he whirled to see Bobby coming down the stairs. The blond youth carried a brown-paper parcel under his arm. His face lighted with pleasure as he spied the gambler.

"Hello. Glad I caught you. Before you got away, I mean. I . . . well . . . that is, I wanted to give you something." He extended the parcel.

"You're very kind."

Before Kincaid could say more, he heard an auto horn in the alley. He grabbed Bobby's hand.

"That car's honking for me. I have to rush." He held up the package. "Thanks for this. I'll open it later. Take care of yourselves, you two."

There was a chorus of good-bys, and he was gone.

Nancy had the door of the Packard open. Rogan tossed the suitcases behind the seat. As he followed them into the car, Nancy let in the clutch. They passed a policeman at the mouth of the alley. He scarcely gave the gray Packard a glance, and the girl drew a deep breath of relief.

"Whew! I was afraid he was laying for us. Where were you?"

"Saying good-by to Bobby Chatterton."

Nancy laughed, the comfortable laugh of a woman for whom things have turned out well and who, in consequence, finds everything amusing.

"Don't laugh at Bobby," Rogan admonished. "I'm laying bets he had John Frant's murder figured out within an hour after it happened, only he was too shy to say much for fear he was wrong. Besides, he gave me a going-away present." He held up the paper-wrapped bundle.

"What is it?"

"I don't know yet. It feels like a package of laundry, but it's too heavy for that. Also there's something hard . . ." He had been untying the string, and as he spoke, the 'something hard' slipped out and clattered to the floor. Rogan picked it up. Nancy took her eyes from the street ahead long enough for a quick glance.

"For heaven's sake! It's a monkey wrench. Are you supposed to use that if the car breaks down?"

"Hardly. I gather this is what Tethryn used to bend the bolt on my door. Bobby was the one who figured out the solution of the lock trick. He probably brought this along to prove he was right about the method."

"Dan told me *he* solved the door business."

"Lots of girls have made mistakes through believing Dan."

"If Bobby's so smart, why didn't he find out what it was that choked you?"

"It was Tethryn."

"It didn't sound like him. Not the way you told it."

"Oh, there was a trick to it, too. But remember I'd spent the evening listening to stories about Od and about how undines came out of the sea, huge and shapeless, like monster jellyfish. Then Miss Makepeace showed me the sea water Tethryn left on the floor of the living room and suggested that it might be the track of an undine. No matter how good your nerves are, that sort of thing makes you feel like Robinson Crusoe finding a footprint from the spirit world. To cap it all, I got back to my room and the thing dropped on me out of the dark. Do you wonder I couldn't think of anything but undines? I was like a kid imagining bears every time he hears a mouse in the wainscot. If we knew the answer, it would probably be something very simple."

"I don't believe it," Nancy demurred. "You said this thing gave when you touched it and yet was strong enough to strangle you. What in the world could do that?" She shrugged. "Well, we'll never know now. What else did Bobby give you?"

"I haven't looked yet." Rogan finished unwrapping the paper and then held up the object it had enclosed. "Good Lord! It's a poncho."

"What's a poncho?"

"Sort of combination waterproof blanket and raincoat. Boy Scouts use them."

Nancy sniffed. "Is that Bobby's good turn for the day? The thing looks like a rubber sheet to me."

Suddenly Rogan began to laugh. He laughed until the tears rolled down his cheeks, and it was several minutes before he could reply to Nancy's insistent demand to be let in on the joke.

"Don't you see?" he chuckled. "This is It. When we were talking about what strangled me yesterday Bobby said something about a wet blanket. I didn't understand him then, so today he gave me this to make the point clear."

"It's not clear to me."

"No? Well, Tethryn must have been wearing this poncho last night when he went out to tie John Frant to the phone cable. The poncho got wet. Tethryn still had it with him while he was waiting for me in my room. When I came in, it was dark and he threw the thing over my head. My imagination did the rest. The wet rubber was slippery, and it gave when I hit at it, but it kept me from moving freely. Once I was under it, all Tethryn had to do was to put an arm around my throat and strangle me from behind. That's why I couldn't feel anything solid in front of me, even while I was being choked."

He laughed again. "Tethryn's technique was fine, only he lost his nerve when Miss Makepeace screamed. If he'd held on a little longer maybe he wouldn't be where he is now, and"—Rogan glanced at Nancy—"it's certain I wouldn't be where I am."

The girl threw him a swift smile. Then she took her right hand from the wheel and placed it in his lap, palm up.

"Miss Makepeace has her uses," she said.

The End

RAMBLE HOUSE's

HARRY STEPHEN KEELER WEBWORK MYSTERIES

(RH) indicates the title is available ONLY in the RAMBLE HOUSE edition

The Ace of Spades Murder
The Affair of the Bottled Deuce (RH)
The Amazing Web
The Barking Clock
Behind That Mask
The Book with the Orange Leaves
The Bottle with the Green Wax Seal
The Box from Japan
The Case of the Canny Killer
The Case of the Crazy Corpse (RH)
The Case of the Flying Hands (RH)
The Case of the Ivory Arrow
The Case of the Jeweled Ragpicker
The Case of the Lavender Gripsack
The Case of the Mysterious Moll
The Case of the 16 Beans
The Case of the Transparent Nude (RH)
The Case of the Transposed Legs
The Case of the Two-Headed Idiot (RH)
The Case of the Two Strange Ladies
The Circus Stealers (RH)
Cleopatra's Tears
A Copy of Beowulf (RH)
The Crimson Cube (RH)
The Face of the Man From Saturn
Find the Clock
The Five Silver Buddhas
The 4th King
The Gallows Waits, My Lord! (RH)
The Green Jade Hand
Finger! Finger!
Hangman's Nights (RH)
I, Chameleon (RH)
I Killed Lincoln at 10:13! (RH)
The Iron Ring
The Man Who Changed His Skin (RH)
The Man with the Crimson Box
The Man with the Magic Eardrums
The Man with the Wooden Spectacles
The Marceau Case
The Matilda Hunter Murder
The Monocled Monster

The Murder of London Lew
The Murdered Mathematician
The Mysterious Card (RH)
The Mysterious Ivory Ball of Wong Shing Li (RH)
The Mystery of the Fiddling Cracksman
The Peacock Fan
The Photo of Lady X (RH)
The Portrait of Jirjohn Cobb
Report on Vanessa Hewstone (RH)
Riddle of the Travelling Skull
Riddle of the Wooden Parrakeet (RH)
The Scarlet Mummy (RH)
The Search for X-Y-Z
The Sharkskin Book
Sing Sing Nights
The Six From Nowhere (RH)
The Skull of the Waltzing Clown
The Spectacles of Mr. Cagliostro
Stand By—London Calling!
The Steeltown Strangler
The Stolen Gravestone (RH)
Strange Journey (RH)
The Strange Will
The Straw Hat Murders (RH)
The Street of 1000 Eyes (RH)
Thieves' Nights
Three Novellos (RH)
The Tiger Snake
The Trap (RH)
Vagabond Nights (Defrauded Yeggman)
Vagabond Nights 2 (10 Hours)
The Vanishing Gold Truck
The Voice of the Seven Sparrows
The Washington Square Enigma
When Thief Meets Thief
The White Circle (RH)
The Wonderful Scheme of Mr. Christopher Thorne
X. Jones—of Scotland Yard
Y. Cheung, Business Detective

Keeler Related Works

A To Izzard: A Harry Stephen Keeler Companion by Fender Tucker — Articles and stories about Harry, by Harry, and in his style. Included is a compleat bibliography.

Wild About Harry: Reviews of Keeler Novels — Edited by Richard Polt & Fender Tucker — 22 reviews of works by Harry Stephen Keeler from *Keeler News*. A perfect introduction to the author.

The Keeler Keyhole Collection: Annotated newsletter rants from Harry Stephen Keeler, edited by Francis M. Nevins. Over 400 pages of incredibly personal Keeleriana.

Fakealoo — Pastiches of the style of Harry Stephen Keeler by selected demented members of the HSK Society. Updated every year with the new winner.

RAMBLE HOUSE's OTHER LOONS

The Case of the Little Green Men — Mack Reynolds wrote this love song to sci-fi fans back in 1951 and it's now back in print.

Hell Fire — A new hard-boiled novel by Jack Moskovitz about an arsonist, an arson cop and a Nazi hooker. It isn't pretty.

Researching American-Made Toy Soldiers — A 276-page collection of a lifetime of articles by toy soldier expert Richard O'Brien

Strands of the Web: Short Stories of Harry Stephen Keeler — Edited and Introduced by Fred Cleaver

The Sam McCain Novels — Ed Gorman's terrific series includes *The Day the Music Died, Wake Up Little Susie* and *Will You Still Love Me Tomorrow?*

A Shot Rang Out — Three decades of reviews from Jon Breen

A Roland Daniel Double: The Signal and The Return of Wu Fang — Classic thrillers from the 30s

Murder in Shawnee — Two novels of the Alleghenies by John Douglas: *Shawnee Alley Fire* and *Haunts*.

Deep Space and other Stories — A collection of SF gems by Richard A. Lupoff

Blood Moon — The first of the Robert Payne series by Ed Gorman

The Time Armada — Fox B. Holden's 1953 SF gem.

Black River Falls — Suspense from the master, Ed Gorman

Sideslip — 1968 SF masterpiece by Ted White and Dave Van Arnam

The Triune Man — Mindscrambling science fiction from Richard A. Lupoff

Detective Duff Unravels It — Episodic mysteries by Harvey O'Higgins

Mysterious Martin, the Master of Murder — Two versions of a strange 1912 novel by Tod Robbins about a man who writes books that can kill.

The Master of Mysteries — 1912 novel of supernatural sleuthing by Gelett Burgess

Dago Red — 22 tales of dark suspense by Bill Pronzini

The Night Remembers — A 1991 Jack Walsh mystery from Ed Gorman

Rough Cut & New, Improved Murder — Ed Gorman's first two novels

Hollywood Dreams — A novel of the Depression by Richard O'Brien

Six Gelett Burgess Novels — *The Master of Mysteries, The White Cat, Two O'Clock Courage, Ladies in Boxes, Find the Woman, The Heart Line*

The Organ Reader — A huge compilation of just about everything published in the 1971-1972 radical bay-area newspaper, *THE ORGAN*.

A Clear Path to Cross — Sharon Knowles short mystery stories by Ed Lynskey

Old Times' Sake — Short stories by James Reasoner from Mike Shayne Magazine

Freaks and Fantasies — Eerie tales by Tod Robbins, collaborator of Tod Browning on the film FREAKS.

Five Jim Harmon Sleaze Double Novels — *Vixen Hollow/Celluloid Scandal, The Man Who Made Maniacs/Silent Siren, Ape Rape/Wanton Witch, Sex Burns Like Fire/Twist Session*, and *Sudden Lust/Passion Strip*. More doubles to come!

Marblehead: A Novel of H.P. Lovecraft — A long-lost masterpiece from Richard A. Lupoff. Published for the first time!

The Compleat Ova Hamlet — Parodies of SF authors by Richard A. Lupoff – New edition!

The Secret Adventures of Sherlock Holmes — Three Sherlockian pastiches by the Brooklyn author/publisher, Gary Lovisi.

The Universal Holmes — Richard A. Lupoff's 2007 collection of five Holmesian pastiches and a recipe for giant rat stew.

Four Joel Townsley Rogers Novels — By the author of *The Red Right Hand: Once In a Red Moon, Lady With the Dice, The Stopped Clock, Never Leave My Bed*

Two Joel Townsley Rogers Story Collections — Night of Horror and Killing Time

Twenty Norman Berrow Novels — *The Bishop's Sword, Ghost House, Don't Go Out After Dark, Claws of the Cougar, The Smokers of Hashish, The Secret Dancer, Don't Jump Mr. Boland!, The Footprints of Satan, Fingers for Ransom, The Three Tiers of Fantasy, The Spaniard's Thumb, The Eleventh Plague, Words Have Wings, One Thrilling Night, The Lady's in Danger, It Howls at Night, The Terror in the Fog, Oil Under the Window, Murder in the Melody, The Singing Room*

The N. R. De Mexico Novels — Robert Bragg presents *Marijuana Girl, Madman on a Drum, Private Chauffeur* in one volume.

Four Chelsea Quinn Yarbro Novels featuring Charlie Moon — *Ogilvie, Tallant and Moon, Music When the Sweet Voice Dies, Poisonous Fruit* and *Dead Mice*

Five Walter S. Masterman Mysteries — *The Green Toad, The Flying Beast, The Yellow Mistletoe, The Wrong Verdict* and *The Perjured Alibi*. Fantastic impossible plots.

Two Hake Talbot Novels — *Rim of the Pit, The Hangman's Handyman*. Classic locked room mysteries.

Two Alexander Laing Novels — *The Motives of Nicholas Holtz* and *Dr. Scarlett*, stories of medical mayhem and intrigue from the 30s.

Four David Hume Novels — *Corpses Never Argue, Cemetery First Stop, Make Way for the Mourners, Eternity Here I Come*, and more to come.

Three Wade Wright Novels — *Echo of Fear, Death At Nostalgia Street* and *It Leads to Murder*, with more to come!

Six Rupert Penny Novels — *Policeman's Holiday, Policeman's Evidence, Lucky Policeman, Policeman in Armour, Sealed Room Murder, Sweet Poison,* classic mysteries.

Five Jack Mann Novels — Strange murder in the English countryside. *Gees' First Case, Nightmare Farm, Grey Shapes, The Ninth Life, The Glass Too Many.*

Seven Max Afford Novels — *Owl of Darkness, Death's Mannikins, Blood on His Hands, The Dead Are Blind, The Sheep and the Wolves, Sinners in Paradise* and *Two Locked Room Mysteries and a Ripping Yarn* by one of Australia's finest novelists.

Five Joseph Shallit Novels — *The Case of the Billion Dollar Body, Lady Don't Die on My Doorstep, Kiss the Killer, Yell Bloody Murder, Take Your Last Look*. One of America's best 50's authors.

Two Crimson Clown Novels — By Johnston McCulley, author of the Zorro novels, *The Crimson Clown* and *The Crimson Clown Again*.

The Best of 10-Story Book — edited by Chris Mikul, over 35 stories from the literary magazine Harry Stephen Keeler edited.

A Young Man's Heart — A forgotten early classic by Cornell Woolrich

The Anthony Boucher Chronicles — edited by Francis M. Nevins
Book reviews by Anthony Boucher written for the *San Francisco Chronicle,* 1942 – 1947. Essential and fascinating reading.

Muddled Mind: Complete Works of Ed Wood, Jr. — David Hayes and Hayden Davis deconstruct the life and works of a mad genius.

Gadsby — A lipogram (a novel without the letter E). Ernest Vincent Wright's last work, published in 1939 right before his death.

My First Time: The One Experience You Never Forget — Michael Birchwood — 64 true first-person narratives of how they lost it.

Automaton — Brilliant treatise on robotics: 1928-style! By H. Stafford Hatfield

The Incredible Adventures of Rowland Hern — Rousing 1928 impossible crimes by Nicholas Olde.

Slammer Days — Two full-length prison memoirs: *Men into Beasts* (1952) by George Sylvester Viereck and *Home Away From Home* (1962) by Jack Woodford

Murder in Black and White — 1931 classic tennis whodunit by Evelyn Elder

Killer's Caress — Cary Moran's 1936 hardboiled thriller

The Golden Dagger — 1951 Scotland Yard yarn by E. R. Punshon

Beat Books #1 — Two beatnik classics, *A Sea of Thighs* by Ray Kainen and *Village Hipster* by J.X. Williams

A Smell of Smoke — 1951 English countryside thriller by Miles Burton

Ruled By Radio — 1925 futuristic novel by Robert L. Hadfield & Frank E. Farncombe

Murder in Silk — A 1937 Yellow Peril novel of the silk trade by Ralph Trevor

The Case of the Withered Hand — 1936 potboiler by John G. Brandon

Finger-prints Never Lie — A 1939 classic detective novel by John G. Brandon

Inclination to Murder — 1966 thriller by New Zealand's Harriet Hunter

Invaders from the Dark — Classic werewolf tale from Greye La Spina

Fatal Accident — Murder by automobile, a 1936 mystery by Cecil M. Wills

The Devil Drives — A prison and lost treasure novel by Virgil Markham

Dr. Odin — Douglas Newton's 1933 potboiler comes back to life.

The Chinese Jar Mystery — Murder in the manor by John Stephen Strange, 1934

The Julius Caesar Murder Case — A classic 1935 re-telling of the assassination by Wallace Irwin that's much more fun than the Shakespeare version

West Texas War and Other Western Stories — by Gary Lovisi

The Contested Earth and Other SF Stories — A never-before published space opera and seven short stories by Jim Harmon.

Tales of the Macabre and Ordinary — Modern twisted horror by Chris Mikul, author of the *Bizarrism* series.

The Gold Star Line — Seaboard adventure from L.T. Reade and Robert Eustace.

The Werewolf vs the Vampire Woman — Hard to believe ultraviolence by either Arthur M. Scarm or Arthur M. Scram.

Black Hogan Strikes Again — Australia's Peter Renwick pens a tale of the outback.

Don Diablo: Book of a Lost Film — Two-volume treatment of a western by Paul Landres, with diagrams. Intro by Francis M. Nevins.

The Charlie Chaplin Murder Mystery — Movie hijinks by Wes D. Gehring

The Koky Comics — A collection of all of the 1978-1981 Sunday and daily comic strips by Richard O'Brien and Mort Gerberg, in two volumes.

Suzy — Another collection of comic strips from Richard O'Brien and Bob Vojtko

Dime Novels: Ramble House's 10-Cent Books — *Knife in the Dark* by Robert Leslie Bellem, *Hot Lead* and *Song of Death* by Ed Earl Repp, *A Hashish House in New York* by H.H. Kane, and five more.

Blood in a Snap — The *Finnegan's Wake* of the 21st century, by Jim Weiler and Al Gorithm

Stakeout on Millennium Drive — Award-winning Indianapolis Noir — Ian Woollen.

Dope Tales #1 — Two dope-riddled classics; *Dope Runners* by Gerald Grantham and *Death Takes the Joystick* by Phillip Condé.

Dope Tales #2 — Two more narco-classics; *The Invisible Hand* by Rex Dark and *The Smokers of Hashish* by Norman Berrow.

Dope Tales #3 — Two enchanting novels of opium by the master, Sax Rohmer. *Dope* and *The Yellow Claw.*

Tenebrae — Ernest G. Henham's 1898 horror tale brought back.

The Singular Problem of the Stygian House-Boat — Two classic tales by John Kendrick Bangs about the denizens of Hades.

Tiresias — Psychotic modern horror novel by Jonathan M. Sweet.

The One After Snelling — Kickass modern noir from Richard O'Brien.

The Sign of the Scorpion — 1935 Edmund Snell tale of oriental evil.

The House of the Vampire — 1907 poetic thriller by George S. Viereck.

An Angel in the Street — Modern hardboiled noir by Peter Genovese.

The Devil's Mistress — Scottish gothic tale by J. W. Brodie-Innes.

The Lord of Terror — 1925 mystery with master-criminal, Fantômas.

The Lady of the Terraces — 1925 adventure by E. Charles Vivian.

My Deadly Angel — 1955 Cold War drama by John Chelton

Prose Bowl — Futuristic satire — Bill Pronzini & Barry N. Malzberg .

Satan's Den Exposed — True crime in Truth or Consequences New Mexico — Award-winning journalism by the *Desert Journal.*

The Amorous Intrigues & Adventures of Aaron Burr — by Anonymous — Hot historical action.

I Stole $16,000,000 — A true story by cracksman Herbert E. Wilson.

The Black Dark Murders — Vintage 50s college murder yarn by Milt Ozaki, writing as Robert O. Saber.

Sex Slave — Potboiler of lust in the days of Cleopatra — Dion Leclerq.

You'll Die Laughing — Bruce Elliott's 1945 novel of murder at a practical joker's English countryside manor.

The Private Journal & Diary of John H. Surratt — The memoirs of the man who conspired to assassinate President Lincoln.

Dead Man Talks Too Much — Hollywood boozer by Weed Dickenson

Red Light — History of legal prostitution in Shreveport Louisiana by Eric Brock. Includes wonderful photos of the houses and the ladies.

A Snark Selection — Lewis Carroll's *The Hunting of the Snark* with two Snarkian chapters by Harry Stephen Keeler — Illustrated by Gavin L. O'Keefe.

Ripped from the Headlines! — The Jack the Ripper story as told in the newspaper articles in the *New York* and *London Times.*

Geronimo — S. M. Barrett's 1905 autobiography of a noble American.

The White Peril in the Far East — Sidney Lewis Gulick's 1905 indictment of the West and assurance that Japan would never attack the U.S.

The Compleat Calhoon — All of Fender Tucker's works: Includes *Totah Six-Pack, Weed, Women and Song* and *Tales from the Tower,* plus a CD of all of his songs.

Totah Six-Pack — Just Fender Tucker's six tales about Farmington in one sleek volume.

RAMBLE HOUSE

Fender Tucker, Prop.

www.ramblehouse.com   fender@ramblehouse.com

228-826-1783   10329 Sheephead Drive, Vancleave MS 39565

Made in the USA
Middletown, DE
14 February 2022

61080699R00118